D1053041

The Daughters

LIVERIGHT PUBLISHING CORPORATION

A Division of W. W. Norton & Company

New York • *London*

The Daughters

A Novel

Adrienne Celt

Vasko Popa, "Last News About the Little Box," translated by Charles Simic, from *Homage to the Lame Wolf: Selected Poems.* Copyright © 1987 by Oberlin College. Reprinted with the permission of Oberlin College Press.

For information about permission to reproduce selections from this book, write to Permissions, Liveright Publishing Corporation, a division of W. W. Norton & Company, Inc., 500 Fifth Avenue, New York, NY 10110

For information about special discounts for bulk purchases, please contact W. W. Norton Special Sales at specialsales@wwnorton.com or 800-233-4830

Manufacturing by Courier Westford
Book design by Abbate Design
Production manager: Anna Oler

Library of Congress Cataloging-in-Publication Data

Celt, Adrienne.
The daughters : a novel / Adrienne Celt.
pages cm
ISBN 978-1-63149-045-3 (hardcover)
1. Sopranos—Fiction. 2. Mothers and daughters—Fiction.
3. Grandmothers—Fiction. 4. Family life—Fiction. I. Title.
PS3603.E465D48 2015
813'.6—dc23
2015005829

Liveright Publishing Corporation
500 Fifth Avenue, New York, N.Y. 10110
www.wwnorton.com

W. W. Norton & Company Ltd.
Castle House, 75/76 Wells Street, London W1T 3QT

1 2 3 4 5 6 7 8 9 0

For my grandmothers, Constance and Ewa,
who are beloved.

• Last News About the Little Box •

The little box which contains the world
Fell in love with herself
And conceived
Still another little box

The little box of the little box
Also fell in love with herself
And conceived
Still another little box

And so it went on forever

The world from the little box
Ought to be inside
The last offspring of the little box

But not one of the little boxes
Inside the little box in love with herself
Is the last one

Let's see you find the world now

—VASKO POPA (trans. Charles Simic)

The Daughters

Prelude

All my grandmother's important stories took place in the Polish countryside. Like this one:

A woman sits nude on the branch of a tree and lets her brown legs dangle into the open air. The bark ridges cut pleasantly into her thighs, and she presses her palms down, curls her fingers around the bough.

A man walks towards her through the woods, pushing aside whip-thin limbs of birch and beech, sidestepping shrubs as he searches for his lost path. The woman hums a song, and the man's feet begin to fall in time with the music. He does not realize that this is happening, does not yet feel his body in thrall to her.

It is a surprise, then, when he catches sight of her legs. He's far from his village, tired and thirsty; the last thing he expected to find here was another person, particularly a woman who is naked and glorious and alone. Her feet are callused, the soles covered in dirt, and they hang before him like clothes left to dry in the wind. He follows the smooth blue ridges of her veins up to her calves, her fingers, her breasts, her neck. To the soft and downy lobes of her ears. When he looks into her face, she smiles, and his surprise becomes recognition. His thirst disappears as the scent of a nearby river fills his nose and mouth, wets his tongue. The man knows that he's met the love of his life, and she is going to devour him.

This is an old story. While the aroma of clean water lingers in the air, the woman asks the man for a gift of bread and salt, which he will feed to her with his own fingers. He's already trembling, imagining it. His body is vibrating with desire.

The man shimmies up the trunk of the tree and swings onto the branch beside his beloved. The closer he gets, the more she smells of river currents, the rush of waves over mossy rocks releasing the green musk of water plants. Tilting her head to the side, the woman beckons him with her fingers. He leans in to kiss her: closer, closer. He bobs his head in time with her song, and as they embrace, her humming rumbles through him. He has never felt so entwined with someone, so protected. After a moment his heart stops beating, and his body drops to the forest floor with a muffled thud.

W hat happened next? I asked my grandmother, my baba.

That, she said, depends on who is telling you the story. Most people don't understand the *rusalka*, and so they wouldn't tell you that she has tears in her eyes as she jumps down from the tree and lands softly in the leaves. They wouldn't tell you of her heaving sobs of regret as she walks back to the river, her body light as air.

But then again, my baba said, what most people *would* tell you is also true. That she will find another man; that she will do it again. She will sit in the trees and sing her song as often as she needs to, take as much strength as she requires to survive.

Part One

1

Last night I woke up in a panic, convinced our apartment building was beset by tornadoes. My bed shook beneath me in response to a distant *whump*, and in the cup of water by my nightstand I saw rings echo outward on the liquid surface. The whole room retained a shimmer of movement, the afterglow of impact; a hint of wind groaned through the trees outside, and my eyes filled up with tears. I've always been afraid of storms.

We live on a high floor, among the top branches of the courtyard ashes and oaks, and if I peer through the bedroom window I can usually see a sliver of Lake Michigan, sometimes the indistinct forms of people running on the lakeshore path. But from my pillow I could only see the sky. Dark and roiling, bleary with water. Another strong shake hit the building, as though every front door were slamming at once, and I winced. Beside me in the dark bed, John turned and mumbled something unintelligible, tugging the blanket over his ear. And then Kara began to whimper.

I'm still not used to infant cries, which always sound, to me, terribly lonely. As if they know they can't be understood, and this is the larger part of their woe. Kara's were soft, though, uninsistent, and I waited to see if they would melt away. Perhaps she'd just woken up to find herself unfettered in bed, the swaddle tossed off by her own sleeping limbs. I held my breath.

Another *thump thump*.

She might not hear it, I thought. She might be too tired to really care, and fall back asleep with her head resting beside her fist. My heartbeat sounded in my ears, drumming in time with the rain and wind. During elementary school tornado drills, we were taught to shield our faces behind elbows and forearms as we filed into the cold concrete shelter below the gym. I wanted to pull the pillow over my head or tug John's arm over my eyes and ears to mute the sounds and give me some measure of protection. But I lay still, listening. And hoping: *don't let her really be awake*. As though being unaware of a storm could save you from it. As though sleeping babies were routinely picked up by twisters and set back down gently, unharmed.

I could lie here, afraid, and watch the windowpanes shatter inward. I could watch the ceiling rise, prised off by giant unseeable fingers. I could feel time slow down and then speed back up, the certainty of death upon me. I could do this, if only she went back to sleep and kept up her deep, unshuddering breaths.

Something banged against the window. A tree branch maybe, wrenched free by the violent air. Kara inhaled sharply and then really cried, a begging, a bellow in the moonless night. The sound seemed to come from my own chest, and I jumped up, grabbed Kara from the cradle to try and fit the cry to my lungs. If anything broke through the windows now it would slam into my back, sticking me with glass shrapnel. I wrapped my head and shoulders over my daughter so we were one body, double-face hidden below the curve of the torso.

But nothing came. John continued sleeping, air easing through his lips. And Kara, snug against my shoulder, shushed. Her eyes trembled shut. The building quivered. And I found my wish granted, me the only sentinel against the night.

The truth about possibility is that it is boundless. I could just as easily have been sucked into the sky to fly with cars and billboard shards as ignored by the gods for another day and left to fall asleep in a chair with a child clutching my hair in her sweating fingers. I admit that singing opera provides me with a taste for the dramatic. But in my daily life I prefer a degree of peace—time to luxuriate in the shower or bath, space to run scales until my voice is warm and elastic.

I just happen to know that sometimes the world gives a little twist and everything changes. A shout percussing across the mountain stones until one falls down and the rest tumble after. There is danger in small things.

This morning I woke up to an electronic *bip*. John stood above me holding my phone, flipping through the settings.

"There you go." He handed it to me—I shook the stiffness out of my fingers before accepting. "Volume is up to the max. You should be able to hear it from anywhere in the house now."

"Oh joyous thing." I yawned. Then I caught myself. "Wait. You found my phone?"

"Wasn't lost." He shrugged and smoothed a navy blue jacket

over his shoulders. "We're doing an open rehearsal for a set of local elementaries today. And then I have to meet with Stan, so maybe seven?"

"Okay." I scrolled through my missed calls. Nothing essential. At least, nothing I wanted to return.

Nothing from my baba Ada. Though that was natural.

Kara stirred, and I adjusted her so she could begin nursing. Her quiet supping sounds. John leaned over and kissed her ear and then, after a split-second pause, mine. I couldn't help but shift. So many mouths occupied with my body.

One possibility is that my husband knows the child we've just brought into the world is not his. Another possibility is that he doesn't. After all, John loves her. That is not in dispute.

I watched him pull his gray wool coat over the blazer, wrap a scarf around his neck, and make sure he had the right music in his leather satchel before putting on his gloves. Then he waved. Slipped through the door and was gone.

Most people in my position would take comfort in the fact that conception dates are approximate at best. The, shall we say, soft-focus view of my daughter's provenance is that no one can be sure about it. And there are moments when I can almost imagine him at the source of her. Hollows left in the pillows by the weight of a head, John hefting himself off the mattress to walk naked into the kitchen for a glass of tap water.

Still, I can't help but know what I know. I know when my heart rate increases by a single point, know the placement of my ribs with chiropractic precision. Feeling a child wake up inside me was as obvious and instantaneous as a slap to the face.

What I didn't know was where my phone had gotten to, and it disturbs me, the ease with which John plucked it from the ether. If he's aware that Kara's blood is not his own, then the question of what he might do next is still an open one. Why hasn't he said anything? Why does a part of me wish he would? I'm sitting on the edge of a precipice, legs dangling into the dark.

Small things: a lost phone, the unnaturally blue eyes of a child.

Outside the storm is still raging, the sky shedding snow. Not as loud as last night, perhaps, but just as angry.

A cross the room, out of my reach, our stereo sits on a shelf with recordings and ruffled sheaves of sheet music. A thin smattering of selections on vinyl, which is John's pretension, not my own. I've never understood his fascination with how music is preserved. I'm interested in how it's made. Living inside music that lives in me, so that we, the song and I, are a continual unfolding out of one another, a growing vastness, an emerging pattern.

John left this morning to rehearse *La Bohème* and I did not. For now, this is the way of things.

It seems odd to me to think of my voice scratched into a wax cylinder, trapped like a spirit caught in a jar. Worse still a computer chip: the tip of my tongue striking my teeth, the glottal contractions in my throat, even the air that circulates through my lungs and my blood, all somehow frozen onto a thumb drive that I can toss into my purse. A song is best sustained through performance, where it can respond to the world around it. Be shaped by its surroundings. Made new. In that way it's like a story, never so alive as when it's being told.

From my seat I take stock of the operatic scores I've lined up to read as I nurse, each with a variety of recordings tucked beside it. Just tools. Their usefulness predicated on the belief that this pause in my career will end, and end well. When I take on a new role, I like to read the full score of the opera first, sing it through, to let my body interpret the notes on the page. Then I listen to all the recordings I can get my hands on to make sure I'm not imitating someone else's voice.

Kara observes me, fighting off sleep, and I wonder what I could say to her to help her relax. Release her hold on the details she's drinking in from around her so we could both get a moment or two more of rest. The doctor, after all, told me that rest was what I needed. "Your body has been through a struggle," she said. "You need to take some time off to get your strength back."

I could tell Kara a story. She has a lot to learn about me, about the past. Where she comes from, where she's going. And anyway, isn't that the function of stories? To teach our brains to dream? It would be daunting to fall asleep into the noise of complete darkness, infinite probability. Without the guide of a little narrative, a little magic, how would we know where to go when we closed our eyes?

Despite her restiveness, the baby barely makes a sound. Sometimes soft snufflings, yawns that expand her entire body so she seems to be unkinking at the joints. We named her Karina, but I haven't called her that since John and I made the official declaration for her birth certificate. She's Kara, plain Kara. In the muted light of day, she doesn't mind that it's snowing outside, that a slick mix of sleet and ice and rain is tapping on the tall windows of the living room. To her, the entire world is the chair I sit in, or perhaps just the length of my arm where she lays. To her, the sun is a bent lamp at my elbow, and the whole of existence is quiet, because I made it that way. Tappings, stockinged footsteps, hush, the baby is sleeping.

Since Kara was born I haven't sung a note. I've lain in bed with her soft weight splayed across my chest, and I've inhaled the milkfat scent of her hair. I've passed her to my husband and watched him press his nose against hers, stare cross-eyed into her pupils, smile his smallest, truest smile. I've seen other, more complicated shifts in his expression too, but we don't talk about them. I wrap silence around myself like a blanket, like I'm always cold. Looking at my scores makes me shiver. Waking up with *Tosca* in my head fills my lungs with ice. Kara is so small, just a creature of cheeks and folds, eyes and rumples. I wrap silence around her, too, and tell myself it is to protect her. To keep her core temperature high, so the breath she sighs out at me will heat my neck in tiny bursts.

My grandmother Ada, *babenka Adelajda*, tells me that when I was first born I blinked my eyes with the regularity of a metronome. As a child I ran down the tiled aisles of the grocery store leaping in time with crescendos in the piped-in music. If the song was up-tempo I got mischievous, pinching all the grapes in a bunch to find the crisp ones and popping them in my mouth when no one was looking. Sometimes I tried to sneak one bite of every kind of fruit and vegetable in the store: a bean sprout; a lettuce leaf, with its torn green taste; an apple, bitten down to the white on one side and placed back on the pile with its shiny, unadulterated face forward.

If the music was slow, I lost the will to walk. My baba Ada held my hand and asked, "Is that the weight of the world I see on your shoulders?" I leaned into her, burying my face in her side and letting my knees buckle ever so slightly. But it wasn't sadness, exactly, that stilled me. I wanted to lie on the floor and progress at the same pace as the chords. Toss an arm out, then rest. Roll onto my stomach, then rest. My body was starting to ascertain that the quiet moments between notes, between sounds, were as important as the sounds themselves.

The wind blows water against the window in waves, as if it were a body heaving backwards and thrusting itself into the glass, demanding entrance. We're close enough to the beach to be a target for the lake effect, frozen raindrops assaulting our building in droves, snow accumulating at a magnitude. Ours is a nice neighborhood in the north of the city, but there is no protection anywhere from the weather. You just get used to it. The pounding is so regular it's almost soothing, at least with a radiator near my knees, hissing steam in concert. My spine cracks as I stretch in my chair, and the child stretches her fingers, which look boneless.

I'm on hold. Alone with a baby girl I have reason to be wary of, a baby girl whose birth I can't remember. Her first hours are a black space in my body's history that leaves me feeling as if I woke up in the wrong skin.

John asked me yesterday if it was really going to be okay for him to go back to work and leave me alone. He was worried, he said, about me not rehearsing.

"Doctor's orders," I told him. As if he didn't know. When my contractions got intense we hailed a cab to the hospital, and I hoisted my bulky body into the car easily enough. But partway through the drive something went wrong. I felt warmth spreading over my thighs and cursed, thinking that my water had broken, and we would have to pay the cleaning fee for the cab. When I touched the wet spot, though, my hand came up red. I remember the earth tilting. Inside me something gave way, clicked, cracked, and I can't recall anything else until the moment I found myself in a hospital bed, strange hands affixing an IV to my arm. Then I lost consciousness again.

"She was a little too eager to come into the world," my doctor said later. She sat beside me with her hand on my arm while John slept in a chair nearby. Apparently this is what happens when you trip unknowingly close to death—you cause physical sympathy. The baby was in an incubator, the doctor explained, for observation. "Tried to push through the wrong way." She pressed lightly on my stomach with her free hand, checking the dressing, and I gasped out an *aah*. "You see. It's unusual. But not unheard of." She frowned. "You'll have to be careful with yourself. Are you in a position to do that?"

The proper term for what happened to me is a *rupture* or *dehiscence*, an event usually reserved for flowering plants. Spontaneous opening of the fruit. Splitting to spit out seeds and flesh. Dehiscence also occurs with old wounds.

When I draw a very deep breath I can feel the place where my body is torn, a hairline scoring in the womb. By now it's supposed to be healing, but I can't picture it that way. I can only imagine the tear as fresh and electric. After all, it responds to me with great sensitivity, whenever I do the things I most wish to do. Like breathing in. Exhaling. Reaching for a high, clear sound.

Supposedly I will absorb this pain like a gong absorbs a blow. First it will radiate through me, in waves. Then I will settle into its absence, perhaps a little warmer with the memory of the vibration. Supposedly I'll wake up one day soon and my lungs will open as sails do in a high wind. I won't need to worry that singing will cause *renewed dehiscence*. Or that there is something dangerous about my daughter. Something inherent, that she cannot control.

The doctor couldn't tell me exactly how long this process of healing would take though. Every body is different, she said. Our estimates only exist because people ask for them.

To fear my own child: a ridiculous thought. But in this case, not without its reasons, its precedent.

John woke up when he heard me and the doctor whispering, and he said, "Oh, Lu." I thought he was just happy to see me, happy I had opened my eyes. But then I blinked and saw him afresh—there was something fragile in my husband that hadn't been there before. John tells stories, is sarcastic. He makes the world what he wants it to be. It troubled me to see him that way, unable to hide his pain.

He ran a hand over his face, heavily. As if to pull it off and replace it. His smile was strained. *Why not?* I thought. He had every reason to be uncomfortable—the discs of his spine crushed by the awkward chair he'd slept in, the plain dumb fact of where we were, and why.

Still, I couldn't help but worry that maybe the doctor had been waiting to share something with me. Some terrible news.

"She?" My lips trembled as I spoke. I was tired, I realized. Still so tired. "Did you see her?"

John looked at the doctor, his head cocked to the side, in a way I didn't like. He came over and crouched beside my bed, lay his chin down on my arm so he had to speak through his teeth, with the weight of his skull bearing down on his jaw. I held my breath.

"Every piece just where it should be. She's a trouper."

"Oh." I closed my eyes in relief. I wanted her there in my arms, but I wasn't sure I could hold her. My head was so light on my shoulders. So heavy on the pillow. Kara was barely real to me yet, but I knew that first I wanted her safe.

"Sleep would be a good idea." John took my hand, kissed it. "And sweet dreams."

I was already halfway gone, the swell of my exhaustion rising up and drawing me towards a black slumber. But a thought flashed into view then, just briefly.

"Is Ada here?" I asked.

If John hesitated, I couldn't tell.

"She was," he said. It was a sensible reply. And with sleep there to take me, I had no time to mull over its vagueness, or the guilty sound that hung, hangdog, under it.

*O*h, *Lu*. I should have known there was something more; should have heard it in the long woe of the *Oh*, the *who* inside my name, *Lu*. But I fell asleep and didn't wake up again until the next morning, when I found a face hovering inches from my own under the hospital lights.

"Just checking, sweetie." The nurse, I realized, was holding my wrist, measuring my racing pulse. I'm not certain if it was her touch that jarred me out of sleep, or something in my deep unconscious. After all, there was nothing between them—the tension of incomprehension and the tension of awareness.

When she was sure my heart could withstand the rate at which it was pumping my blood and had satisfied herself that I was not about to swallow my tongue, the nurse brought me a cup of water and instructed me to sip, to cool me down and to help the saline drip in rinsing the anesthesia from my system.

"People fight the drugs," she told me. "That's what gets your pulse up so high; you're reacting against it like a virus. Except"—she paused in thought—"sort of psychologically."

It didn't feel psychological. My limbs grew lighter and heavier of their own accord, and my stomach churned what little water I'd been able to swallow. John was gone, though he'd left his jacket balled up on a bedside chair.

"My husband," I said. "Is he with the baby?"

"Oh." The nurse wrote something down on a clipboard. "No. Well, I'm not sure. But I think I saw him somewhere with a phone book. The funeral home, you know." She pinched her mouth up. "You poor thing."

The room was so pale, the light so white-green, that for a nauseous second I wondered, *Am I dead?* I lifted one hand to my cheek and ran my fingertips over the surface of it. Tiny prickles, the heat of skin responding to skin.

So I was alive. But then why did John need to plan a funeral?

"Where *is* the baby?" I asked, my voice small.

"Still in the pediatric ICU." The nurse picked the cup of water up off the tray beside my bed and stuck the straw between my lips. "Drink. Yes. One more sip. All right." She set the cup back down and sighed. "Honey, do you remember anything that happened?"

I shook my head.

"Well," she said, "from what I hear it was kind of a mess. Your husband thought the baby was coming early, and the doctors thought she was coming late"—I cringed, since I was the one who'd lied about my due date to John—"and he called your grandmother, and that's when things got all helter-skelter."

Ada had blown in faster than seemed possible—"Like she was waiting right outside the door," the nurse told me—and she and John got into a shouting match. The nurse didn't say what about, and I didn't ask. I breathed up towards the ceiling of my room, where a water stain bloomed out from the corner. Rusty orange with hints of green.

The pitch of the argument had risen, apparently, until Ada tried to push her way into the area where the doctors were attending me. She was surprisingly strong for, as the nurse put it, *a woman of a certain age.*

Then it all happened at once. Perhaps she caught sight of my body, torn open, blood red. Perhaps she saw Kara and mistook the tubes and monitors for more than just precautions. There were shouts. She fell down. And though they tried to revive her, it was too late. No hand, no voice, could call her back.

My great-grandmother Greta made it a tradition in our family for the women to sing each new girl into life. Ada always said we were *lending them our voices*, which gave me a shiver, since my voice is everything. After all, it's also been the tradition in our family for the singer, the mother, to lose something.

When I was a child, Ada was the one who steered me to sleep, past fear of oblivion, around monsters in the dark. Baba Ada with her pinned-back hair, Ada with her careful clothing. I remember how her hands seemed infallible to me, psychic: they knew where I would be the most ticklish, knew in which pocket I'd hidden an illicit treat. Ada studied opera from books so she could teach me. Pulled threads of knowledge out of the air just so she could stay one step ahead of the precocious girl in her charge.

And every night while my mother, Sara, robed herself in silk and went out to sing and sip whiskey in bars, or practiced jazz standards with a crackling record player in her bedroom—even after the day she went out and failed to come back again—Ada would tuck me soundly into bed and tell me stories of her own *matka*, Greta, the fierce Polish mother of us all.

Greta, Ada, Sara, Lulu. My lullaby, my lineage.

The Greta I heard about then was a young woman, ferociously proud of the fact that she never shrank from work. With her brown arms she rolled bread loaves, hauled lumber, spanked naughty children. She was equal to the challenge, so common in her time, of a woman's double burden: family and field. She was formidable, tobacco-spitting, knuckle-handed, and when she kneaded bread in her kitchen she hummed. With a baby dandling, she hummed. And when called upon, she could sling a whole calf over her shoulder and bring it, puling, to the slaughterhouse with a song so low in her throat she might be mistaken for a growling bear, dragging her prey to its bloody end.

But there was also something uneasy about the Greta of my childhood, a hint of tragedy and lack. That was what made her so compelling: she had true love, she had power, and she traded it all for the prize of a daughter. Like the *rusalka*, poor wraith in the trees, Greta drained the life force from all that she loved in order to fill a yawning, indefinable need. According to my baba Ada, she made a deal with the devil. According to my mother, Greta's crime was betrayal.

Whomever you listened to, though, it was clear: Greta brought us gifts, at a cost for which there's no accounting. We were destined to daughters, and to giving something up. Ahead of time, we can't know what.

Ada wanted me to sing to Kara and bring her in, bind her to our family's stories. She believed in it quite sincerely, that act. That it tied us together, all the way back to Greta.

Picture the scene: a mother, flushed, serenading her infant. The girl, swaddled, drinking it in. Something passes between them like a bit of fire. You can't see it, but you can feel the heat. They are both connected to something now, to the give and take of history. And it's the mother's singing that has done the job.

Did I believe? Certainly I thought it was a lovely tradition. Like a little religion we could hold in our throats. I agreed that

Kara's christening was the natural time to make an official show of the thing. That much I would give to Ada happily.

But now Ada is gone, and I think, *Still just one step ahead of me?* I look at Kara, sweet one, and I wonder. To bring her into the world I lost my grandmother. If I lend her my voice, can I trust her to give it back? Perhaps not. She might take it, and my life too, in the bargain. Without wanting them or knowing what to do with either.

I want to sing, more than anything. But. I am getting a new sense of the sacrifices required of me.

So I keep our apartment in a state of hospital silence even though John says it's unsettling. Normally he allows me my privacies—if I want to wear green every day for a month, or develop a sudden aversion to dairy, he doesn't make a fuss about it. Just cleans out the refrigerator, trashes the yogurt. After all, he has his own proclivities, which I allow in turn. But this, he claims, is different. I refuse to sing Kara lullabies. I don't hum in the shower.

"I know what the doctor said." Last night, before the storm rolled in, he leaned across the bed where we sprawled with Kara between us. "But she doesn't understand you like I do. As long as we've known each other, you've never gone a week without singing. Maybe not a day. You're going to blow some kind of gasket if you can't rehearse."

I let him stroke my tense jaw for a moment, then pulled away.

"Technically, I'm going to blow a gasket if I do."

"You know what I mean, Lu." John took his hand back. He looked annoyed, suspicious. I closed my eyes and rearranged my head on the pillow, unsure whether I was collecting my thoughts or feigning sleep.

"Yes," I said. "I know what you mean."

I thought about Kara's baptism. The date chosen, the ceremony and the singing planned.

After a few minutes I peeked out at John from between my eyelashes and found him running the back of his fingers over Kara's belly. His love for her is so strong that if I squint I can see it issuing off him in ultraviolet rays, a beatific suffusion of light. Part of me wants to take that love away from him right now to make things easier for all involved. He would be a good father. He is, in general, a good man. But it terrifies me to see that he's ready to give her everything, when he doesn't really owe her anything at all.

And it leaves me wondering: am I?

2

Until my mother disappeared when I was nine, the three of us—Ada, Sara, and I—shared an apartment in Ukrainian Village, a neighborhood of Chicago that has since been taken over by the young and the chic, walking their dogs. Then as now there was a Polish grocery store where Ada picked up items she found essential: spiced sausage, pickled herring, water carbonated by a spring in her hometown in Poznań. But in my memory, the differences between past and present are stronger than the similarities. Instead of twenty-three-year-olds with razor-cut hair, I remember the neighborhood porches populated by old men with piercing eyes, smoking cigarettes that they held, pinched, half an inch away from their mouths. The scraps of conversation that whipped by in the breeze were as likely to be in Polish or Russian as English, and the air smelled like wood varnish, and pickles, and wool.

This is where Ada chose to raise my mother, and then me. In an old world, hidden within the new.

I didn't mind. What child minds a home when they know no other? My bedroom in the apartment was small, but it faced the yard. We didn't have a remarkable garden, since it takes a special sort of madness to do much planting in Chicago, where the winter cold is obliterating and the ground can be covered in snow through April. But on summer nights I could look out the window and see lightning bugs skimming over the lawn. If I sat still, I could hear the murmuration of neighborhood cats as they stalked through the bushes, calling out to prey.

That window was also instrumental in one of my first conscious realizations about sound—that it changes depending on its environment. I must have been very young, maybe four years old, not yet in any formal training for my voice. But I was big enough to reach the window latch and raise the sash, and proud enough of my independence that I didn't mind struggling a little bit to do so. I was singing something silly—a little do-re-me, a trill, a scale. I had to shove the weight of my shoulder underneath the sash to get the right height, and when I did I was thrilled with myself: I stuck my head outside and bellowed my song into the open air.

Immediately I knew: something was different. I was so surprised that I hit my head as I pulled it back in and felt my tongue gulp up against the roof of my mouth. In the safety of my room's four walls, I turned and sang the same few notes, feeling the air rush up from my lungs and strum through my throat. My eyes widened as I listened. Inside, the notes ricocheted like pinballs, without room to open up and spread out. But outside, the sound had space to flex. A C might waver and become a D as it hit a patch of wind and lifted into the sky. A high note, instead of sounding slightly bossy, was clear: it cut like a knife through the traffic and barking dogs.

In a different house I might have been encouraged to take on a wide range of activities. Maybe, seeing my interest in the urban wildlife in our yard, the kind caretaker in my alternate universe would have bought me books on anatomy and helped me articulate the skeleton of a vole from an owl pellet cleaned in ammonia. I could have attended ballet lessons and enrolled in the Girl Scouts, extending my toes into a perfect pointe and earning merit badges for insect identification and a facility for starting fires.

Idly speaking, it sounds nice. But it would have been the wrong approach with me. I'm not the sort of person who benefits from having her excess enthusiasm drained, and I was never the sort of child who got bored easily. It's true that I had a lot of energy. But it wanted focus, not dispersion. If I'd been taught wilderness survival skills, I might be a feral arsonist by now.

Ada knew just what to do with me because she anticipated my love of music before I was ever born. When my mother, Sara, was pregnant and woozy with size, Ada sat her down next to a record player and let Chopin's nocturnes rumble through her. She played Polish composers first—Paderewski minuets, Lutosławski concertos—but soon realized that I moved around more to vocals.

"It gives me heartburn," Sara complained. Apparently I had a special fondness for Mozart and Dvořák and expressed this affinity through acrobatics. I know now what it feels like to be stretched to capacity—a drum skin, a bulging bag—and have your passenger decide to start kicking, so I can imagine my mother's troubled expression as she readjusted to move her ribs out of the line of fire. She would've been reclining on pillows, sipping tea. At some point, when Ada wasn't looking, I'm sure she reached down and gave me a few sharp flicks.

With or without my mother's explicit approval, my cells were coaxed together in arpeggios and crescendos. I was born, much to Sara's dismay, with a large head and a strong jaw, giving my very first scream a breadth and tonality that stopped my doctor in his tracks.

So I'm told. My baba Ada was always big on stories. And her chronicles leaked into my life before I was even conceived, even considered, by way of the people who lived them.

Ada recounted her stories with the unwavering faith of a missionary, and so as a child I never questioned how she came to know so much about what her mother thought and said and did in her absence. The stories about Greta and Ada just existed, they just *were*, like Baba Yaga and the Dragon of Krakow and Peter Rabbit. I cried at night for *more Greta, just one more Greta*, in the small purple bedroom where I discovered my voice, where poster versions of Lucia Popp smiled her pristine soprano smile down at me under a bouffant hairdo.

Greta's story followed a path that wound and split like a road on a map. It diverted into variations, forded streams, ducked through trees. You could step off it and run any number of directions, but eventually, no matter how far you wandered, it ended up in the same place.

A woodland clearing marked with a dark cross.

A blue girl, unbreathing, wrapped up in a shawl.

And here's where the story always started.

"There was a party." Ada perched on the edge of my bed, one knee balanced neatly on the other. I settled beneath the covers and could see the threads of the narrative occurring to her: inspiration weaving together with myth, the certainty of the tale mingling with surprise. "The *fabryka Łozina,* the factory of pianos, invited all the young people by to hear the voice of their instruments and to dance."

She repeated herself often, looking for just the right word. Drifted between English and Polish so that from her mouth I heard them both as the same language.

"A large room. A hall. A loft."

Her tongue tripped from the *l* of *loft* to the *f* in a broad arc, as though saying *lolly* or *lopped,* halfway to *loop.* I was thirsty, but I didn't want to ask for water. If Ada got up, she'd fuss around about something. Find that all the glasses in the kitchen were dirty and tie an apron on with a sigh. Or she'd come back with the water but lose the thread of the story and maddeningly embark on something different. The spit in my mouth was heavy and thick, and every time I swallowed I felt my throat getting drier. But I wrapped myself around Ada's arm and leaned my weight into her. Listening.

She stroked my hair, and then she truly began.

"Someone had swept the wooden floor so it was as clean as it would ever be. The window was tall, *kolosalne,* prodigious. Let us look at it. The harvest moon glinting through the glass. Snips of wire lit up around the room by the moon's beams. Like fireflies.

"Then what do we see? The doors open up and in rush the young people, stamping their feet in excitement. Hitting each other with an elbow, a knee, in their hurry. Young people are always in a hurry, you see, and sometimes it gets them where they're going faster than they ought to go."

Ada smoothed her skirt.

"But our young people didn't know that. They rushed from place to place and looked around. The boys huddled over a table of apples and bread, adjusting their ties, while the girls swarmed and dispersed with—well. They were light on their feet and they chattered. They followed the same logic as birds.

"By chance the bird girls were all wearing blue dresses, and each of the dresses was brand new."

In my mind, these antic girls were clear, tugging at one another's hems and judging the geometry of waistlines, the pristine nature of pressed fabric. Any piece of dirt or dust was carefully picked away by fingernails, which were themselves buffed and polished to a diamond gleam. I could hear the matching dresses flutter.

"Then," said Ada, "came the music. There weren't cassette tapes then, and no radio. So if you heard any music at all it was either an accident—walking by a lucky window—or the music was being played just for you. For your pleasure. In the *fabryka* there was a little bandstand, a stage, with a piano and a fiddle and a clarinet. The players looked into each other's eyes to make sure they started playing at the exact same time. In the space of one heartbeat.

"The sound got under everyone's skin, so the young people were terribly overexcited. A girl and boy cracked their heads together reaching for the same slice of apple, and the whole room burst out laughing. They didn't know what to do with themselves."

Ada unpeeled me from her arm and laid me back onto my pillow. Twitching her mouth into a secretive pout, she leaned an elbow on her knee, her chin on her palm.

"You'll probably want to know, why were they so . . . provoked? Why was every heart beating so fast? The whole room was full of energy. The whole factory was. Up in the ceiling beams, there was a colony of little gray birds, little starlings, and when the musicians played they swept around the roof, going crazy. They beat their wings all at the same time, and the young people could feel the wind those birds stirred up.

"*Shoosh*," she said, sweeping her hand through the air and then smacking it against the other one. "*Boom*.

"And why? Why? No one knew. They just felt their breath coming fast and short. And they decided they should fly like the birds—or at least they should do the next best thing. The boys bowed"—Ada tilted her chin—"and the girls curtsied"—she flicked her chin back up. "And they all flooded out onto the dance floor. Like petals," she said. "Like petals in a rainstorm.

"As the boys and girls danced, the room filled up with the heat of their bodies. Steam curled off the girls' naked shoulders and from under the collars of young boys' shirts. The dancers' faces were covered with little beads of sweat, like jewels, and instead of annoying them it just made them more eager. They shook their hair to get out the water. And they danced two-steps. Foxtrots. Every type of dance they knew. Until the boards under their feet got so hot they glowed.

"Just as the heat was really raging, just as the room was about to flash and erupt into flames, just as the factory inhaled a breath to release up the walls with a *woof . . .*"

Ada paused.

"What?" I squirmed, tapping her leg with my toes through the blanket.

She clamped a hand over my feet and clicked her tongue. Pinched her eyes into slits and peered at me, half smiling.

"Do you really want to know?"

"I *do.*"

"Well, all right. Just then a gust of wind blew the door open with a *bang.* Standing in the doorway was a girl. She wore a dress as red as holly berries."

"Is it Greta?" I asked.

"Of course," Ada said. "Of course it's Greta. And when she crossed the threshold into the hall, the heat was snuffed out"— she licked her thumb and pressed it to the pad of her index finger—"like a flame. One moment the dancers were pink in the cheeks. In the next, they were frozen into sculptures of ice."

I closed my eyes and smiled. Tried to breathe in a whiff of winter air.

"But this forces us again to ask a question: Why did Greta choose to freeze them? What need did she have for such silence, such a chill? They were her townspeople, after all—familiar with her dirty childhood feet and uncombed hair, the wildness of her arms and legs.

"Was she jealous of them for the heat of their dancing? Maybe she was.

"For the townspeople also knew that Greta was a strange girl, who prickled with lightning when she was angry and hummed in time with the bees in the field. But they didn't know her as she was that night, wrapped in red linen and tapping her clean, fresh shoes on the floor. Greta wanted something, wanted it deeply, and she knew that she would never find it by standing on the edge of a cloud of dancers. Outside.

"With the townspeople frozen, she could walk among them. She was careful not to disturb the statues, not to knock against them and upset their precarious balance, send a young girl or boy crashing to the floor. But she got as close as she could without touching. Peered into their faces: the *oh*s of surprise and the tongues stuck out just a bit, with exertion.

"She wanted something, but she wasn't sure quite what it was. So she looked everywhere. At the arch of a foot rising out of a shoe, at the symmetry between the fingers on twin hands. None of the girls or boys in the room seemed quite right though. They didn't have it—this thing that Greta desired."

Ada paused and rolled her shoulders. She worked all day bent over, mending clothing, so I often saw her stretching out to the fullest capacity of her spine—vertebrae clicking unlocked, bones popping away from their sockets. Normally I liked to imitate her, pulling on my joints until the tendons tugged back. But during a Greta story? I had no patience for it.

"So?" I said.

"So." Baba Ada gave one last stretch. "She was angry. Frustrated. Yes? It's difficult, not getting what you want to get. Just as she was becoming really furious though, something caught her eye on the other side of the room. An ice man, taller than the other dancers, slightly stooped. As if he didn't want to be seen."

"By Greta?"

"No. By anyone else. His hair was shaggy, hanging down against his neck, and he looked somewhat disheveled. A little bit wild. But his eyes were warm even through the ice. Greta stood right next to him and held her breath so he wouldn't fog up. The ice man had strong hands and an untucked shirt.

"Greta looked him up and down and then pressed her thumb to his fat bottom lip. Her warm thumb left a print, and the skin stuck slightly as she pulled it away. And then. Can you guess?"

I gave a little scream.

"Just *tell* me."

"All right, okay. As soon as Greta stepped back, the room burst back into its noisiness and its scuffling. The ice man—well, the man—fell to tapping his toes, and he held a hand up to his mouth. The lip Greta touched had a new dark bruise, and do you know what? It was bruised for the rest of his life. Saul knew he was to become her husband, and he held out his hand and invited Greta to dance."

I pulled the sheet taut over my fist and sucked on the knuckle of my thumb through the fabric, imagining my fingers clasped by someone I loved. In my head Greta appeared, standing in front of Saul while the rest of the now-unfrozen girls in the room shook their heads, like colts, to clear them. Her red dress was a blot of blood against the inky blue cotton and twill around her. Saul took Greta in his arms, and the skirts twisted and swayed together, their colors melding, so that from above you might track their movements by the purple streak tailing behind Greta through the crowd.

"What are you thinking about?" Ada asked me. She always seemed to ask after my thoughts when she already knew what they were, seeking confirmation. Or seeking to correct. I sunk my teeth into the sheet, to slice through it like scissors, but my incisors just rubbed blunt and dry against the threads.

"Did they live happily ever after?"

"Hmm." Baba Ada frowned and tucked the covers around me until I was as immobile as a mummy. "Did you think we were at the end of the story? Do you think that's where it ought to finish?"

"Oh." I lay still. "I guess not?"

"Good," Ada said. "Because the most important thing is still to come. Even with the dancers melted and dried off, even with the flames of their dancing banked, the *fabryka* still sizzled. And Greta felt it all over her body. She was awake in a new way, her ears tingling and her spine straight, in the arms of her marked man.

"She looked at Saul's face, which was stern and serious, heavy with concentration. As though he'd never danced before but had been studying the art of it all his life, from afar. His fingertips put just a bit of pressure on her back, telling her which way to turn, which way to move. Greta let him lead her around and around the floor. She closed her eyes.

"And she felt the music. The fiddle yawning. The starchiness of the clarinet. And the piano running lightly, very lightly, over its notes, as a brook runs over pebbles.

"Her heart pounded. Like a knock at the door. *Klapać, klapać, klapać.*"

Ada ran her fingernails down my arm. I shivered.

"Do you know what it feels like," my baba asked me, "to be someone's darling?"

She knew the answer: yes and no. I was her darling, but that wasn't what she meant.

"It's like sinking into a bed. Sinking into a bath. Knowing there is no better place for you on earth. Greta and Saul's feet made light scuffs on the floor, which were swept away by the scuffs of the other dancers. The band played on, and the dancers twirled.

"A drop of sweat trickled down Greta's face, over her forehead from the hairline, between her eyes and nose, to the lips. The heat in the room was once again rising. And now Greta was a part of it, part of a pair.

"This should have made her happy, yes?" I nodded in response to Baba Ada's raised eyebrow. "But for some reason it made her nervous. As she and Saul moved in time with the other young men and women, couples scattered slightly, avoiding them. They seemed to remember, somewhere deep down, the feeling of being as still as stones. Cold to the very center of their bones.

"Greta wanted to dance forever, here in the center of a happy crowd. But you cannot change your nature. If you are a lonely creature, this cannot be undone. Something will always crop up to remind you."

"Like what?" I asked.

"It might be simple. Just a noise across the room. A cry."

"What kind of cry?"

Ada laughed.

"Like you, *lalka*. Like you when you don't get your way. *Wah wah.* When you scrape your knee. There was a cry like this coming from the other side of the factory floor, and it cut through the music and went straight for Greta's ears.

"No one else seemed to hear a thing. Or anyhow, they heard the band playing and that was all. Greta shook her head, stuck a pinky in one ear, but the noise wouldn't go away. Saul looked at her strangely. With a question. But he didn't notice that cry, that wail, any more than the other dancers.

"Greta began to feel frantic. Her heart threw itself against her rib cage as she craned her neck and scanned the room for the source of the sound. But she couldn't see anything out of the ordinary. How could it be? An invisible mouth? An invisible throat? An invisible misery? She was desperate to hear the music, to feel again the simple pleasure of dancing. But she couldn't ignore the weeping, the sobbing, that called to her and her alone from somewhere close by.

"So what else could she do? In the middle of the song, in the middle of the dance, Greta broke away from Saul's arms and ran into the crowd. Saul made a sound of surprise, but Greta didn't turn around. She didn't dare until she could find the cry that was tugging at her heart and still it.

"She pushed her way through the swarm of bodies, knocking girls and boys out of place as she went. And do you know what she found?"

I held my breath. Shook my head.

"There was a *man*. He was wearing a suit as gray as ashes. And he was holding a baby as small as a cat. It was shrieking with all its tiny might, its face red and blotchy with despair.

"Greta stopped. The man saw her and he smiled. As if he knew she would come, as if he expected her. Then he held a finger to his lips and handed her the child."

"Who was it?" I asked.

"Who?" Ada shrugged. "A little girl."

This wasn't the answer I was looking for. I meant, who was the man? The man as gray as ash? But Baba Ada had a hard look in her eyes that didn't invite further questioning.

"Greta held the little girl, and the child's face started to clear. Her mouth nestled on Greta's shoulder, her sack of a body on Greta's breast. And the gray man, standing nearby, smiled.

"His smile was like a lock. As it widened, the child quieted down, and Greta held her more firmly, feeling a sudden need for her slight weight. Where she might have come from didn't matter; this was where she belonged. The rest of the room seemed to disappear around them as Greta pressed the girl to her chest, tighter and tighter. The room was silent. The room wasn't there."

Ada brushed a lock of hair away from my eyes. She sighed through her nose.

"It was a moment of enchantment, *lalka*. But such things don't last forever. There came a tap on Greta's shoulder, and she turned to find Saul standing there, his brow all wrinkled up in concern. After all, she'd run away from him as if he were on fire. It was normal that he might worry about such a thing as that.

"Greta tried to hold the child out to Saul, as an explanation. But she found her hands were empty. The child was gone. And when Greta looked, the gray man was gone too, with not so much as a footprint remaining where he'd stood.

"Saul scratched his head and touched his lip. Greta just stood there. What could she say? But Saul knew better than to ask a woman like Greta to justify herself. He nodded at her. Whatever it was, it didn't matter, he seemed to say. He would be her husband anyway."

I considered silently the meaning of this understanding.

Baba Ada sat with me for some time and at last took my silence for a slide towards sleep. She stood up and crept towards the hall. As she flicked off the switch by the door, though, and set one foot outside, I called her back.

"Baba?"

"Yes, darling?"

"So *did* Greta and Saul live happily ever after?"

"Oh." Ada frowned, leaving me with a feeling I couldn't place. "In a way," she said finally. "You could say they were happy. But every so often Greta turned Saul once again into ice."

"Why?"

Ada slid out the door, so only her head was still visible to me.

"To try and get back what she lost the first time. To make the world bring back that child."

3

Let me suggest that all events begin much earlier than they seem to. The real reason, the first cause, is rarely what you think.

For instance: when you drop a plate, it's only superficially the fault of the floor when that plate shatters. And I'd argue, too, that it's hardly better to blame your hand, hardly better to blame your exhaustion, or the late night spent soothing a child that brought you to that wearied state.

So what about Ada? Did her death really begin in her heart, as the medical report suggests? A muscle choking, a ventricle blocked by debris? Too easy, I think. And yes, one can look a little ways further, to the way she ate or the days she chose to take the bus instead of walking to the store. Or to the cells that made her, the air she breathed, the way the earth turned years before. But as long as I'm speaking for her, I know she would never allow something so mundane to undo her. And in her honor, I can say: her death began in the Sonoran desert.

The request came late: I was to fly into Tucson for a two-night stay and a birthday party in an outdoor amphitheater. A solo performance on a ranch where the air that drifted through my bedroom window would be laced with creosote and the sweat of horses. I was out to dinner in Chicago when my agent called, and John told me to put my phone away. In fact, he implored me. Between my travel and both our rehearsal schedules, we hadn't been able to make time for a dinner out, together, in weeks. But I answered, giving him a guilty look out of the corner of my eye, as he took a long sip from his glass of water and crunched a bit of ice between his teeth.

What I had planned to tell my agent was this: my presence on such short notice would be impossible. There are rules, after all. There is the reality of my calendar. But as Michelle described the stage—which, in either arrogance or prescience, had been erected just for me—my body prickled all over. The scaffolding was warm wood, in a canyon. I could feel the acoustics already, on my skin.

As I say, though, things begin before they begin. So let me start a little before the desert. Let me start with why I was ready to go before I was even invited.

I fell in love with John because he knew how to look beyond the veil of his life and see something ideal. He's a storyteller: like Ada, like everyone I've ever given my heart. Before he moved to Chicago for a spot at the Lyric, we saw each other only infrequently, when and wherever our schedules aligned. There is something about that distance—the rushes together and then apart—that we will never recapture. It was an era, an epoch of sweetness that couldn't be sustained. Once, we walked along the shoreline at Huntington

Beach during a break from an engagement at the LA Phil. The sea beyond us was unquiet, littered with incongruous oil wells.

"Eyesore," I said. John shook his head.

"Nah."

His pants were rolled up, his shoes and socks in one hand so he could step into the water and feel the cool sand. He paused, digging in his toes, and I stopped beside him. A wave rolled in all the way to my calves, eliciting an *oh* as it moved like an animal, up and around my legs. John's hand went to the small of my back, making a counterpoint against the water on my skin.

"It's like . . ." His fingers moved against my spine, drumming out a pattern. "It's not natural, I get it. Like a lightbulb. But those are islands in the middle of the ocean that help me see you in the dark. They make power." He turned to me, smiling at himself. At his own romanticism. "That's magic."

We both dissolved into the water then; that's how I remember it. Just so much sugar on the tongue.

But things change. Or at least they should—a person should. Moving with the tide of life, up and down. Letting yourself expand and shrink as the situation merits. You can become just as stuck in good stories as in bad habits, and then when things don't go your way you fall hard. Tumbling through open air when the wave goes out from under you. I should know.

That night at dinner, before I got the call from Michelle, John had been complaining about his career. He wouldn't call it complaining, just talking. He might even have thought he was being elegiac, telling me about some old tour from years ago. I'd heard it before, but I listened. Trying not to pay attention to the keen in his voice that asked, *What happened between then and now, what changed?* He wouldn't have wanted me to tell him. He would have found it a strange interruption.

You can think about it like this. When singing a scale, the real difficulty is not in hitting the high notes or the low, regardless of range. The recognized test of a voice is its navigation of the *passaggio*: the space between the head, the middle, and the chest. The ability to move between different modes of being.

In a less-experienced singer, the *passaggio* transitions are all too noticeable; they jar like the gear shifts of a new driver. The timbre in the singer's voice stutters and breaks, and the listener— probably incorrectly, but still—assumes they could do better themselves.

John has this trouble, and it costs him parts. Not as noticeably as in a beginner, but still. He takes the easy path into his head voice and ends up in a breathy falsetto that lacks support from his whole body. His whole range of possible sound. And he complains about it, making a case against the world. I know this about John: that he can be hard to listen to just as often as he is dramatic, heroic. A marvelous tenor. I am bound up in it too. My stories exist in his mouth, and I exist in them.

The man who requested the Tucson concert, the man whose birthday it was, had tried to book me before, once or twice. Though this was the first time he'd built me a stage.

"He heard you sing in Paris, I think," Michelle told me over the phone. "He likes the best and brightest, you know the type. Richie Rich." It didn't matter to me, I said. It sounded too good to pass up. An experience, at least. "Just be careful with him," she advised before hanging up.

"Careful? Why?"

"Oh, I don't know." Michelle was quiet for a second; I could hear her choosing her words. "He just strikes me as a collector."

"A what?"

"Never mind." She laughed. "I'm sorry, you're right. It'll be something, I'm sure."

Ending the call, I curled my phone into my palm.

"I'm going to Arizona tomorrow," I said. "Some guy's party."

John speared a long purple bean pod on the left-hand tine of his fork, considering it with more seriousness and focus than it quite deserved.

"You'll have a good time, I bet," he said. It wasn't clear if he was angry or just thinking about something else. A musician of his caliber, though, is trained to control his voice and use it to express whatever emotion he needs in a given moment. No matter what he feels. He bit off one end of the bean and observed the steam piping out of the flesh that remained. "It's nice to be impulsive."

He wasn't done talking, but I didn't know that yet.

After deplaning in Tucson I was shuttled quickly into a Mercedes, plush with black leather. The assistant who'd been dispatched to fetch me handed over a bottle of cold water and asked if I was familiar with horses. She didn't really appear to be listening so much as checking things off a list in her head.

I sipped, then frowned. "Should I be?"

She frowned too.

"It was part of the agreement." Her voice kept an even pitch, but she crossed her legs so hastily that the heel of her boot snagged the cuffed edge of her jeans. Unhooking it with a thumb, she began typing into her phone with the other hand. I waited for a moment, but she didn't look up.

The ranch, it turned out, was inaccessible by car, nestled in a

valley between mountain crags. We arrived at the end of a long
dirt road—the literal end, where the dirt track wavered and
diminished into weeds and shale—and I stepped out into the
sharp desert light, not sorry to be rid of the assistant. Guests were
milling around in the dust, while ranch hands cinched soft leather
saddles onto the horses.

The birthday gentleman, who went by Finn, came up and
kissed my hand. He took off his hat to introduce himself as
the owner of the ranch and wrangler of all the *fine country folk*
around us. Finn's hair was dark and disarrayed by sweat, his
body thick but muscled. A 1950s sort of physique to match, it
seemed, his manners.

"I heard you weren't comfortable on pack animals," he said.
So he had to have a phone, hidden somewhere in all that rustic
apparel. Full of urgent texts about me and my city-slick ways.
"Perhaps you'd prefer to travel by carriage?"

I squinted at him, then at the stone and spiny plants around me.

"Is that even possible?"

"We can make miracles," Finn said. "For your delicate sensi-
bilities. The rest of us are basest cowboys." He turned my hand
over and kissed the soft skin of my wrist.

I pulled away.

"I can ride." This was not true, but I didn't think it could be
very difficult—all the animals seemed sleek and gentle. And I
didn't like the way Finn looked at my skin like it was milk to be
lapped up from a saucer.

His eyes were blue and inscrutable.

"As you wish," he said.

Luckily the horses themselves were mild, because the passage
was not particularly straightforward. There were many dips and
divots in the trail; dry logs to jump over; spontaneous wells in the

sand; and always, Finn riding up from behind me to make some obscure observation. He was a wellspring of information, pointing out the differences between the bleached skull of a dairy cow and that of a deer. The deer's head was smaller and more tapered, but made to look somehow more substantial by still being attached to a ribbon of vertebrae. Finn called the cow a beef, and let his horse clatter its hooves over the half-smashed remnants.

"That one we call Bob or Bobo." Finn pointed to a saguaro cactus some thirty meters off the trail with bubble arms growing off it in every direction. "We like to keep track of the freaks. There's one about fifteen miles that way"—he waved a cupped hand behind him and to the left—"bent over like a horse, with a yucca growing right up through a hole in the middle. Damnedest thing." He nodded to me, just a hint of a smile on his mouth. "Pardon the language, of course."

Finn rode up and down the line of horses, laughing with some guests and favoring others with wild stories, making all of us stop dead and peer into the sun at a coyote loping across the middle distance. He seemed to transform depending on whom he was regaling, and so everyone loved him—a man who could pick people up and make them shine with his own reflected glow. Most of the time he left me alone; I wasn't the only one there, not hardly. But every so often he spotted me and smiled, as if discovering me. Against my better judgment, his attention drew me in. The ebb and flow of it. The rare flashes.

A collector, Michelle had said. I could see it. The thing was, when Finn set his toys back down they disappeared—out of sight, out of mind. That was why I felt new each time he turned in the saddle and met my gaze. In a way, I was. And in a way—even though it meant he forgot me each time he turned his back—I liked it.

That night Finn started a large fire in the brick-lined pit in the ranch's courtyard. The next day we would walk to the amphitheater in the midafternoon, and from there the real party would commence. Although I was not in fact obliged to do more than smile and retreat to my room, I lingered beneath the darkening sky, skirting away from the smoke of the fire.

"*I hate white rabbits,*" people chanted whenever they saw me ducking another cloud. "*I hate white rabbits, I hate white rabbits.*"

I thought they were making fun of me, but the wife of an architect I'd ridden with before assured me that it was a kid's game meant to chase away the smoke. I put a hand up to my throat.

"I just have to be careful. If I inhale too much, I'll sound awful tomorrow." I rubbed my fingers down the crest of my neck, where an Adam's apple would have been on a man. "I can already feel it building up."

"Of course," the wife said. She took a sip of whiskey-laced tea from a delicate teacup. All around us people sat on logs, balancing china plates on their knees while the fire illuminated their faces erratically.

Just as I decided that I ought to sneak away, someone brought out a few guitars, and to my surprise the group converged around them. I thought my presence was just a whim of Finn's—an embellishment, like the china and the beef bourguignon. My concern over tomorrow's performance was half a put-on: it was true that I didn't want to inhale too much smoke, but the show I was worried about would take place in New York a week hence. This was the desert. These were desert people, at a party for their wealthy friend.

As the instruments were strummed and tuned, the crowd reshuffled themselves and began to sing. Country songs, old James Taylor, Johnny Cash. Then they veered towards folk songs, or so I assumed anyway, being unfamiliar with absolutely all of them. The songs seemed tied to the singers' bodies, borrowing rhythm from hands slapping or feet landing against the dirt while couples danced. I settled myself on a stone bench some distance from the fire and watched them. Listened. While two women wove a harmony so sleek I could feel their voices rolling through one another like strips of silk being tied into a knot. While the guitars bantered, and skipped, and ran. While Finn played and sang, a smile opening his face so wide it became another face entirely.

Easy to read. Empty of expectations, save one.

I don't know how long the music went on, but by the time it stopped the cold from the sky had settled down over our shoulders, dampening the fire. I shivered, sitting lonely on my stone bench, and the shudder in my body startled me properly awake. Standing up, I stretched my arms to the stars and shook out my hair, taking one last look towards the bonfire. Finn was sitting with a guitar flat across his lap, the fingers of one hand stroking the strings, the fingers of the other hand muting them. He stared at me and I stared at him until finally the night was so fully quiet that I walked back to my room just to hear the sound of my footsteps falling.

And, when Finn followed behind me, his.

In Chicago, after ending my call, I'd made a show of powering my phone all the way down and tucking it into my purse. John seemed pleased, growing more gregarious as we ate. When our waitress brought over the dessert menu, he asked her for a split of champagne to accompany our almond pra-line macarons.

"To what do I owe this sudden joie de vivre?" I accepted a glass from the waitress but didn't take my eyes off John. He took his own glass, tasted it. Smiled.

"To impulsivity?" he suggested. "Impetuousness? Impishness?"

I couldn't help but laugh.

"Infatuation?" I offered. "The attitude of an infantile, indulgent impresario?"

John toasted me. "Indeed. At your service."

"All right," I said. "All right." We sat quietly for a time, listening to a Bach fugue playing over the stereo and sipping our champagne. I let my gaze travel out the window, around the room, but my eyes kept drifting back to John. His hair was thinning away from his temples, something I'd never noticed. It looked good on him. A slight tightening. But I felt a little hollow pocket in my chest, knowing this was something I should have seen before.

When you're young and your love is new, you map the geography of a person's body inch by inch. You want to know them so well you could make another version of them, one wrought out of gold and filled with light. And so when you touch your lover, you're also molding and reshaping their avatar. This rib slightly lower down. The birthmark higher, above the hip. Later, you don't look so hard. After so much careful scrutiny, you come to believe that you know all the secrets of your beloved's skin and bones. You run your hands over the golden version in your head, thinking it is the real flesh. Thinking you can do everything by memory. We were only four years married, that night. And yet his hair seemed like a revelation.

"I'm going to tell you something," John said.

I raised my eyebrows. "What?"

"Oh, I think the story of the man who'll take you away." He ran a nail down the stem of his glass. "What do you think this time? Zeus the swan, or Zeus the bull?"

A little sigh of relief escaped me, though I couldn't have said why. I suppose I thought he was going to reveal something terrible, something that I could never unhear. After all, there had been times lately when I caught John assessing me carefully, slantwise. Like I was a creature invading his home, which he was afraid to startle.

My touring frequency had risen to an alarming pitch—I flew to a different performance every few weeks, sometimes jumping from one to the next and staying away for a month at a time. More. When I came home, John seemed surprised to find me there, doing what I always do. Lounging in bed, reading a score in a state of undress. Picking a plum out of the refrigerator and eating it.

But the stories of my kidnapping were old standards. John used to tell them often, to make me laugh. When he wanted to say that I was beautiful. A god sees a maiden on earth and can't stand to live without her. Steals her while wearing the skin of a beast and takes her essence for himself.

"Well," I said, "I'm going to Arizona, right? Some rich so-and-so with a ranch."

"Okay." John tilted his head, waiting.

"So the bull, I'd think? Southwestern?" I could see that something about my answer didn't sit right with John. A little frown crossed his face, then disappeared. "Or maybe Greece doesn't translate well to contemporary American landscapes?"

"Not an inspired choice," he agreed. "Maybe it would be better to pick something new. Go down an uncharted road."

He sat back in his chair, tilting it onto two legs in a way that always makes me nervous. One false move and *crash*, we can't come back to this restaurant, ever again. On the stereo, Bach changed to Vivaldi.

"Someplace," John continued, "remarkable."

"All right," I said. But I felt, again, that little shiver.

The wonderful thing about Bach is that his music always says what it means—his exploration, his sense of exercise, is plain in each line of notes as they ascend and then descend in turn. And in Bach's case, clarity is not at odds with transcendence. They are one and the same: a pure thought, a wordless feeling. Vivaldi is more of a piece with the backways and canals of Venice. His tone is light and seems to follow—as his titles promise—the seasons. But under the sunlight of it, under the whiff of clean snow, I've always felt something lurking. People laugh at me when I tell them this, but I maintain that Vivaldi is untrustworthy.

"Well." I spoke carefully. "Like what?"

"We have to decide on the rules of the world," John said. "First of all, you'll be gone there for a long time. Maybe it's even somewhere you've been before?" His eye caught mine in a flash, then flicked away. Sounding me out. If I hadn't noticed what he looked like, what else might I have missed? Submerged signals. Signs of displeasure when I talked about a conductor in Berlin, the broad chest of a basso profundo in Carnegie Hall.

"I go where I'm asked."

"Yes." John let his chair descend with a thump and I looked around, embarrassed, but no one was paying attention. "But who's asking? A, shall we say, rich so-and-so. Debonair type, who keeps a whole storeroom full of jewels to drape around the shoulders of the women he lures in."

"John," I said. But he put up a hand, one finger aloft. *Let me continue.*

"What you see when you look at him isn't the whole truth.

But at first that won't be what's important, because he'll want to look at you. He'll give you a necklace to wear when you sing, one that clasps at the top and bottom of your throat. And there will be jewels—rubies, probably." John raised an eyebrow at me, daring me to critique him.

I shook my head. If we were going to really go for it: "Garnets."

"Ah, ha," he agreed. "Even better. Garnets then. To mark each gulp." John traced a vertical line down his neck, running over the Adam's apple. "A row of jewels up and down, a collar of jewels at top and bottom. That will be your welcome gift."

"Not a very good gift, if he wants me to sing."

"Why not?" He looked wounded, and by way of explanation, I made a choking motion, hands a V on my collarbone.

"Too restrictive."

"No, it isn't."

"Yes, it is." I could feel my blood pressure rising—a dial twisting, turning by centimeters. I wanted John to stop, to look at me and say he was sorry for letting himself get carried away. But he didn't.

"Well, that's just the point," he said instead. Then he smiled. Wide. And with that smile, I felt him pull something out of my hands. The rope that tied us to shore. The mooring. "He'll have had it designed just for you. So it doesn't obstruct your throat, it moves with it. You see? He's a man who likes to watch." He took a drink of water. "Watch you sing, that is."

I stared down at the plate of macarons, which our waiter had slipped on the table unobtrusively. They were arranged beautifully, and I picked one up but couldn't quite bring myself to eat it. My stomach had gone off. Too much rich food with dinner. Too much wine.

"I thought the man wasn't what he seemed," I said. "That was your premise."

"No, you're misremembering." John reached over and took the cookie from me, ate it clean in two sharp bites. "I said that what you saw of him wasn't the whole truth. That doesn't mean that what you saw was a lie. Just that"—he glanced towards the ceiling, considering—"I don't know, he has lizard skin underneath. Or feathers. A reverse swan, if you will. Zeus on the outside."

"I don't know," I said. Drummed my nails on the table.

"Oh?" John licked his teeth.

"You make him sound so wretched, but really, what is he? A rich man who loves music? I've heard of worse."

"Well yes, but—" John mimed my earlier choking motion. "You know. His perversions."

I shrugged. John put his hand over mine. I flattened it against the table, and he flattened his own, to keep the contact. "We're just playing. Don't get upset."

"You don't listen to yourself," I said. "Do you?"

We looked into each other's eyes.

"Well, I'm going to go pay the bill." John stood up and caught the attention of our server. His voice had gone tense, his jaw set. "You come when you're ready."

"You don't listen to anything," I said to his back. "It's no surprise you don't get invited to tour anymore."

He didn't turn. Small wonder.

Outside a group of people walked by, laughing. It was spring, the city beginning to thaw. I sat still and finished the last of my champagne. Considered drinking John's too, but thought better of it. At the front of the restaurant, John laughed with the waitress as he handed her a credit card and signed the slip. To look at him, you'd never know he was angry—would never know he'd ever been angry in his life.

The day of Finn's party I woke up early, the sun softer and warmer in the dawn than it had been the afternoon before. I was alone but hadn't been for long—the pillow beside me was depressed in the telltale shape of Finn's head, and still smelled like him, dust and musk. There was a shape lodged in my throat, making it hard for me to draw normal breath. A heart, beating. A small animal, curled in a ball. I rolled into the hollow Finn had left in the sheets, masking his scent with my own.

The fire, the smoke. I'd known it would cause problems. Sinking into the mattress, I pulled the duvet up over my ears, hoping that a little more rest would clean me out. Wash away all remnants of the previous evening.

On its surface, the ranch was rustic—it told the story of a Mexican hacienda, with small orange and pink casitas dotting the land around the main estate. When I first rode into the courtyard, my gameness for adventure had stuttered, as I imagined scratchy woven blankets and hard wooden chairs. But the antique touches were just for show. One layer down, everything here had been built for comfort.

Still, I couldn't find sleep—still, despite my bed and its deep well of feathers, despite the crisp sheets. No matter how I arranged myself, I was too aware of my body. Tiny hairs crackling on the back of my neck. Ribs abutting stomach and spleen. The memory of a finger tracing a line down my back. I felt too alive, too touched to drift off.

And then there was the issue of my throat, that shadow shape. *Get out,* I thought. But it sat firm, small bean. Silent passenger. With a sigh, I sat up, holding the blanket around my shoulders.

A window beside me allowed in streams of light where a triangle of curtain had been folded back—when? Finn had wanted to show me constellations. Finn had crept out in the morning, perhaps before the sun bled into the sky.

Outside nothing tempered the landscape. Cactus and rock, bone and tree, jutted from the earth where and how they wished. Contradictions refused explanation: the sky through my window was clear, but the sand was speckled with rainwater, the scent of which lay over the morning like a shawl. *What are you doing here?* The question came to me from the air. And I remembered.

The stage. A real reason, a good reason, to have come all this way. To have pushed and pulled John into a fight, and then tumbled down after him, much further than I expected to go.

I pulled on jeans and a long cotton shirt, hasty dress against the wind. My plan was simple, if vague: find the right path and reach my destination. If there was a path, that is. Knowing what I did about Finn, it was entirely possible that the stage was hidden and we'd need to be led there by some sort of native guide. He liked a show. Though at least he had no trouble admitting that. No hesitation about telling you what was a performance and what was real as breathing.

As luck would have it, I slipped outside without meeting anyone else in the hacienda. An hour later and the other guests would all have been out to waylay me. Polite hellos. Curiosity. I'd have had to look at their bodies and try to map the sensations in mine to possibilities in theirs. Like coded words being translated back to ordinary meaning.

A bruised lip. The strange heat on my thighs. My neck, cooler than usual where the wind hit it. And my hair, which felt tugged— my whole scalp loosened. My body raggedy and strange, and beautiful.

That's what I felt, anyway, when I only read the pleasure.

Outside I looked around myself for some orientation. There was a promising path down by the fire pit, and lacking any greater insight, I began to walk it. I had an absconding schoolgirl feeling, of being alone when and where I shouldn't. The roads on the ranch were just brushed dirt, so every step crunched beneath me like crackers in my teeth. But when I looked over my shoulder, no one was following my noisy footfalls. No one seemed to care where I was going.

Shadows fell from the mountains, but to the northwest the desert was already bathed in sun. Elevation changes were rumpled into the hills like clothing discarded on a bedroom floor. Around me everything looked identical and mischievous. Tall spiked spires covered in green leaves, flat paddle cacti spitting needles. If it hadn't been for the path, I would have lost my way immediately in the blur of brush and flora. As it was, I had a difficult time believing that I was making any progress—indeed, that there was progress to be made. A stage, here? Would it sit on top of the boulders, or beside them?

Then I turned a corner and saw it.

The canyon narrowed, funnel-like, towards a passage that was fit only for rib-thin coyotes. In front of this passageway sat the stage that my agent had promised me, embraced by the canyon walls. Posts poked up from each corner like turrets, perhaps to support a canopy that hadn't yet arrived. One half of the structure, still shaded by the overhanging rock, was wet with dew. And on the other side, in the sun, sat Finn. He had a hammer in his hand. A few nails scattered around his feet.

I stopped, surprised somehow to find him there. The stage was supposed to be for me. *Don't be ridiculous*, I told myself. *Didn't you want this?* I brightened my face into a smile.

"Really?" I called out, hands cupped around my face to make a megaphone. "You're building it by hand?"

But Finn didn't seem any more delighted to see me than I was to see him. His face remained blank, officious, as thin wings of discomfort brushed against my neck. Perhaps he had come here specifically to be alone. Here, on his birthday, with his dawn thoughts. Perhaps we were the same in that way. A kinship, but not a fellowship, or a comfort.

My throat tightened up and I coughed.

"Sorry," I said. The shape in my throat twitched, moved. Reshuffled. Finn just stared.

When I was a child, I used to play games, imagining myself transformed into a rabbit or a cat, urging my spine to flex out and my fingers to withdraw into paws with hot, dry pads where my palms had been. I hadn't thought about those games in years, but now I felt the same urge bubbling up in me—to change and become unrecognizable. My arms might fuse to my sides, my legs harden into a single stalk. My body shift until only a hint of my head and neck remained—the suggestion of shoulders that cowboys leading trail rides would point to as a minor landmark. The lady cactus, the canyon ghost.

Finn looked down at his hands and, as if in afterthought, held a nail up to a board and hit it in. Three hits. Neat.

"Since you're here, why don't you sing me something?"

He didn't glance up when he spoke, and so it took me a ridiculous moment to realize he was talking to me. But when I did, something inside me responded to the idea, as it always did. Loosening up, relaxing. Singing, after all, was simple. In that act I had no need to speak, or to remember the night before. I could simply disappear inside myself, go deep inside my body, my voice. Escape, for a short time, the weight of my life.

Become airborne.

I was thinking of the stringy skeleton of a saguaro cactus; Finn had pointed some out on our ride. He said that small animals bore inside the cacti to make hidden colonies, and I couldn't tell if he was joking. But I liked the idea of birds nesting within me, moving through my bones. On the outside, my body would be a fortress, and inside I'd house an army of gilded flickers.

Well, that would *be amazing,* John's reply came to me unbidden, and I heard also his sardonic laugh. The shape in my throat shifted.

"All right," I called back to Finn, then walked to the stage. There was a stairway on the side, just four steps high. I walked skyward. "You want a preview?"

Finn shaded his eyes from the sun. "Equipment test, ma'am."

The boards on the stage were unfinished. It was, I realized, a temporary structure. And no wonder—out here, the wood would degrade in the sun or end up nibbled to scraps by passing animals. Maybe, in time, it would become a nest.

Love is a rebellious bird—so says Bizet's tragic heroine Carmen. She cries out: *Love is a gypsy's child who has never known the law. The bird you hoped to tame beat its wings and flew away.* Just then John, at home in Chicago, was probably waking up for coffee. Using that same thick-bottomed mug he always liked, and washing it out so it would be ready again whenever he wanted it. He used to tease me that I sang like a sparrow, and when he did I'd hit him with things—pillows, a single shoe—because a sparrow has no range. Has no power.

And yet here I was, in the middle of the desert, and all I could think about was birds. A rush of feathers brushing against one another in my mouth, like slips of silk. And then a river of bodies sailing into the air. *Flick-flick-flick-flick-flick.* Leaving something behind so that I wouldn't forget them. A seed. A feather, tickling my abdomen. Or, to call her what she is, a child.

So you see. I was wrong to think that I could run away and make my life lighter. If I hadn't been there, hadn't left John alone to wonder about me, if I hadn't sung for Finn and watched his eyes dance in the firelight, there may have been no Kara. No birth. And so Ada wouldn't have been in the hospital either, wouldn't have fallen to the cold tile floor.

On the ranch, I opened up my mouth and let sound rumble from my deepest well. Not knowing, then, who I was really singing to. *Si je t'aime prends garde à toi!* I thought it was a wake-up call for the sleepers in their beds. I didn't know it was a warning.

If I love you, you'd best beware.

4

I heft Kara onto my naked waist and check the temperature of the shower with one wrist. Among the things I cannot yet do is walk to the gym and swim laps in the beautiful pool there. I pay a considerable monthly fee for access to the facility, though I never use any other piece of their equipment. Why run on a false rubber sidewalk? Run from what? Why lie down on a piece of foam that is saturated with sweat and body toxins, only to lift a heavy bar above my head? The pool, though, is unique.

Sixteen floors high, the gym's building has an atrium on its penthouse level, a bubble of steel and sea-green glass. Beneath this dome is a grotto lined in white and blue mosaic, the water never too warm and never too cool. I asked the front desk girl about their arrangement once: how had the gym's management convinced the building owners to let them install a pool in that premium space? The girl leaned across the front desk, her eyes sparkling. *It was already there*, she told me. They had simply remodeled a bit, adding new tile and revamping the showers.

Baba Ada used to take me swimming with her at the YMCA—not as plush, but it was enough. She sat on the concrete edge of the pool and tucked her hair into a bathing cap, swung her arms around a few times before sliding into the water. Instead of letting me run to the shallow end and splash around with the other children, she insisted on keeping an eye on me. When I was very young this meant sitting on a chair and watching her curl into a ball below the surface, pushing off the wall like an otter. When I got older, it meant pacing her in the next lane. Each stroke I swam could be counted into measures and bars, a slow crawl allowing me to play out a cello sonata, breaststroke popping like tango.

Sopranos are not, as such, required to be beautiful. But I've never found that it hurts to keep my limbs slender and strong, darken my eyes with liner and just a smudge of shadow. Swimming is part of my life's rhythm. A legacy from Ada. But it's also—how did the doctor phrase it?—*taxing*, and so for today, this is the best I can do in terms of water. A warm shower in the morning. A hot bath at night.

Kara's mouth is open as I step under the stream, and she widens it slightly, closing her eyes and screwing up her face. Her forehead wrinkles with a special intensity as she's drenched, and I turn so that my own back occupies the majority of the flow.

"Shh," I say, jogging her gently up and down. This is good practice. After all, in another week she will be baptized, a priest cupping cold water over her skullcap. Perhaps if we spend enough time in the shower beforehand she won't be daunted.

As it's planned, I'm supposed to join the choir at the ceremony, which I gave Baba Ada free rein to arrange. When she told me this I shrugged—I'm more than proficient in "Ave Maria." But she made her preparations, and I agreed to them, when I was only halfway through my pregnancy. When she was still alive, and I thought I would sing to Kara, lullabies and arias, from the very day of her birth. Now I think about my lungs and twist a bit, trying to feel them behind my ribs. I take half a breath and huff it out, part of a warm-up I've used since I was six and enjoyed pretending that I was a dragon. It doesn't hurt much but sends my pulse racing anyway. I imagine walking up the nave of the church and splitting in half across the altar.

At this moment, my *babenka*'s body is in the ground. Not festering, as we had her cremated, but still buried. I found it very hard to believe that the small box of ashes they gave us was *her*— even if we all lose some essence at the moment of death, it didn't seem to weigh enough.

I was in the hospital for six days, and when I was released we went to visit her in the mortuary, where she had been arranged and clothed and powdered. Apparently they do these favors even when a body is earmarked for fire—that, and keep it in cold storage up until the very hour of its conflagration. We were nervous on the way over, as if by waiting even those few days to present the baby we'd violated the basic rules of decorum. When in fact, bringing her at all was unusual, at least according to the mortuary staff. John called ahead to let them know we were coming— polite, it seems, in all circumstances—and when we arrived we were ushered into a small room that was not unlike a suite in some anonymous hotel. There was even an electric kettle and a selection of inexpensive teas. Baba Ada had been laid out on a table, wrapped up to her chin in an acrylic comforter that matched the wallpaper. Green and gold whorls. I laid my head on her chest, and it crinkled. A plastic, stuffed animal sound.

Tissues had been provided for our convenience. The institutions of life and death are nothing if not thoughtful, prepared.

I barely remember her funeral. John says it was lovely, but

then again he arranged the whole thing—amazing how quickly an event of that size can be thrown together, when needed. I do remember that it was cold. The doctor recommended that I be wheeled up in a chair, since there would be a fair amount of standing and moving about, and I was still quite freshly opened. So Kara and I sat wrapped up in our respective blankets, just two bundles taking condolences from a faceless line of mourners. You'd think some great and specific accident had taken place. Ada dead. Me, near crippled. And then this baby, hale and pink, but totally helpless. Lying in my arms as heavy as a handbag.

In the shower, Kara begins to squirm. "Shh," I say to her again. Her many layers and rolls are slippery, and for one heart-stopping moment I feel my grip slide. Kara cries out just twice, warning shots fired across the bow, and with great difficulty I kneel down, resting her in my lap as I grope for the bath tap. From this angle I can see the majestic difference between *then* and *now*, the way my stomach slopes and bunches in new patterns, my skin the color of sickly milk. The angry scar.

When I was nineteen, in a hotel room far away, I stood in the shower with a man twice my age whose hair streaked dark beneath the water. We were in Rome, and he was a stranger, more or less. He had spotted me from the audience of a performance of Massenet's *Cendrillon* while I pranced around as one of the spirits who send the opera's lovers into an enchanted sleep. A minor part, but I caught his attention. His hands ran down my slick side, over my ribs, and into the hollow of my waist.

I can't remember his name. Perhaps I could if I tried.

He whispered to me and I closed my eyes so that the water seemed to be rain. Soft and warm, his voice tickled the coiling hollow of my ear, brushing the small hairs deep inside, near the drum. What did he say to me? Only silly lovers' nonsense. *I'm totally disarmed, I'd give you anything.* What did he do, when he wasn't wooing young women in the dark of night? I never knew. He might have been a banker, a preschool teacher, a surgeon. *I'm naked of myself,* he said. *You have everything. I don't want anything for myself anymore.*

Later that night I climbed out of bed onto my toes. Hair still wet and starting to curl. He slept, the stranger, his face crushed against the pillow, while I pulled on snagged silk stockings and tugged a dress down over my nose. I picked up my purse, made sure my own hotel key was inside, and left him sleeping, empty and new.

Now I clutch Kara, water rushing around my feet and down the drain, and beneath me my legs quiver with the unaccustomed strain of crouching. Resting the heel of my hand against the rim of the tub, I hoist myself into a standing position and wrap a towel around Kara, tufting it up the back of her head. I'm not sure if I've ever felt so keenly the various strengths and pressures of my toes against the ground, the balls of my feet against the tile. I could easily slip.

For some minutes I stand still, taking shallow breaths, afraid to move lest we both fall down.

My daughter's face reminds me of past lovers. How do you live with that? How do you let yourself feel that complicated rush of adoration and not lose your mind? It happens every day, every time.

And of course she also calls to mind the better people I have known, the ones who wouldn't cringe away from the task of singing to a newborn baby. The ones who were glad to sacrifice what they had so their children could live. Kara and I, we go on in spite of them. We breathe the air they gasped out with their last exhalations, swallow their dust by the happy accident of being in the world.

So, I tell myself, *think of a lesson. Something Ada taught you about living.* I remember being six and frankly annoyed that my *babenka* had signed me up for the children's choir at a church in Pulaski Park. Up to that point I'd only sung for her or my mother at home, and I wasn't entirely sure that music should be so widely shared. Not when it made me feel so open, so undone.

"It will be healthy for you, darling," Baba Ada told me, "to sing in front of a crowd. You need to learn presentation."

She was right. Sight and sound have a natural link, since sound is a primal trigger, an indication of where to look for signs of danger, water, food. We peer into trees to find hiding predators and watch dancers to see how their limbs correspond to the strain of a cello, the beat of a drum. A deaf man, if properly trained, could track the progress of a song by the flicker of a singer's throat, the clench of muscles around lymph nodes and collarbones.

But I was young and single-minded and didn't want to learn. Walking from the train on the way to my first rehearsal, I dragged my feet, scraping the toes of my once-polished Mary Janes. It was March, and gray snow still gathered in the corners of the streets where it had been thrown by snow blowers over the course of the winter. The sidewalk was perpetually wet and salted, and my shoes were already near ruin, white-streaked and saturated.

Baba Ada seemed to have decided to ignore my attitude and walked in brisk steps, her nose pointed upward into the crisp air. She held my hand, my cotton gloves sticking against the mended suede of her own. And she quizzed me on sounds, quick, like a drill sergeant.

This was a game Ada had devised, based on her assumption that my whole body—mouth, lungs, brain, and tiny ear bones—had operated as a precision instrument from the time of my birth, and perhaps before. Very likely she whispered to my mother's pregnant stomach and listened for phantom reactions, as if her very hope was sonar.

The game was simple. If we were sitting in a restaurant and someone accidentally struck their knife against a glass, Ada would turn to me with an expectant gaze until I said "B minor?" Or whatever the note might be. That was how I won.

Perfect pitch, to Ada, was part of my birthright, written in my blood. Which wasn't to say I could be casual about it. She was irritated if I hummed a song just a shade flat in her presence, even if I was mimicking something I'd heard on the radio. And since she was proud, she liked to show me off. In church I named the organist's key changes; walking down the street with Ada and one of her friends, I called out the different pitches of car horns. People laughed and admired me and handed me candy. Adults, anyway; none of the hauteur or exactitude I learned from Ada earned me many friends at school. But I didn't mind, because I had her. Once, when I was ten, a waiter in a café dropped an entire tray of glasses near our table, and when the shock in the room wore off I said to Ada, "Shostakovich?" She stared at me for a moment and then laughed so hard her eyes leaked tears, which cut tracks through the pale powder on her face. Then she signaled the clumsy waiter back and ordered a piece of chocolate cake, which we shared, occasionally breaking into renewed giggles.

On this day, however, as I sulked along the sidewalk, she pointed to things—a squeaky gate hinge, a bookshop's entrance bell—without so much as a command, and I named them in an insolent monotone.

Near the entrance to the small rehearsal room, which we

reached by way of an alleyway door and a dusty hallway that wove through the church, a round-cheeked woman stood, taking names as each participant arrived. She was particularly tall, milling around with the adult chaperones, so I could see the ribbed archway inside her mouth when she threw back her head and laughed. In the middle of such a laugh, without warning, she sneezed three sharp reports from her nose, and I felt a creeping sensation up the back of my neck. I turned to glare at Ada, hoping that my expression would communicate something cutting. *See, I'm going to catch my death of cold.* But she just shooed me forward.

I placed myself on a low stool and watched the other children. The boys had formed a pack to one side, leaving only their backs visible from where I sat. The girls simply looked uninterested— one was zipping and unzipping her jacket, while another slowly unraveled her glove.

"All right!" The sneezing woman, who seemed to be in charge, looked at her watch and walked to the front of the room, hopping up on a small wooden box. "I'm Mrs. Baker. You can call me Noreen, or Noree." She beamed at us and wiped her nose with one finger. My stomach pinched slightly, but I stayed still. *Baba brought me here*, I thought. She must have known this woman, must have trusted her.

"*Hi, Noree.*" The children around me all spoke in unison, as if they'd been prepared for this exact interaction, this bubbly woman standing before us. The boys had assumed seats, interspersed with the girls, and looked calm and composed.

"Now tonight we're not going to start with anything too tricky. Remember, we're here to have fun." I shifted in my seat. "I know it's almost springtime," Noreen continued, "so first I thought we'd do one of my favorites. You might know it. It's called 'I'll Be a Sunbeam.'"

As she spoke, Noreen hopped off her box and walked around the room with a stack of pink and yellow mimeographed papers. She handed one to each child and gave a few to the adults who were shifting from foot to foot in the back of the rehearsal space. My paper was yellow and slightly smudged. It smelled like old silverware. In the top right corner was a picture of a grinning sun, and below that was a list of verses intercut with the chorus.

Ada was only beginning to teach me to read, but I didn't need to read to see that something was wrong. I raised my hand.

"Yes, sweetheart?" Noreen smiled at me and bent down, putting her hands on her knees. I tried to lean away imperceptibly, but this only caused her to move closer.

"Where's the music?" I asked.

"Honey, it's right there in your hand."

"No, it's not."

"Yes, honey, it is." Noreen reached out and took the page from my fingers, wagging it in front of me. "See?"

I pinched my lips together and nibbled on them slightly. Ada was always telling me to be polite, but she never let me talk nonsense to her either. And this woman was talking nonsense.

"That's just words."

Noreen stood straight and looked at me.

"What's your name, honey?"

"Luscia."

"Well, Luscia, what a pretty name. You see, these are the words that go with the music. So I'm going to play the piano, and we'll all sing these words along and make the song. Okay?"

She smiled at me again, and I could tell she thought that I didn't understand. But as I glared with all my childish might, her face took on an aspect of bland menace, something shifting below the surface and recategorizing me as trouble. Noreen gave a short nod and turned back towards the group, opening her mouth to give further directions.

Well, fine, I thought. Or something like it. Some inarticulate, foot-stamping approximation of indignation and despair. If she wanted trouble I could certainly provide it.

My hand shot, shaking, back into the air, but before Noreen could so much as acknowledge it, it was grabbed by a larger, softer version of itself. Baba Ada stood beside me, looking severe, and tugged me to my feet. She turned to Noreen only when we reached the door.

"My apologies. We seem to be in the wrong place."

"Where are we going?" I asked, once we were safely outside, safely on the train. My relief at escaping *Noree* and her sickly sweet voice had left me briefly giddy, and now I felt exhaustion creeping up. I was also a bit nervous, having openly and publicly defied my grandmother, rendering dead her plans for my choir career.

I had expected to be dragged straight to my room and left there to think about what I'd done. But we didn't seem to be heading home. The car creaked below us and I leaned my face against the cool window, watching brief snatches of apartments appear and disappear as we barreled past. People's lives, here and gone.

"What a revolting woman." Ada sat beside me and squeezed my wrist. "Although," she said, looking down at me, "you knew perfectly well what that sheet of lyrics was."

I took my hand away and fiddled with the collar of my coat, so it pushed my scarf up, warm over my chin.

"I thought you might enjoy it." Ada spoke as though in

response to something I hadn't said. Her brow was knit. "Your mother thought so too. We should have known."

"Mama did?" My mother's moods and choices seemed to come like weather, blowing warm, then cool, then gray. She could, even then, be gone for days at a time, and I held any scrap of information about her close to my chest in the hope that it would lend some sense to her inscrutable patterns. Stretched-out hair ties left on the sofa arm, a broken teacup thrown in the trash: they were all meaningful to me. But Ada, who understood her better than I did, wasn't interested in my archeology. She gave me a look, and I changed my question. "Known what?"

We skittered past a brightly lit series of brownstones, and I made a mental list of what I saw. A man swirling something in a glass. A dog curled up on a blue couch, alone. Two women standing front to back, one pulling up the zipper on another's dress.

"That little group." Ada gestured upward, away. "Such a silly thing to do. You don't need anything to belong to." She put her arm around my shoulder. "You're already part of something bigger."

I saw a mostly dark building with one bright room. It appeared in the distance like a beacon and seemed to grow warmer and warmer as it approached. A radiant den in a stone tomb. Just as we slipped by, I saw there were gauze curtains hung across the window frame. Light blue curtains, moving slightly, as though unsettled by the train. I was seized by a sudden urge to reach out and touch whatever lay behind them, because it was alien, because it wasn't mine. But though I looked hard, the world behind the curtains remained indistinct, and we were gone too soon for me to see if I could peer into the space between them.

At some point in our ride I fell asleep, my cheek crushed

against the hard plastic window frame. I awoke to Baba Ada pulling on my elbow, ushering me quietly to my feet. In sleep I'd tucked myself up into a circlet, knees and hands all compressed into my coat for warmth. The train's lights flickered momentarily off as we pulled up to an elevated wooden station, and I stood on creaky knees, trying to maintain my balance.

"*This is Lawrence*," declared the car's speaker.

"Hmm?" I asked Ada.

"I had an idea." She tightened her grip on my elbow, and the cold night air rushed around us. When we reached street level, she stopped and instructed me, "Close your eyes."

I was still only at the edge of consciousness and followed her lead through the streets as through lukewarm water, not really paying attention. Ada took care that I didn't slip on black ice or ever feel the looming of a mailbox or parking meter in front of my forehead, and I trusted her to do it. As though she were my own subconscious, ferrying me across the boundary of sleep.

"Keep your eyes closed," she said, as my senses were enveloped by a sudden breath of cigarette smoke and body heat and human noise. "Stay here for a second."

I stood blind and still in the middle of a wooden floor, swaying with the crowd, locking and unlocking my knees. "Who's that?" I heard from a strange voice nearby, making its way out of the general bubbling of conversation. But if a reply came I never heard it. Ada returned and took my hand again, guiding me forward. Whispering, "Excuse me, excuse me," I brushed by soft, invisible bodies. I banged my knee on something hard. And then I found myself seated in a too-tall chair, instructed to open my eyes at last.

It was still like a dream. Except that around me every face was amused, as though my presence was some wonderful joke. I was in a large and low-lit room, surrounded by tables full of men and women in evening clothes, facing a stage. Behind me, as I saw when I craned my neck, stretched a long rectangular bar, backed by mirrors and stacked with many-hued bottles of varying heights.

The conversation stilled and the hushing of a drum brush called my attention to the front of the room. Somehow, without my noticing, a band had taken up residence in front of the red curtain. A bassist leaned against his upright, picking his teeth, while the trumpet player and pianist opened up the room with a low tune, tossing handfuls of chattering notes out over the drumbeat. The bassist cracked his knuckles and started plucking away, layering his soft *haum haum haum* under the present melody.

And then she came, slipping out from a slit in the curtains I hadn't seen. Her dress green and shimmering with sequins. My mother slunk across the stage, saying hello with her hips. She leaned briefly over the piano, hopped forward with a smiling "Oh!" when the bassist plucked out a few loud notes behind her. She hummed along with the song, audible even though she trapped the music under her tongue, feeling it out like a hard candy.

"*Mama*," I said under my breath. She didn't see me, and didn't hear me. Instead she sang and tossed her hair—just a lock at a time over her left shoulder, as though keeping inventory or marking time. As the song rose—crescendoed, ascended the scale— she ran her hands, fingers open, down her hips and then lifted them slowly into the air with upraised palms. I felt the song invade behind my shoulder blades. Imagined her fingers on my cheeks.

"I thought this might be a better way," Ada whispered. Her breath a distraction, a hot intrusion in my ear. I twitched away from her, but she leaned in and lifted my chin to her face. "Now you understand." Her voice was firm. "Presentation."

She tilted my head back towards the stage, using her thumb and index finger.

"Presentation."

When the song was done, my mother melted back into the curtains, barely moving them as she slipped through. And we all sent our hearts back with her.

Some of my memories are like this, half soft, half sharp. My whole small self leaning towards the stage, leaning towards the invisible whatever that lay behind it, hiding my mother. My mother, most beautiful, who is never in my mind without bringing her whole complicated self.

She is awash in connotation. She is transforming. She doesn't exist. She is the only real thing in the world. How can I still feel this way when I'm a grown woman, with my own child? It was the hidden truth of my life for so long—this love, this longing. Ada knew better than to let me bring it too close; even the night of her great *presentation* she kept my love on a string. Led me with eyes closed, ushered me to bed before my mother stumbled home.

But now Ada is gone. And the doors she guarded are coming unlocked. Who was Greta, really? What did she mean? And where did my mother go, and why?

5

Greta and Saul married in late fall, in the middle of a rainstorm. Ada told me about it every year on the anniversary of their wedding—November 15. It was important, she said, to understand that Greta and Saul were in love in light of everything that came after.

The rain that day, according to Ada, was strange. It obscured the entire sky, including the clouds, with its sheer weight and its audacity. People huddled together inside, but the rain infiltrated after them. It slipped through their walls in the form of a mist and clung to their clothes, dripped on the floorboards. Outside the rain fell like sheets of needles, shivering, silver, and sharp. When anyone poked their head through the door to check for signs that the weather might yield, they saw nothing, nothing but those undulating waves.

Until they saw Greta.

If her guests were nervous about going outside, the bride was elated. No one could remember seeing an announcement, and certainly no one had been formally invited, but most of the town recalled catching sight of her, and once they did they were enchanted. Greta greeted the water like a friend and raised her nose to the mineral smell, the clean air each peal of rain left behind. With her white dress hugging her closely, she walked along the black dirt road and made no attempt to cover herself up in the face of the storm.

The pounding of the water on the earth was a drum, and Greta paced its rhythm towards the forest. She didn't seem to mind that she was alone. The cottage Saul had built for them was at the edge of town, and that was where she knew she'd find him. People peered out their windows and watched her go by: a speck of light, a candle flicker in the gloom. The vision of her drew them like the scent of fresh fruit. They followed her hungrily from pane to pane.

For despite its obscuring of everything else, the rain revealed Greta. The cotton of her gown became translucent and sticky, luminous against her flesh. The townspeople could see the curve of her shoulder blades, feel their fingers aching to run keystrokes down her spine. They wanted to pinch her thighs, bite her thumbs, suck the water off her hair. They wanted to blow warm air against her belly and unbutton her clothes, feeling the *pop* of each release. Greta shook her head and shot silver spray in all directions, a halo of movement and mercury. People everywhere opened their doors and walked out into the storm, carrying flowers.

At the border of the woods and the road, Greta paused, halting the crowd that had formed behind her. Everyone was soaked, and solemn. Beyond Greta was nothing but the same gray water, hanging like a curtain that roared and reared. But then there came a light.

It seemed to those looking that Saul had opened a door in the very rain. Behind him glowed the warmth of golden wood, the scent of a cookstove. He stood, perfectly dry, in the doorway and looked out at his bride: a living wave. She bade him come forward and he did, the rain plastering his hair against his head and turning his clothes as dark as pitch. Standing in the space where civilization melted into the trees, he wrapped his arms around Greta and kissed her until she almost wasn't there. The crowd's ears were full of the howl of the storm, their stomachs gnawing with joy and envy. Greta pulled away and placed her thumb on the bruise of Saul's bottom lip. *I choose you*, her eyes said. *You only.* And if it was a half-truth, still hungry for the child lost at the dance, it didn't seem so at the time.

Saul picked Greta up in the driving rain and ascended the unseen steps to their home: just a rectangle of warmth in the storm, an outpost on the edge of the forest. When he closed the door, no one could see where the couple had gone, and they could only throw their flowers to the ground in the hope they'd be found when the sun reemerged.

All day I've been walking into things. My toe slammed so hard into the leg of a chair that I had to set Kara down and grab on to it—I was sure the nail had split, but it did no more than blush purple. I knocked another bruise onto my arm just walking through a doorway, and scraped my tailbone against the corner of a dresser drawer while picking out clothes after the shower. That one bled, red blooming through the flakes of skin as I bit my lip and contorted my spine to get a look. I can never resist inspecting an injury, although until recently I almost never had any to look at. Perhaps wounds have gravity, and draw their own kind. Like the sun draws the Earth, and the Earth draws the moon.

What would Baba Ada think of my sense of presentation today? I laugh even to imagine it, which hurts just a little below my navel. Yes, I put on makeup and blew my hair dry, but my face is only a veneer. I have no control over my body at large, the instrument I've spent my whole life honing. Did Ada know that giving birth would be so disastrous? She must have guessed, must have had some sense of it—after all, she herself was Greta's only daughter, come after three sons and a number of miscarriages.

Proximity between birth and death runs in every family, but it seems to run especially close in ours. Ada didn't like to tell the dark side of a story though. As far as presentation goes, that was her method, her modus. Still, I wish she were here now. I could tell her things that would make her hair curl, and she would listen. I could ask her what comes next, how scared I need to be that these little cuts and bruises aren't the end of my troubles.

Old habits: I half look for her, my baba, perched on a chair or leaning against the door. But there's only Kara, lying on a blanket on the bedroom floor. Burbling as she moves her head—it would be wrong to say she turns it, but it bobs a little, gives a healthy jerk. Her limbs move too, spasmodically. This is what she's been doing all day, either in my arms or laid out somewhere. I almost resent her calm unawareness, the blank canvas of her. She doesn't know that my heart skips every time the phone rings from the other room, as if it were always John, calling to accuse me. Kara could still be convinced to become anything. Anyone's. Whereas my life is scribbled over, a garbled language with no one left to understand it. I miss Ada. Ada, who knew me.

"Let's go outside," I say to Kara. "Hmm?" Making my voice soft.

I pick the baby up, and her back bends gracefully under the pressure of her own weight, muscles too foreign to themselves to support the bones. It's exquisite, how close my attention adheres

to the details of her body. One false move and I could snap something, tweak some tender part of her so it grows awry. Carefully I
bundle her, trying to meditate on each piece of clothing. The soft
knit cap into which I tuck Kara's hair fits snugly down over her
ears, so tight that it seems to promise a bit of extra skull for these
days of early life, as well as a barrier against cold air.

Good thing, too. A gust of wind roars against the window,
which audibly strains. The day is still stormy. A part of me knows
we really shouldn't go out in it at all, but then again, my phone is
still ringing. I think about Greta and Saul, married in a rainstorm.
I think about my own husband, turning up his collar this morning
against the cold.

I think about myself, and when I can't anymore, I think about
my daughter.

Supposedly infants can't see well. The world to them is made
up of dim shapes and vague shadings of light. Not unlike a surgery
patient wrapped up in gauze. Or a theater patron, once the house
lights have gone down, who can half sense that places have been
taken onstage but doesn't know where, or who, or why. *Is that
how things are for you?* I wonder to Kara. She seems to be watching closely enough, more so as she unwrinkles from her time in the
womb and her eyes lose their perpetual sleepy squint. I touch her
cheek and she immediately sniffles towards my finger. I snap on the
other side of her head and she wobbles around trying to get a look.

Not so gauzy then. She is already a creature of sound and
scent, full of anticipation and eagerness. She wants to hear. And if
she hears enough, someday she'll want to speak. To see. To know
everything.

But not yet. For now, there's still just one person I can whisper my secrets to, even if they don't quite reach her. One person
who can tell me if the face I'm showing to the world is the right

one. I need that today, if I ever want to be strong enough to hear Kara's secrets in turn. Otherwise I might keel over, a ship in a gale, no help in sight. I pull the cap more carefully around her ears and enclose her in a downy blanket the color of the sea. Out we go. We're on our way.

To the only place I can think of worth going, right now. To the only person I've ever known who could always see light when faced with darkness.

G reta and Saul were early with their sons. First was Andrzej, towheaded at birth but later dark as dirt. Then Fil, who tagged after his brother and begged to play; Fil who was smattered with freckles and stomping with mischief. Finally came Konrad, blond as a bell ringing.

"My brothers," Ada said, "were a tribe. Always together. They moved with one body, like a herd of deer. They sniffed in the grass, and they butted their heads together, pushed each other around in the yard. Sometimes they nibbled food from the vegetable patch. Just a bite here or there." She slit her eyes at me, sidelong. "Like some other people I could mention."

We were walking along Lake Michigan, summer wilting the grateful city around us. I wore a pink dress, my favorite color when I was eight, and sandals that left white lines on my feet through the tan, as if I'd been born palomino. It had been more than a year since I saw my mother sing at the Green Mill, and in that time I'd developed a sense that my opinions were powerful and important. At school a girl I despised had announced that her favorite color was pink too, and I took her aside at recess and talked to her using my sweetest tones. She leaned closer to me with every word, and by the time the bell rang her new favorite color was gray.

In Edgewater, a few blocks from the lakeshore, there's a grand pink hotel, wedged like a slice of cake. We never went inside, but that summer I insisted on taking our walks up north so I could watch the water glint off the windows. I was waiting for an opportunity to get closer to the ground-floor doors; I imagined finding one mysteriously open and slipping through without Ada noticing. Inside would be a society of magicians who would recognize me as one of their own by examining some insubstantial element of me. The color of my bones. The weight of my lungs. I'd run through the empty hallways, waited on by eager and animate pushcarts, brooms, and pieces of cutlery.

But we never got close enough. Instead we crossed Sheridan, maneuvering around a complicated freeway exit, and then strolled along the large, cracked concrete stairs that border the lake.

"They were good boys." Ada held my hand and stared out into the waves, which smelled like bathwater and diesel. Farther down the shoreline lay a beach dotted with towels and studded with white lifeguard chairs. "Did what their mother asked, mostly. And loved her very much. Very deeply. They were her champions."

"What were their special gifts?" I hopped carefully over the seams in the concrete. If I was going to be denied my hotel, I wasn't going to miss out on the best part of the story. "You said they had gifts."

"Well, *lalka*." She didn't shift her gaze. "They were spirits of the forest. They could disappear into the trees, camouflage themselves in leaves. That kind of thing. Just for starters. But they each had a particular talent. A gift, as you say.

"Andrzej could hear footsteps from twenty miles away. Sometimes we would be sitting on the porch talking and he would tilt his head to the side"—she cocked her ear towards the water—"like this. As though someone were whispering something to him. He could tell the direction a person was walking, and the weight of their body, and even what kind of mood they were in just by the sound of their feet on the earth. *Smak smak*, if you were angry; *flek flek*, if you had something to hide. Anyone else would make themselves crazy trying to hear what he heard. But Andrzej didn't even have to try. Listening came to him as naturally as a heartbeat.

"Fil was shiftier." She smiled. "He could smell anything, taste anything. He'd have made a wonderful knight to a king, because he could have detected poisoned food without even having to take a bite. It made him a fussy eater. But it was useful."

"How?"

"Planting, for one thing." Ada squeezed my hand. "He could always smell water in the ground. And his father, Saul, of course, was a woodsman—he cut down trees to make his living. Saul was already very clever at picking out which trees to cut, to harvest, but Fil could smell an infestation of ants. He could smell a bird's nest in the top branches of an oak and would climb up to pick it out before the tree was felled. The thing about Fil, though, was that he was always looking to play a trick. If he wrinkled his nose and you asked him what he smelled, you had to be ready for him to say it was you."

We walked along the steps for a ways, coming close enough to the beach that I could hear the jingle bells of an ice cream truck. "C major," I said, not to anyone in particular. "What about Konrad?"

Ada stopped at the edge of the concrete stairs, where a series of smaller steps led down into the sand. At the lake's edge, a group of children were throwing buckets of water at one another and shrieking with laughter. For a moment I felt a tug behind my navel. I wanted to run down the steps and onto the beach, letting the dirty sand get in my shoes. I would head straight for the water and dive in, soak my dress, float on my back, and look at the sky. But Ada's fingers were still interwoven with my own.

"Konrad was a beacon," she said finally. "He called things to himself."

I stared at the gang of children. "What kind of things?"

Ada blinked in the sun.

"Light. Animals. If Konrad sat still, he would be surrounded by birds. They fluttered out of the trees and landed all over him—on his shoulders, in his hair, on top of his feet. And he called rabbits. Not"—she looked pointedly at me—"by shouting or whistling. Not anything like that. I mean they came to him. First the smallest creatures, but then larger ones too. Once Greta walked into the woods at the edge of our land, looking for Konrad. She wanted to bring him in to dinner. And she didn't see him in the first clearing, so she went a little farther, and then ahead of her there came a sound. A rumble. A growl. On the path stood a bear the size of a house, and right next to it stood Konrad. His fingers were wound up in the bear's fur, and the bear's eyes were closed. It was, well, *purring*.

"Greta ran towards her son, and the bear's eyes snapped open. The three of them looked at each other for a long moment. Then Konrad whispered something to the bear and scampered into his mother's arms. Greta watched the creature lumber away, but it never turned around."

We ourselves turned to walk back the way we'd come. I stole a last glimpse at the children over my shoulder, as they played on the beach, sunburned across their noses. Loud and ordinary, not one of them looked up at me, content as they already were with one another.

The one thing Greta didn't have in her family of strong sons was a creature of songs. That is to say, a creature like herself. She had never minded living apart in her small town, hearing the whispers of those who said she was a witch, a water spirit. That the songs she hummed everywhere she went would draw men to her so she could drain them of life.

But after the dance at the piano factory, she couldn't shake the memory of the girl she'd held there—a child who had blinked into existence to the tune of a piano. And then blinked back out again, disappearing with the gray man to who knew where. Greta loved her sons, but when she held them she could feel the girl's absence.

She hated being alone in her own home. Saul was a gently giant man, hunched over at the table as he ate his soup, back bent in the woods to avoid hitting his forehead against low-hanging branches. But with his softness came his silence. He regarded his wife with an always-quiet admiration and never got caught up in her humming. In fact, he seemed not to hear it at all: the rhythms, the buzzing, the vibrations in her throat were as nothing to him. They were too insubstantial. He loved her for her weight and heft and hands.

The boys ran relays around their home. They pitched war games and threw mud balls and called up storm clouds and held congress with foxes and elk. Saul dragged trees down and planed off their rigid bark, and the boys queried wood larks, teased the nanny goats in the yard. Inside, Greta baked bread, and to herself she hummed. She took pride in her household and family, but she knew deep down that there was something missing from it, without which she would never be satisfied. Behind the cottage was a small plot of land fenced off near the trees to protect it from wild-life. The grass was so green it was practically purple, and dabbed here and there were spots of white, which, from a distance, could easily have been flower bushes. Saul carved each slim cross him-self, after the wood was consecrated by the church.

Greta vibrated with music, so much that it was hard for her to believe that neither her husband nor her sons noticed it. Some-times Konrad paused in his games when she walked by as though he had been struck by an idea. But he never sang a note, never hummed along with her; for all his affinity with animals, he never caught a small bird and brought it to his mother trapped in his hands, singing. To even want this, Greta knew, was selfish. He was his own child. He had his own path to follow.

The cottage that the family shared was built of redolent pine, the walls always dripping slowly with sap. It seemed to be a sturdy and impenetrable structure, but when Greta was alone and looked around herself she always felt the forest encroaching, the trees returning to reclaim their material selves. Greenling stalks coiled around into the backs of chairs, and trunks like spines erupted from the floorboards: a thicket of men turning their attention to the distance. From the ceiling sagged branches so robust that Greta knew they came from trees almost too large to fathom, and despite the careful chinking Saul had done, wind seemed to slither through the timber limbs.

When they grew out of their cribs, each boy went with his father into the woods on what Saul called a hunting expedition, the purpose of which was to find the boy's bed. They would spend a full day, sometimes two, searching through gnarled branches, assessing the benefits of each possible contender. Andrzej chose a mighty pine because the tree had impressed him in the back-bone of his house, and because upon leaning his ear to its trunk he heard something inside that he chose not to describe. Fil settled on ash after telling his father to close his eyes and then sneaking a taste on the tip of his tongue.

And Konrad, who was often inscrutable, spent two days of fruitless hunting. When his father was nearing exhaustion and despair, a sudden wind picked up and began blowing leaves around the forest floor. Konrad held out his hand and snatched something off the breeze. By the river's edge, he and Saul found the willow that the leaf belonged to, and Konrad hid his eyes behind the roughing knuckle of one hand until the tree had been felled.

During these expeditions Greta stayed near the house or barn, usually wrestling with a new presence in her belly. *What tree will you choose?* she hummed and asked the air. When Andrzej was on his quest, it was a cheerful question; with Fil, uncertain. And by the time Konrad stepped into the woods, Greta's mind sat balanced on a careful scale of fear and joy as she contemplated the red mess of a child coagulating within her. For between each boy there had come a girl, at least one, for whom there had also been a careful selection of wood grain. But instead of a bed, Saul cut the somber boards of a box, inside which each girl would nestle like a jewel while she rested silent beneath the trees.

It wasn't until I was eleven that I realized what these sleeping girls meant. Who they were. They'd shown up in various Greta tales over the course of my life as anything from vital talismans to mere window dressing, their grave markers landmarks on the grassy ground my great-grandmother walked. But from the way that Ada spoke about them, it hadn't occurred to me that they were my flesh and blood—Ada's sisters.

Once the thought came to me, it took up residence. For weeks the dead girls hovered around my head like summer flies; I had to blink them out of my eyes and bat them away from my hair. Anytime I managed to distract myself—slipping bread into the toaster for a sandwich or leafing through the libretto Ada had given me for my birthday—one would pluck at my sleeve until a thread came loose. And as soon as I acknowledged one, the lot would be upon me, whispering their insubstantial opinions in my ear.

The haunting took its toll. I began to toss and turn in my sleep, and the food on my plate lost its savor. Whatever the meal was—pierogi, pizza—it appeared sallow to me, lacking in essential nutrients. My cheeks hollowed out. I looked like a ghost myself.

One day Ada was sitting across from me in the living room of our apartment, correcting my posture as I warmed up with a series of minor scales. She held a yardstick like a conductor's baton, waving it back and forth to keep time. Occasionally she would press it to my shoulders or stomach to make sure I held an erect carriage. This was how I spent my time after school, on weekends. Other girls came over sometimes, but few returned. They made vague noises about being too busy, and most of the time I didn't mind—we didn't have much to say to each other. But it would have been nice to have someone to whisper to about the ghosts.

Baba Ada's approach to my training was unscientific—she encouraged a straight spine that looked disciplined but is not technically correct for singing. At an age when most of my peers were still inventing games with plastic horses and sneaking makeup from their mothers' purses, I was singing Puccini. But the maturity of my voice outstripped my emotions by several years. Inside I was still young enough to want to believe that my *babenka* always knew best.

Today, though, the short wooden flicks began to irritate me.

It was already taking all my attention to focus on the transition from an ascending melodic minor to a descending when my mind kept drifting to the graveyard behind Greta's house. Each tap of the ruler against my abdomen felt like a gentle reminder: *you're breathing*, it said, *that must be nice*. We started every rehearsal session with at least fifteen minutes of scales, and today there seemed to be no end to them.

Ada switched the ruler to her other hand, and in doing so cracked a nail.

"*Matko Boża*," she said under her breath. And she set the yard-stick on the sofa while she went to find clippers and a file. In the meantime, I was meant to take a short rest; this was the agreement made through countless sessions of voice lessons—while the cat's away, the mouse must save her breath. I walked over to the couch and picked up Ada's ruler, flexing it between my hands. Not very strong. With one swift bend, I snapped it.

Baba Ada rushed back into the room.

"What do you think you're doing, *lalka*? Do you think rulers don't cost money?"

I was ready to start yelling at her. To tell her that her rules were crazy and that my posture was fine and that I was tired. But instead my lower lip began to tremble.

"What happened to Greta's daughters?" My voice came out in a whisper. "Her *other* daughters?"

"Oh." Ada looked surprised, turning the nail clipper over and over in her hand like there was some important part of it she was missing. "You're worried about that?"

I nodded. Ada walked over to the window and looked out of it, and for a little while I thought she wasn't going to answer me at all. My anger started to heat back up, but before it could boil over, she spoke.

"Konrad used to pick flowers for them."

"What?"

"Well, they all did. Konrad and the others picked flowers, and Greta buried the girls in their own little yard and kept them safe." She turned towards me and looked thoughtful. "Except one. But you know that. It's part of the story."

It was true. The girls' graves, the boys' gallantry—all that was part of the story. I troubled each piece smooth over time, from Greta's appearance in the factory door to her fight for the sacred ground of Poland when the war came. Ada told me her mother was a warrior, and that when she was tired she went and lay down with the girls underneath their house, ready to wake up again when the time was right. Safe and protected.

All this should have comforted me. It had, in fact, many times before. But today something nagged at me. The ghosts, who wouldn't let me go.

"So where's Konrad?"

Ada just blinked at me.

"And Fil? And Andrzej? Where did your brothers go? Why aren't they here?" *If Greta is safe*, I wanted to ask, *and you're safe, why didn't she save them too?*

My baba pressed her lips together, considering. "Darling," she said. "I think you're trying to put me off. I think you don't want to practice your scales."

I shook my head. She knew that wasn't true. Her eyes told me so.

"I think you need to go to your room and think about what you're saying. Maybe when you come back out you'll be ready to practice again, like a good girl."

We stared each other down for a moment; then I spun on my heel and ran out of the room. Lying on my bed, I did exactly what she asked—thought about my questions, and thought about Ada's answers too. All the girls, buried in the yard. All the girls, safe with Greta.

Except one.

It's unsettling to think that I'm still looking for my lost family all these years later: one more of Greta's daughters tucked into the soil. I know it's crazy, but part of me thinks, *There'll be a sign*. Ada wouldn't just leave me. As I step outside the apartment building, my phone rings again from the bowels of my purse, and I think, *It's starting*. I answer without even checking the caller ID.

"Lu?" On the other end of the line, John sounds frantic. "Are you all right? I've been calling."

"I'm fine." I feel a little numb—just John. What did I expect? "I was in the shower."

I hear him sit down as he says, "Oh," and can in an instant imagine him exactly. On break from rehearsal, hiding from the elementary school audience in the singer's greenroom, sitting on the old leather couch. Stirring honey into his midday cup of peppermint tea. His flushed cheeks. The chintzy tinkle of a cheap steel spoon in a microwaveable ceramic mug. He never really liked children before Kara was born, which is one reason his sudden devotion to the image of our perfect family unnerves me. That, and the fact that it can't last. Once the truth is out, then what?

"Well," he finally says, "any plans for the day?"

"Yes." I readjust Kara with one hand, tuck the phone between my chin and shoulder with the other. "Ada."

"What?" Concern creeps back into John's voice.

"We're going to see Ada." I pause, letting him think I'm crazy. "Bring flowers." I pause again. "To the *cemetery*, John."

"Today? In this?" I imagine him gesturing to the weather, which, from his windowless room, he can't see.

"We'll be fine."

John hesitates.

"Be careful, Lu," he says. "Be gentle with yourself."

He has no idea how much loss a person can stand.

Of course, I haven't lost him yet. So maybe neither do I.

6

Kara's infant form switches around in every Greta story; she's bundled up inside them like a tiny egg. In Greta you can see us all, descending from her like wooden nesting dolls. But when I was a girl I thought the view stopped with me. That when my baba Ada braided my hair or led me through scales, I was the last note in the song, the last line in the tale. The little queen our family machine was built to make.

In her time, my mother, Sara, thought so too. I couldn't know, as a child, what a surprise I'd been to her. All I saw was that she was suspicious of me. That she wanted to keep me close, but didn't know how to stay.

If she was bored she picked up my hand, so much smaller than hers even I could see it was delicate, and clipped off the raw, smiling ends of my nails. If she was in a good mood, she'd file them down with her many emery boards, each possessing its own subtle use. And she'd pick a candy color she felt suited me and paint my nails until they resembled jelly beans.

"Okay," she'd say. "Now blow on them. And don't move. You can't move until they're dry because you'll muck around with something and mess them up." Then she'd frown. "I'm not doing this over again. So you'd better keep them neat."

So I would sit. Sara disappeared into her room or out into the day, but I remained perfectly still, to show her I could. When Ada happened by—ten minutes later, sometimes an hour—she would find me in my small wooden kitchen chair, practicing my mother's frown. My hands would be laid out on the table in front of me, itching on the palms and starting to twitch impossibly, with my fingers each separated by the width of a cotton ball.

The first time she discovered me this way, Ada sat across from me and smiled as if we were playing a game.

"What are you doing?"

I didn't look up. It seemed important to maintain focus on my nails.

"I have to wait for them to dry. Otherwise I'm going to mess them up."

Ada made a small *aah* and came over to me, picking up one of my hands in her own. "So when will these be dry?" she asked. "They look dry to me."

I scowled. "You can't tell by looking."

"So touch one."

"I'm not allowed."

"Oh," she said. "Well."

We sat quietly together for some time. The beams of sun coming through the window traveled across the waxcloth on the table and crept up my wrists. At last Baba Ada stood up and stretched her arms, pressing her nails into her palms and then wiggling her fingers, balling her hands up and then extending them so her arms looked like wings.

"Sitting here is making me stiff, *lalka*. I'm going to go get a hot chocolate," she said. "I was going to invite you, but I can see that you're busy. So I suppose I'll just have to go alone." She walked out into the hall, still talking back at me as she put on her coat. "It's too bad. A long way to go by myself, since I don't have a book to read on the train ride. And I'll be awfully lonely if I have to wait for a table. But there's nothing to be done."

Before she had fitted her key to the lock, I sprang from my seat and threw myself against the door. Ada came back in and wrapped me up against the wind outside, making sure that my scarf and hat matched the new grown-up color of my nails. Sitting pressed together on the train, rocking back and forth as we traveled towards a bus exchange, Ada told me about Greta's home in Poland: about what had been and what was to come. I leaned into her on the turns and let the words seep beneath my skin, as the light had in our small kitchen.

I knew that Ada was trying to make me feel better about the fact that my mother had left me alone. What I didn't understand was that once upon a time, my mother had heard these stories too. That she'd been petted and painted and made to believe she was whole, until one day she cracked open and out I came: a smaller doll with a sleeker voice.

Ada taught us both that Greta's magic set our family line in motion: women who came from women, women who came with music. Each woman a better singer, a more perfect form. When I was a girl I couldn't see that in these stories, Kara was implied by my very existence. That I was required to improve on my mother, and that the day would come to improve on me.

My first major role was almost Mélisande from Debussy, and it was so boring that I cried the first time I ran through it with Baba Ada, who was at that point still my de facto voice coach. You barely need a soprano for the part, and I just think the libretto is ridiculous, with its all-too-fragile heroine and her darkly fated loves. I was an apprentice at the Lyric back then, allowed occasionally to fill in soubrette roles, like the Massenet, and pretend I wasn't biting my fingernails to pieces every time a new show was being cast. So when they decided to give me a genuine debut, whispering the news in my ear and giving me a champagne toast, I was meant to be very grateful.

The only justification I could fathom for the casting was that I was young and knew how to hold back my sass onstage when the moment demanded it. They didn't want a mezzo-soprano, they wanted someone really innocent, and after spending twenty years under Ada's watchful eye, I suppose I appeared to qualify. She hadn't been careful with Sara, because Sara's voice is low and easy, waves against a boat and wine dripping down the neck of a bottle. But my voice is limoncello, steam from a kettle, flint. It can be dangerous if you turn your back on it, and Ada knew better than to make that mistake again.

The first day of rehearsal was a disaster. Or at least it started out that way. I'd been working over the role phrase by phrase, picking it apart with Baba Ada in our living room, while outside the snow melted and then froze back up in rigid bulges. We could have worked in my mother's empty room—had, in fact, intended to turn it into a studio. But that didn't pan out. Her absence shuddered through it, always. When I crossed the threshold I couldn't sustain notes and started breaking out in nervous sweats. My throat closed up, growing thicker and thicker from the inside, and I swallowed with great glottal gulps until Ada couldn't take it anymore and swatted my bottom. I felt smoke rising behind my eyes. So we moved back into the living room.

I stood onstage at the Lyric beside the piano and drummed it with the pads of my fingers. The pianist gave me a dirty look—I was nowhere near the tempo of the section we were rehearsing. *Pelléas et Mélisande* has no real arias, but there are two brief solos and one of them belongs to Mélisande. A foundling from the woods, she marries a prince and falls in love with his brother but is too stupid to understand quite what she's done. Her song from the tower is all about her long and long-suffering hair—shades of Rapunzel—very waiflike and full of dull quavering. That was what we were starting our day with. I tapped out the rhythm but sped it up to triple the appropriate pace. In my rehearsals with Ada, I'd sprinted through the song to keep myself motivated, and it left us both rolling on the floor with tears in our eyes. *My long hair awaits you in the tower*—it sounds much better frantic, as maniacal as its meaning.

"Ehm, I think we should get started," said Rick. These days, I've come to love Rick. I love that his name sounds like it should belong to a bricklayer instead of an accompanist. And that he can hold a casual conversation while playing Tchaikovsky's first concerto. But that morning I did not love him yet.

"I am started," I snapped at him. "All warmed up and nowhere to go."

"Whatever." Rick yawned. He's used to dealing with divas, actual divas. I barely weighed enough to legally give blood.

"All right," said the director, Martin. He was parked in the fifth row—not the house's best seats but close enough to be audible when he wanted to start dissecting our work. Beside him sat Philippe, who was overseeing the whole season, and looked crassly intimidating in a black mock turtleneck and blazer. It was unusual for Philippe to attend a first run-through, and I pushed away the feeling that perhaps his presence had to do with me. The feeling that this was perhaps a test.

"From the beginning. We'll run through the tower song a few times at least so we can"—he waved a hand above his head—"get calibrated, really make sure Mélisande feels right. She's the key to setting the tone here. Remember"—Martin swiveled to face me directly—"in her head, she's still lost in the woods, even though technically speaking she's up in the castle. And she's about to get a lot more lost, though she doesn't know it yet."

He leaned over and whispered something to Philippe and then settled back in his seat, hitching one ankle over his knee.

"Okay, Mellie, let's take her for a ride," said Rick. I glared at him but said nothing, just curled my fingernails up into my palm so I wouldn't be tempted to tap them on the piano shell. I rested my other hand briefly on my stomach, checking my own posture since there was no ruler here to keep me in place. Then I breathed, and sang.

Mes longs cheveux descendent jusqu'au seuil de la tour;
Mes cheveux vous attendent tout le long de la tour,
Et tout le long du jour,
Et tout le long du jour.

I had just about reached Mélisande's list of saints when Philippe tilted over and started whispering to Martin. I stared at them without breaking my pace, then glanced back at Rick, who shrugged. It's not a long piece, and we were through it before I had time to really worry. Without looking up, Martin flicked a hand at us.

"Again."

And so we started from the beginning. *Mes longs cheveux descendent*, and all the rest. The two men had their heads pressed together as if they were teenage boys planning a conquest. They flipped through something, and then Martin looked up briefly.

"Again," he said.

So we did it again. And again. And again. Repetition, obviously, is par for the course in a rehearsal, especially an early one, but you usually get some sort of direction to stop you from tearing off into the same mistakes over and over. By the fifth go-round, I was tapping my foot against the stage as quietly as I could, swaying my hips just a little to see if a hint of the sultry would get some kind of response. *Très innocent*, they'd said. *Très jeune*.

On the sixth repetition, Martin and Philippe were still deep in congress, and my heart was beating hard. *Well*, I thought, *give them something worth whispering about*. I caught Rick's eye just before he went into the opening and released a quick thrum of nails on the piano, then two more, double time. He winked at me.

At first I'm not sure either of the men in the audience noticed our slight edits to the score, but by the tenth bar I'd substituted out Mélisande's quiet liquid rippling for a tremulous jazz, and by the time we turned the corner into our seventh repetition, Rick and I were racing each other to see who could control the tempo. I had unsettled him by taking the whole piece up an octave, and he retaliated by trilling shamelessly at the end of a phrase.

"Enough!"

The voice startled us so thoroughly that we cut off where we were, Rick letting two or three last notes trickle out before he took his hands away from the keyboard and folded them in his lap. It wasn't Martin who had spoken, but Philippe, and now that he had our attention he turned back away from the stage.

"Do you see?" he said, addressing himself to Martin but talking loudly enough that we could all hear him. "This is what I was talking about."

Martin frowned. "She's too young?" There was a question in his voice. His hand strayed up to his throat, as if it could discern with subtle fingertips the nodes young singers develop on their vocal cords by pushing too hard, straining too soon. I wanted to scream at them. *Not me. I'm different.*

But Philippe spoke for me.

"She's wasted on Debussy. This girl is a born *Reine de la Nuit.*"

A gong went off inside my head, and in its aftermath I couldn't hear Martin's reply, could only track the movement of his hands as if they were showing me the way somewhere. Mozart's Queen of the Night, in *The Magic Flute,* is his best witch, and I prefer to sing the songs of witches. The Queen is impossible for most voices, and quite wicked. She's ready to eat her own young.

"Darling." Philippe leaned forward in his chair, chin seated on his laced fingers like a soft-boiled egg. He was known to devastate debut singers. Make them cry. He purred at me. "Do you think it would be too much?"

Rick barked out a single laugh, then stared straight ahead as if it had been someone else. It was then that I truly began to adore him. I allowed my hand to stretch and flatten against the cold bulk of the piano's hood, for balance. Raised my eyebrow.

"If anything, I may be too much for her."

Martin sighed.

"You're going to owe me," he said to Philippe. And then, looking me up and down, "And spoil her rotten."

Philippe just smiled.

"You know," he said, "I quite intend to."

hat night I could barely hold my keys as I jammed them against the door, only tumbling into the apartment when Ada stood up from whatever she was doing and put me out of my misery by unlocking it from the inside. She was already an old woman then, my *babenka*, but you'd never have known it. Her hair was dark brown and piled on her head in an impressive bun, and she was wearing a wool pencil skirt that gave her the shape of a girl. Ada always said I kept her young, and it certainly seemed true that night. I bounced from one foot to the other and infected her with the aura boiling around me until she started to do a little shimmy of her own.

"What?" she asked. We were both laughing, though she didn't yet know why, and I spun around, allowing her to pull my coat off my shoulders.

"Three guesses," I said. And she considered, poking her tongue out thoughtfully to touch her upper lip and wrangling my coat onto a hanger. We had pathetic little wire hangers, from thrift stores and the odd dry cleaning mostly, bent into oblongs and suffering greatly under the weight of their burdens. *First thing to go*, I thought. *Wooden hangers forevermore.*

"You found a pile of gold," she said. I clapped my hands as I bounced.

"Not exactly. Two more guesses."

"It turns out that your shoes are magical dancing shoes, which will skirt you away to the land of the eternal ball, where you will dance faster and faster, until at last you light on fire."

Ada made eyes at me, but I tucked my chin down, unwooed. Lowering myself calmly onto flat feet, I shook my head.

"Well, all right then," said Ada. "It can only be one thing."

"Oh yes?"

"Oh yes," she said. She brushed an imaginary beard against her pale skin. "You figured out that Mélisande is not so bad after all and remembered that you're about to sing on a real stage. I will admit, doing away with the silly goosey versions will be a difficulty, but I think, all in all, I can manage."

Baba Ada looked happy with herself. Always upon making some sort of breakthrough in my singing, I'm consumed with a ball of energy. She assumed that the rehearsal onstage, with live accompaniment and professional critiques, had plucked me from my slump and reminded me to thank heaven for the favors I'd been granted.

"Oh no," I said. "Oh no no no."

"Well then, what?" she asked. "I do have to get dinner on, you know. You aren't over the moon about a movie coming out or some other nonsense like that, are you? Because I told you last time, I can only care so much about—"

"I'm going to be the Queen of the Night," I said. "I'm going to sing *The Magic Flute*."

Ada stopped in the middle of hitching up one of her nylon stockings as she turned back to the kitchen. I watched the air leak slowly out of her, only to return, transfused, as if made into champagne. She bubbled upward back towards me and put both hands on my shoulders. They were surprisingly strong, and in other circumstances I might have winced.

"Are you being serious, Luscia?" Her voice was deadly focused, and her eyes shone like gunshots right into my own. I nodded.

Ada rested her forehead on mine, leaning down just slightly. She had three inches on me. "I knew it," she said. So softly I almost couldn't hear. "I knew it."

Her fingers were still digging into my shoulders.

"Can you imagine," she continued, as if to herself, "what your daughter will be like someday?"

I craned my neck back, away from her.

"What?" I asked. But Ada only shook her head.

"Never you mind, child," she said. "We should celebrate."

And so we did.

7

Kara and I walk through the streets of North Chicago and I point things out to her that she probably cannot see. She's almost completely invisible in her winter clothes—out of reach of wind and dirt and water and snow—and yet everything touches her. When a bird skims the air above her, suddenly flight is possible. When she smells bus exhaust, the world loses its semblance of perfect cleanliness. Every time I stroke her cheek, she remembers tenderness.

My stitches feel better than I had expected—much better, considering that I have an extra six pounds attached to my chest. But the day is undeniably frigid, sleet sticking against my coat and wetting my hair, and when I turn the corner and see we're at the end of our journey's first leg, I want to laugh with happiness. Across the street is a florist's shop where I sometimes order bouquets for dinner parties. They do nice window displays—right now, big puffs of hothouse hydrangeas to simulate snowballs and frozen hillsides, as if to taunt the real winter landscape, which is spitting mad. The shop is always warm inside, and they have a counter where you can sit and order coffee or tea while your flowers are being assembled. They'll do something nice for Ada, I know. It's stupid to leave flowers in the cemetery to wilt and freeze, but going without them seems callous to me. Presentation and all that. I look in both directions down the street and begin to pick my way across.

I'm almost at the sidewalk when a stylish woman emerges from the florist's door cradling a tall bouquet of peonies and lilies. Various shades of pink and white and yellow, which she's adjusting with her thumb when she loses traction on a patch of ice.

The woman is wearing inadvisable heels—she was probably planning to walk all of two paces before hailing a taxi—and one toe slips forward while the other slips back. I suck in a breath and hold out my hand, but I'm too far away to help. And do I really want to? Would I really have offered myself to grab if I'd been closer? I pull my hand back and shrink into myself, hugging Kara close.

"*Oh,*" the woman gasps.

She skids her feet around and then falls hard on both knees, the flowers spilling out of their wrappings in front of her.

And she screams.

Wherever she thought she was going—a party, an office building—she didn't expect to make a noise like that on her way. The woman's voice is so shrill that every pedestrian within a block turns to see what the commotion is. But what I hear mostly—what I cannot stop hearing—is the crack of her kneecaps. A sickening crush, palpable as footsteps on glass. I turn back and walk with purpose to the other side of the street and keep going. Tell myself I imagined it; she couldn't have been hurt that badly. People slip on the ice all the time. But a few blocks later, hurrying in the opposite direction with my eyes down, I hear the wail of a siren approaching from somewhere to take the woman away.

Just a little farther, I think. *Almost there.* I rush past coffee shops, antique stores with furniture peeking through the windows. But I can't go fast enough to calm down my frantic breathing.

Wounds have their own gravity—isn't that what I was telling myself before? That injury draws further injury, and a person, once damaged, is never safe. I had believed, though, that the gravity was localized. Attached to its object. Kara murmels against my chest, sucking intermittently on the strap of her carrier, and I hold her closer, imagining an underground rumbling coming from the direction of the accident. A great wrenching moan as the street rips open. Buildings falling away into nothingness. People struck by bricks and swallowed by the void. Even though I know it's not real, a large handful of my heart believes that if I look back, I'll see destruction barreling down the road. That it's only by averting my eyes that I can keep us both from being consumed.

St. Boniface Cemetery is surrounded by high walls, situated on the liminal edge between two neighborhoods—the wealthy one I've just passed through and the penniless one on the other side. In death they move closer and finally meet, the rich and poor alike. I stop when I reach the fence and rest my hand lightly against it, as if this were home base in some cosmic game of tag. I think of all the things Baba Ada saved me from, how close she hewed to me when I came to her crying after school or after a bad audition, any little injury. The cemetery is full of statues of saints, robed figures who peer out at me from their veils of stone and snow. I walk a few more paces to the gate, trying to ignore the nest of anxieties beneath my lungs.

I have no flowers after all, just a child half sleeping, but it's Ada I'm here to see. She won't be angry about something so petty.

She'll take me in her arms, put her hand to my cheek. That's what she always used to do. Listen to my troubles. Tell me a story.

In the distance I hear some scratching, shuffling steps, but there's no one in sight. Maybe it's a stray dog, or a teenager avoiding school. The statues are perfectly silent, as statues tend to be. The snow has picked up, still wet, hitting hard against my skin, and I curl my fingers around one of the bars on the gate, the iron freezing even through my gloves. Somehow, I can't bring myself to step inside. Ridiculous. What am I afraid of?

The saints, concrete and marble alike, stand still and wait for me, eyes hidden under hoods. I shiver and turn away.

All day I've been trying to save Kara, save myself from danger. A curse. The pressure of my secrets and fears building up inside me to a boiling point. Yet this is where I brought my child: not somewhere safe, but to a graveyard, a mausoleum. Maybe I hoped the silence would make me feel at home. This isn't where my baba is, though, not really. Ada hated dead things. Or at least that was my impression. She would never talk about them as they really were. She had a taste for the living, or perhaps the living dead.

I remember. It was, after all, a taste I came to share.

Ada earned our keep doing alterations at the Marshall Field's annex store on East Washington. When she arrived in Chicago in 1938 it was a good job, better than doing tit and tat as a home seamstress, and certainly a vast improvement over anything connected to the city's infamous slaughterhouses, where her cousin Freddie worked until they closed down or until he died—I've never been sure which.

To me the work at Marshall Field's always seemed beneath my *babenka*, who herself wore clothes tailored to make her look like a lady, with precision pleats and hidden darts. None of the other women Ada worked with seemed to know who Greta was, and they took liberties with my baba that I didn't think anyone had the right to: they laughed with her, they scolded her, sometimes they told her what to do.

Basia was my grandmother's particular friend, the only one who ever came to our home. They drank tea out of our two good cups and generally chased me away to discuss "things a child wouldn't understand." So Basia put it.

Not long after the day Ada rescued me from my exile of painted nails, Basia sat in our kitchen listening to me go on about Greta's powers. She turned to Ada and frowned.

"What nonsense are you filling this girl's head with?"

I actually gasped, a terrible piece of theatricality.

"Oh, *lalka*." Ada waved her hand at me. "Go to your room. Give us some time."

"Baba—"

"Go on." She set down her teacup. "I mean this."

As I stalked out the door to what felt like another banishment, I heard her say to Basia: ". . . can't know what she'll make of it."

Basia just laughed and said, "Well, it's no better to hide."

To which my baba said nothing at all.

What I didn't understand was that Ada's two sides— her dignified sense of style and her position as a day laborer; her self-assured domination over our home and her bonhomie at work—were quite inextricably linked. She was able to bring home clothes deemed beyond repair and work them over into sleek statement pieces for herself or else cut them down for my mother or me. And the women at Marshall Field's—most of them immigrants too—provided a community that neither family nor church could give Ada when she first left Poznań.

Despite my certainty that my baba deserved better, the store still drew me with the childish appeal of a factory floor. I marveled at the fact that a bolt of cloth could become a pair of pressed slacks, that a tear could be mended into invisibility. And when they were all collected together, the seamstresses were a captive audience. Why they viewed me as a performer and my grandmother as nothing more than *one of the girls*, I couldn't quite grasp. But it seemed to be what Ada wanted.

I was generally not allowed in the big back room where the women sat with lamps bent towards their handiwork, fingers running nimbly over bobbins, belts, and treadles. It was thought I would be in the way, and I was. On the few occasions Ada capitulated to my whining and snuck me along with her, I raced up and down the aisles between sewing machines and stood in the hallway singing "Amarilli, Mia Bella" until all foot pedals stopped and all hands applauded. Probably Ada and Basia prepared the rest of them for me, those women with their hair tied back, with their sensible dark eyes and occasional arthritic protrusions in their fingers. But as far as I knew they lived their lives there, bent over careful hemming and hypnotized by the constant grinding mumble of the machines. When I ran through the door—shoes making their *slap-slap-slap* against the floor—I pictured myself as a refreshing, avenging wind blowing misery and monotony out the window with my laughter.

After a song or, if I was lucky, two, Ada would give me a handful of Frango mints and tell me to go play quietly by myself. This was the hard part; I was not naturally still. But Ada told me it would be good practice for being a singer when I grew up: sometimes I would have a single aria nestled amid two full acts of opera. I would need to be able to wait in the wings for my moment of glory. That my taste for glory came from Ada too would not occur to me for some time.

The alteration room was on a floor that wasn't open to the public. So when my fists were full of chocolates and I'd been dismissed from the sewing quarters, I was generally able to wander around the hall and find a place to sit all by myself. Any clothing waiting for the clever attention of Ada's ladies was piled in a mountain of fabric in one room; women would come by as they completed projects and peel a new one from the stack, with instructions for hemming, mending, or taking in pinned to the front.

The finished clothing was treated with more reverence. Several of the rooms on the alteration floor were no more than giant walk-in closets with low lighting, as though they housed art that required preservation from the elements. Racks of suit jackets hung beside rows of starched blouses; wool skirts organized by length were suspended beside coats, which were trimmed with mink or rabbit depending on the price. One room was always reserved for wedding dresses sheathed in thin sheeting—the plastic muted the dresses' blinding whiteness and made them glow as they might have in the light of the moon. Often the dresses swayed when I entered their lair; they looked very much like a cadre of sleeping ghosts all hung by the shoulders, effluvial tails dragging gently on the ground.

I dared myself to stay among them. It was a challenge: eat a pile of chocolates in a room of white clothing without leaving any fingerprints. Sit in a quavering pool of spirits without awakening one and raising its ire. I chose a point in the middle of the room and shuffled a few hangers aside to duck between so the plastic closed back around me when I leaned against the wall. I was afraid of the ghosts, but if I closed my eyes I could convince myself that the *shushing* sounds of the swaying dresses were really coming from leaves rustling together in the wind.

The only risk to this tactic was that sometimes I would fall asleep, and then my dreams might take me anywhere.

I remember the last time I ever visited the ghost room, how I pinched my eyes shut and concentrated on the sound of my own breathing because it blocked out all other distractions—a creak in the corner or a suspicious lowing of conversation from the floor below. As with any dream, I can't recall the moment that it began, just that there was a woman roaming in a forest with her skirt brushing against her knees. Daylight leaked through the nearly bare tree limbs, but it was a bleached light, bone-white and arctic. When the woman—for I was the woman, though then again I wasn't—looked up at the sky, she could see a cold bulb dangling there as if from a wire.

Something was following her. Maybe more than one something. The woman picked up her pace but her path was obscured; thorns pricked her shins and left thin scratches on her arms that turned into messages she couldn't read. Lying on the floor of the room full of wedding dresses, I felt the rough carpet rub against my cheek and I tossed in my sleep. The woman felt a tug on the hem of her skirt, but when she turned around there was no one behind her. Just bushes and trees.

Dark clouds rolled over.

They rolled back.

I felt something pulling me forward, away, but the woman either couldn't hear me or wouldn't listen. She paused to look around herself, and I thought, *No. Go faster.* My heart broke into a run. It was stuck inside the woman's body, though, and she was curious about the patterns in the tree bark that appeared and disappeared, changed colors. Changed shapes.

"*Greta-ah-ah-ah.*"

We heard the voice, and her blood froze for both of us. There was another sharp tug on her skirt. A sudden wind scattered a pile of leaves and the woman jumped. Somewhere far away my body was tossing and turning, itching to wake up. But around us issued the soft crunch of footsteps; out of the corner of my eye—or was it hers?—I saw shadows ducking in and out of view.

"*Greta-ah-ah-ah.*"

Closer, the voice splintered into many voices, a hollow harmony that encroached from all sides. Hairs stood up on the back of the woman's neck, tiny follicles prickled on her cheeks. A third tug came, the waist of her skirt pulling away from the skin and snapping back into place. This time when the woman looked down, she saw a beautiful little girl with thick dark hair who took a step backward when she realized that she'd been spotted. Her hands were folded demurely behind her back.

A circle of little girls surrounded the dream woman. And though some of them were larger and some were smaller, they were clearly identical in design—they would grow into the same woman. If they were given the chance to grow.

"We're here so you can eat us."

"Eat us."

"Eat our hearts."

The dream woman spun around and I spun somehow in the other direction so we saw them in stereo, their mouths moving in tandem. Each set of small brown eyes was serene. The voice of the dream woman trembled.

"I don't understand. I don't want to eat your hearts. I was just out walking . . ." She trailed off as she realized that she didn't remember how she got there or why she began strolling through the woods in the first place. I shifted around on the floor of the wedding dress room, feeling like the driver of a runaway car.

"Oh," said the little girls. "*Oh. Oh. Oh.*" They stepped forward, their knees knocking together. "Well, then." The sound echoed: *well well well.* "We will have to eat your heart instead." They stepped forward and grabbed the hem of the woman's skirt as though they were her children trying to keep from getting lost.

The first girl, the tallest, reached up and put a hand on the woman's arm.

"Don't worry." She stroked the woman's arm lovingly. "Everything will be better when we're done."

I awoke screaming beneath a row of white dresses with my baba Ada shaking my elbow. Her skin was pale paper, crumpled slightly and pulled back tight by the set of her mouth. For a moment I couldn't stop my screams—the dresses brushed back and forth around me like branches and the plastic wrappings clung to my skin. Ada grabbed my shoulders and pulled me out into the center of the room, dragging a couple of wedding gowns off their hangers behind me. Standing on my own two feet, I was able to bring the room into focus. I took a few gulping breaths, feeling the hash marks I'd scratched into my throat by shrieking.

"What is it?" Ada kept hold of my shoulders and searched my face as if she would be able to see through it. On the word *it*, she gave me the tiniest shake, so slight I'm not sure she was aware of doing so. "What's the matter?"

A whispering drew my attention to the doorway. There, several seamstresses leaned their heads together, sneaking occasional peeks in my direction. A sick feeling followed: they were talking about me, their eyes full of pity. I tried to straighten my spine. What I wanted more than anything was to burrow into my *babenka's* arms, feel her cradle and soothe me. But the women were watching. I tried to imagine what they'd say if I told them what I'd dreamed—they'd think I was crazy.

And what would Ada think? It wasn't so much the disruption

that made me feel guilty as the fact that my dream had turned Greta somehow sinister. It populated her landscape with threats, which was the opposite of what Ada wanted. My *babenka* didn't always tell me the truth. But when she chose not to, it was because she wanted to let me believe something better. Or because *she* needed to believe something better. She could give that to me, and I could give it to her, too.

"Nothing," I said. "I'm okay. I fell asleep."

Ada looked at me with a terrible little wrinkle in her forehead. But then she straightened up and turned towards the doorway with a shrug that scattered the women who'd gathered there. When they'd gone, Ada picked up one of the wedding dresses that had fallen to the floor in the confusion—it draped heavily over her elbow like a lady in a pose of supplication, arms wafting hopelessly down.

"I'm going to have to press this again." She spoke quietly, inspecting the few almost imperceptible new lines in the fabric. "Maybe you could go sit in the main room with the girls? I think you left a book with Basia."

I nodded tightly and walked down the hall, trying to keep my footsteps quiet. Trying to be good. I'd bitten my tongue thrashing around inside the nightmare, and for the rest of the day my mouth tasted like blood. I found it sitting on my teeth at the gum line and felt myself swallowing it, my stomach filling up with iron.

I try to walk slowly and keep myself calm as I move away from the graveyard, but the weather won't let me. The weather, and the tight fist of my heart. There are too many people on the street, all of them guarding their faces from the wind but still, somehow, seeming to watch me. When I see a bookstore I duck inside, because it looks empty. In the heat of the store, cold fingers of snow melt off my hair and drip down my neck, and I watch the sleet outside, leaning with one hand on a stack of old books with cloth covers. They smell like little museums.

I turn away from the window-paned door and start to gather myself. Or at least I try. What actually happens is that the baby sneezes, and an older man behind the counter looks up and says, "God bless you."

I begin to cry.

"Hey now," says the man. He's half hidden behind piles of merchandise, the corners of his mouth turned down in a frown. "No need for that."

I want to explain myself, but where to begin? Kara has begun whimpering too, and taking a ragged breath, I shush her. Brush a few drops of water off her cap where snowflakes melted. The bookstore man watches as I dry myself off, digging in my purse for a napkin that I use to wipe my eyes and blow my nose, after first dabbing Kara's face. When it seems like the danger of my bursting into renewed tears has passed, he looks down at the open book in front of him and the sheet of paper beside it, which is filled with tabulations. He jots something down with a pencil, but then looks back up at me. I'm still there.

"Is there someone I can call for you?" he asks. I shake my head.

"Actually, if you don't mind me using my phone in here, I can call." I pull out my cell phone and show it to him, as if to prove I'm not lying, and he looks around us at the empty store.

"Not like there's anyone to bother."

He turns back to his book, flipping through the pages and skimming, now and then licking his index finger for traction. I seem to disappear, which suits me fine.

In the back of the store, behind a tall bookshelf, I find a

chair—faded upholstery tacked onto unpolished cherrywood, with curling armrests like cat paws—and I sit, gratefully. Kara lies against me. A store like this would be a nice place to take a sleeping baby sometime. I could pick titles off the shelves and read long passages in this very chair, waiting to see if the words lived up to whatever price the man had penciled into his books. An ordinary world—what must that be like?

As I arrange myself, the chair lets up puffs of dust. The cushions seem too skinny for that, but apparently they have unseen depths. Like everything.

I know what to do. Who to call. I flick through the numbers on my phone, trying not to think what a strange portal it is, a sort of witchcraft. The phone, like the chair, feels thin and insubstantial. But it can bring me all the way across the world. Take the dust of my voice to an ear so far in my past that, by rights, it should be as deaf as stone.

"Hello?" I speak immediately when the line connects.

"Hello?" Echo. Silence. *"Hello?"*

Her voice is so familiar, I could cry.

"Mama," I say. "It's me."

8

The woods encroached on Greta's home—through the lumber, through every window and crack. But they also belonged to her, and she to them. Her people were always killed in the manner of forest creatures; they died as they lived—struck by lightning, poisoned by a corrupted stream, lost in a field of identical birches that confounded a wanderer's sense of direction. People in town said Greta came from nowhere, that she'd been found by a hunter bundled up on the ground and had for the most part raised herself. And for that reason or for some other, she continually slipped back into the woods on rambling walks that led her nowhere.

People also said she pulled trouble behind her wherever she went, but for a long time that was just talk, it wasn't true. Not until she was a grown woman making choices for herself and asking for the things she wanted. Wishes are dangerous things, you see. Start asking the sky to grant you requests and you better prepare for some fallout, red rain.

When a fifth daughter had bloomed within her and faded, this was when she made the deal. The baby lasted long enough inside her to inspire a new glimmer of hope, and to bring a new type of devastation when it was born early, blue and still. Greta insisted on digging the grave herself, and taking the girl far away from her home. She was worried that the voices of the lost girls were getting too loud, and that no child would ever be able to hear past them. She was insensible to protests—deaf to Saul's urging to stay in bed, to the midwife's painstaking explication of the volume of blood she'd lost in labor. Greta took the small raisin of a body and wrapped it in clean blankets with the face left bare. Even close up it was difficult to tell the child wasn't just sleeping.

Greta strapped this parcel to her chest with a long cotton shawl, leaving her hands free to carry a shovel. She allowed Saul to put an apple in her pocket, a crust of bread, and then she kissed the boys on the tops of their heads and walked into the forest, snapping small twigs beneath her feet.

She walked all day. In truth she had no notion of where she was going, what she was looking for. Occasionally she caught a hint of a song on the wind—naturally, she thought she was imagining it. But with no other guiding light to follow, she turned her ear to the sound and walked towards it. By noon she'd consumed the apple and tossed the skinny core beneath a bush. By nightfall she was curled up beneath a tree guarding the waxen infant with the curve of her body.

When the sun came up, Greta found herself in a small clearing full of light blue flowers. She couldn't remember seeing them the night before, though of course it had been dark then, black shadows dripping down from the sky. Now she was covered in dew, her clothing wet and her hair hanging in damp strings. She blinked in the light and spent a moment rubbing color into her cheeks, cricking her back. There was a baby asleep beside her.

"I'm afraid not."

Greta started at the voice but made an effort to retain her composure. A creature that sneaks up on you in the dead of the woods is usually only as dangerous as you make it. Keeping her body poised, she turned her neck to peer behind her. Some ten feet away, just outside the clearing, a man stood, leaning against a tree. He was bathed in shade, with only one leg peeking out into the full light. When he noticed this, the man pulled the leg back, turning his body monochromatic.

But Greta had seen the color of his suit, gray as the ashes from an old fire. Familiar.

"Do we know each other?" she asked.

"Perhaps." The man turned so his spine lay against the tree and his weight rested on his heels. "We may have, once."

He began to whistle, as though he had all the time in the world and this was the most ordinary interaction he could have dreamed up. Almost dull. But the sound sent a thrill through Greta's body, her lungs constricting, heavy and cold.

"I've heard that song before," she said.

"Well." The man smiled at her, a half smile. "It's not uncommon, is it? The kind of song you might hear at a pub." He whistled another few bars. "Or a dance."

A cool wind blew across the clearing, bending stalks of vegetation into sway-backed petitioners. Greta let her weight rest on one hand and listened to the familiar music rebound from rocks and trees. She hummed along, just a little. Remembering Saul's hand in the concave of her back.

The body of her child lay tranquil beside her on its bed of flowers and grass. During the night the child's skin had taken on a bluish hue—peaked, freezing—and, unthinking, Greta tried to warm her. Ran a finger over the small forehead, felt the cheeks with her palms. But the child didn't stir. She just lay there, skin smudging slightly where it was touched.

Greta shivered. When she looked up, the sun had gone behind a cloud and the man was stooping right beside her. His hair was white blond, his eyes slightly lined, as if from squinting.

"Well," he said again, nodding at the shovel. "Aren't you going to get on with it?"

What could she do? What else *was* there to do? Accepting the hand the man held out to her—a clean hand, with trimmed nails and pink skin—Greta hauled herself to her feet and picked up the spade.

"I think," the man said, "that anywhere around here will do."

Greta's shoulders heaved each time the shovel sliced the ground, calling forth a cold *chink* from the soil. She wanted a hole deep enough to muffle her own grief, if such a hole could be had. Soon she was standing in a pit up to her ankles, then her knees. The dirt grew cooler the deeper she went, a chill seeping out from the earth and into Greta's skin. The man just watched, rocking back and forth on his heels.

"Although . . ." Sweat dripped from every inch of her skin, but still, when the stranger spoke, Greta froze. She looked up to see him wearing a thoughtful expression. "It does seem like a shame."

Greta waited. After a minute she asked, "What does?"

"Or a *waste*, really." The man began strolling around the hole, his hands folded neatly behind his back. "A beautiful girl. A terrible tragedy."

"I don't know." Greta looked at the small, still child and wanted with every fiber to be able to breathe her own life into that body. But what she said was "It happens all the time."

The man wasn't listening.

"And of course sons are nice, lovely really, but they're not the same for a woman. I can see you holding a little girl in your arms. I can picture it." The man sighed. "Oh, clearly. Very clearly."

He walked over to the baby, lying in a bed of grass where Greta had left her. The blanket was wrapped tightly around the child, folds tucked cleverly under folds so that the whole package was as smooth as a pillowcase. Crouching on his heels, the stranger picked up the baby and cradled her in his elbow. Greta sucked in a breath. But what could he do that hadn't already been done?

"Yes," the man said. "I wonder if we don't have something to offer one another, you and I." He rose back up, still holding the bundle. "After all, I hate to see you so lonely."

He stood at the lip of Greta's hole and looked down at her. Her shoulders tightened.

"Because you are lonely, aren't you?" he asked. "You have a little family. All those little men. But how happy can you be? With this?"

The man tilted his chin to the cold form of the baby.

"I can offer you the child you really want," he continued. "The child you dream of. You *do* still dream of her, don't you?" He smiled his thin smile again and nodded. "Often. Yes. It would be a good trade."

In her half-dug grave, Greta's ankles were freezing cold. She tried to call up an image of Andrzej's face, then Fil's, then Konrad's. But she couldn't.

"What do you mean, a trade?"

The man looked up into the distance as if calculating a very large number.

"I really dislike waste, you know. Can't stand it. Everything has a *use* if you look for it. But most people don't look, do they?"

Greta scowled. "You're talking in riddles."

"I am, aren't I?" The stranger scratched his ear. "Please forgive me. It's just that I get caught up in my own ideas and I forget what I have and haven't said out loud. What I mean is very simple. You want a daughter, and you should have one. And she"—he looked now into Greta's eyes with a frankness that seemed to fix her in place—"she should really have a daughter too. And her. And her."

He moved the baby so that she lay with her face against his shoulder.

"I'm not sure I understand you," said Greta. But the man was no longer paying any attention to her, caught up as he was in the details of his idea. He seemed to forget that he'd begged her forgiveness for this very sin not a moment ago.

"And the beauty of it is," he continued, "you don't even have to say yes. All you have to do is not tell me no. For a little while, you might think you've dreamed this. Oh, you'll try to convince yourself. Or you'll think I was a madman in the woods. You'll think, sometimes, that you've caught a glimpse of me—in a window or on a busy street. But you don't have to worry. I won't be checking up on you." He tugged his earlobe. "No need."

Greta's fingers tightened around the shovel. The day, she realized, had grown dark, and the sky now seemed to be threatening rain.

"What are you going to do?"

"I told you. Or did I?" The man frowned. "It's just a simple trade. I take a few things that you don't need—a few things I'd like to have—and you get something in return. Something you want very much. Doesn't that seem fair?"

A drop fell from the sky onto Greta's cheek. The stranger looked up at the clouds.

"You'd better hurry," he said. "There isn't much time to decide."

"All right," said Greta. Before she knew what she was doing.

"Really?" The man scraped a nail along the edge of his bottom lip. "You're sure?"

Greta nodded. Another few raindrops fell on her shoulders, a few on the top of her head and her hands.

"Well, good then." The man turned and walked towards the woods, then looked back at Greta. "I won't see you again, you know." When she didn't reply, he stepped into the trees, picking his way through the underbrush until he was gone.

A moment passed and the rain began to drum against the ground in earnest. Then Greta's heart wrenched. The baby. He'd taken the baby with him.

"Wait!" Greta tried to pull herself out of the hole, but the dirt was turning into mud and she slipped and scrambled against it. "Wait!" she cried.

But her voice echoed into nothingness. When she finally managed to get out of the grave, the clearing was empty. There was no one in sight, no matter which direction she turned. Just trees, which looked spindlier and more identical as they receded. Her shawl lay empty on the earth.

Greta sat down and sobbed into her hands. Her whole body was covered in mud, and it slurred into her eyes, so everything looked brown and dead. She waited. Time passed and nothing changed, except that she blinked out the mud and wiped her nose on the back of her hand.

The man was gone. And he wasn't coming back.

Little knowing what else to do, Greta filled in the hole she'd dug. And as strange as it was, with every shovelful she threw down, she felt her fury recede. As if she weren't lifting dirt from

a mound but from her own shoulders. A weight from her mind.
When she was done, she marked the place with a cross of stones
and paused to appreciate it. No one would ever know the difference. *Maybe*, she thought, *I'll forget too.*

But she never did.

9

"Lulu."

Over the phone I can hear my mother light a cigarette, take a drag. Pause and spit a flake of tobacco off her tongue. She doesn't say anything but my name, and that's enough. As always, her voice sounds like it's kept on packed ice. Winter breathing off the water, ice crystallizing on your eyelashes as you stroll the last block home. A Billie Holiday voice, scratchy muslin that touches your skin even before it reaches your ears.

"Mama, I—" My own voice catches. "I was just . . ."

On the other end of the line, she shifts. I can see her lifting her arms to the lights in the jazz bar. Sipping a glass of wine with her legs crossed, dainty, at the ankles. All the poses she made in my childhood, flitting in front of my eyes like a deck of cards. So many of the cards are blank though. Black.

"Lulu," she says again. "What?"

A fair question. I cast around for common ground: history,

geography. "I'm near the Green Mill," I say. The bar is, in fact, close by. "I was just thinking of you."

I'm surprised to hear her laugh.

"Well, first time for everything, isn't there?"

This is fair too—or almost. And it hurts. The bookstore is quiet around me—I can hear the scratching of the man's pencil behind the counter, the occasional flip of a page, but I'm the only real disturbance. Kara has settled down and blinks, her nose rooting around my collarbone. I should feed her soon. I keep forgetting that my time is not my own.

"Don't be mean," I say.

"Am I?" Sara laughs again. I can feel it in my body, like a punctured lung. "If I'm not very much mistaken, you called me. I don't see how that obligates me to all the pleasantries."

My good sense tells me to hang up, make some excuse. But somehow I can't do that, any more than I could walk into St. Boniface and stand on top of Ada's grave.

"I had a baby," I say at last. "A girl. Kara."

"You think I didn't know you were pregnant?" Another deep inhalation, smoke swirling between my mother's teeth. "Your grandmother still calls me sometimes. Which is more than I can say for you."

I catch on the present tense—I make the same mistake too, often enough. God knows, today has been that kind of day. Before I can mention it, though, my mother speaks again.

"Should we pretend something, Lulu? Something fun? For old time's sake."

"Like what?"

"Oh, let's say magicians. Children trained by their next-door neighbor in the art of sorcery. To everyone else, the neighbor's just a shabby old man, but to us, he's twenty feet tall, dressed in silk the color of the sky just before everything goes really black."

"Mama," I say. I can't quite picture her expression. Is she having fun with this? Does she really want to play, the way we used to? It's been ten years since I saw even the shadow of her, the edge of her dress. During my debut run, I thought I spotted her at a matinee of *The Magic Flute*, but whoever it was turned a corner and disappeared too fast for me to be sure. Trick of the dark witch. *Poof.* Gone. Probably I had Ada to thank for that too. I'm surprised to hear they were in touch.

"Okay." I pull Kara closer to my neck and breathe in the soothing scent of her hair where it meets the cap. "Magicians. What's my special power?"

But my mother has lost interest.

"Is she with you right now?" she asks.

"Who?"

"This baby. Did you say Clara?"

I shake my head uselessly. "Kara. Of course. Where else would she be?"

"I don't know," says Sara. "I don't know anything about it."

There is no one in the world like my mother for saying something hard, and then sitting in the ringing silence that follows. I hear her pour a drink: no more than half a glass. I remember how she used to do this, asking for just a splash, and then drinking splash after splash. Ignoring the arithmetic.

"We're having a christening," I say before I can stop myself. "Next Tuesday. Saint Mary of the Angels."

"And you called to invite me? Well. Aren't you a thoughtful girl."

This is too much. Sara hasn't changed at all. Why don't I hang up? My mother seems to be wondering the same thing.

"Was there something else you wanted?" she asks. "Really?"

And just like that, I remember there is. She has always had that ability: to make things true about me with a word, a glance. I sit deeper into my chair and look at the spines of the books nearby. I'm in the *P*s. Poetry. Postmodernism. Poltergeists.

"Do you think I should be worried for myself?"

"About what? About me?"

"No." I wipe a strand of hair off my forehead—it's still wet from the snow, starting to coil up in the heat. "I—you know, because of Greta. The curse."

I find myself holding my breath. If anyone knows, it's Sara. If anyone can tell me what's happening. What comes next. But she doesn't answer me—at least, not exactly. Her voice, when it comes, is distant and distracted.

"Did you say you were at the Green Mill?"

"Nearby. I was going to visit Baba Ada's grave." I'm talking as much to myself as to my mother now. "What a stupid idea that was. No wonder I'm being so morbid. But I can't shake it. This feeling that something even worse is coming."

Another silence. Another inhalation. My hackles are raised, and I laugh, not a pleasant sound.

"I almost died having the baby," I say. "And then Ada . . ." I let myself trail off. "You know. Don't make me say it."

"I didn't know anything." Sara is cold. "No one told me anything." The temperature around me seems to drop, complicit with her. "Where is she? Not in Graceland, I hope. She hated that place. It's tacky."

"St. Boniface," I whisper. And then, in my own defense, weakly: "I was unconscious. I didn't know who was called."

"The hell," she says. I hear her breathing. Then her voice drips once more into my ear. "I'll see you on Tuesday. You and the baby."

My phone beeps as the call is dropped.

barely remember leaving the bookstore. What I do recall next is being in a cab and asking the driver to stop a few blocks from our apartment because I need to walk and clear my head a bit. My whole body feels shaken—literally shaken, as if some giant pair of hands has picked me up and rattled me around. I stop in a neighborhood café and order a glass of wine, drinking it too fast as the eyes of the other patrons bore into me, taking in the baby.

The wine laps back and forth inside me, nauseous, sweet. Heavy, salted foods are stacked under the counter, hanging off the walls. Fat of the goose. Marbled meat of the pig. Pungent cheese dripping from a blood-red rind. I want to be calm, sniff indifferently at the mozzarella and the duck confit. All my favorite foods, and John's too. But the richness just makes me sick—one more indignity visited upon my body. And that makes me angry. I set down my glass and skid towards home as quickly as I can.

It's dark by the time I arrive, and John is in the living room, lying on the couch. As he reads he rubs his feet together, an idle gesture, the wool socks scratching against one another. Velcro, Velcro, tiny fibers linking and wrenching apart. He sees me over the top of his book, and he smiles.

"You bastard," I say. "What the hell is wrong with you?"

He is momentarily too shocked to speak, and I hear this beat, this pause, and I take it.

"You had my phone." I lift Kara out of the carrier on my chest and set her down in a car seat on the floor, which we've been using as a makeshift bed. "For days, I think. So it's not as though you didn't have her number."

"*Her?*" John has gained enough composure to be dubious of my choice of pronoun. It occurs to me that we may be about to have two different fights, but that's all the more reason to push my advantage. I don't know if I'm ready to be honest. But I'm ready to be angry.

"What were you thinking? What kind of a person are you? You just let her go on living, thinking everything was fine, when her *mother* had died? Did you think that would be *better?*"

So far John has not moved off the couch. What he's ready for is not yet clear. He lies back, his neck on the sofa arm and his head hanging off into nothing. I tear off my coat, kick both shoes across the room away from the baby, throw my unwound scarf in front of me, where it flutters ineffectually and falls into a heap. John sits up and leans his elbows on his knees.

"So," he says, "did you go to the cemetery after all?"

"Shut up." My voice is shaking, and it feels wonderful. "You want something *good*? You always want something *good*. But some things are just bad, and you can't talk your way out of them. You can't tell a little lie to make the world look the way you wish it did."

"Who are we talking about now?"

"We are talking about *you*." I reach down into my lungs for the words, giving them enough force to reach back fifty rows in a theater. That's something a good singer will practice for years, being able to intone while still projecting, making yourself heard but still making yourself clear. "Your little stories. Telling me Ada was fine. Telling my mother . . ."

John walks across the room as I talk and puts his face very close to mine. *Here it comes*, I think. He's right next to my mouth, close enough to bite it and take a piece out. For a second I wonder if he might kiss me. He sniffs.

"I think," he says, "that you've been drinking. You always

get like this." He picks up Kara, turns a slow circle while holding her above his head and smiling. Then he looks back at me. "Unreasonable."

He walks to the kitchen and I can hear him take out a bottle of formula that we have on hand in case we want to go out to eat and have a drink, just relax together. Something untarnished for the baby. With her in his arms, he goes into the bedroom and gently, so as not to scare her, closes the door.

We are still frightened, then. Both of us.

10

Everything about me depends on Greta. That's what Ada told me, what she needed to be true. With every word and every flick of the wrist, she made me into something as fragile and hard as cut glass. A lens, through which she could see the world she wanted.

"You are the finest creature yet born," she said to me each morning. We had a ritual: Baba Ada woke me up at seven, and the first thing she did was brush my hair. Light spilling through the curtains in the summer, a soft lamp turned on to help us see in the winter, when the sun was barely up by the time she cracked open the door. My baba Ada sat on the edge of my bed and wrapped the comforter around me, drawing me towards her and kissing the top of my head.

"You are my golden girl, *złota moja, lalka.*"

The brush was brown wood, with many hard bristles, like a horse brush. It brought me into my body. My first sensation on any given day was the sudden sharp pressure of those bristles on my scalp, and the slow tugging that followed them. I let my head fall to the side Ada was brushing, and she tilted me straight with two fingers on my chin.

"You're growing so beautiful. Every day."

She said this to me when I was three, four, five; she said it to me on my fifteenth birthday, when I lay in bed with my colt legs tucked under me. At seventeen I decided the routine left no room for my personal expression and began sleeping naked. It made no difference. In fact, my baba never even mentioned it. She came into my room and brushed my hair a hundred strokes, then stood me up on bare and wobbling knees and led me to the closet to choose between my dresses.

"Before me," Ada told me, "Greta was lonely for a daughter. And when I was born she wept for ten days. As I grew up, she brushed my hair every morning to spin it into silk, and to teach me how to someday brush your hair for you. She understood what a treasure you would be. She dreamed of you even though she had to wake up every morning into a world without you."

The night before Kara was born—not that I knew it, then—I lay in bed with the covers pulled up to my knees and chatted with her through my skin. I wanted to prepare her for coming into the world, explain that I would be gone sometimes for tours but that someone would always be at home to take care of her. I told her that she would resent the way adults treasured her childhood, would always be indignantly trying to explain that her life was difficult, too, and could we please just acknowledge that?

"But we'll have our reasons," I told her. "You'll have something we all want and can't have, and we'll be so jealous of you that sometimes we'll feel like blowing up."

In my dreams, until I was six or seven years old, I lived with Greta in her small cottage at the edge of the woods. When I wanted to be alone, I sat on a footstool in the corner of the kitchen so that I could be near the fire but also smell the sharp resin of the wooden walls. The footstool was covered in scratchy brown wool. Greta reached into the stove and took out fistfuls of flame with her bare hands.

She and I stared at these balls of fire, asked them questions as if they were tiny stars come down to visit. *You must have seen so much*, we said.

Each time I learned a new song I rushed to sleep, to Greta, and sang it for her. Each time I coaxed my voice towards a new high note, I saw her eyes shining with pride. We walked through her Poznań township hand in hand, and the people on the street parted ways for us—they shifted the sea of their movements to let us through, and we walked as though on the sandy floor of the ocean, marveling at all that was around us. Sometimes Greta pointed up to the sky and said, *Look!* And a bird flew past so fast that no one but us noticed it obscure the sun. Just for a moment. The bird's wings a black cape across the clouds.

"We'll want to see what you see," I told Kara. At that moment her eyes were shut against their gentle bath, the warm water I stored for her within me. She saw geometric combinations, Escher portraits of the sounds on the other side of her swaddling wall. Or maybe she saw nothing, since she hadn't yet the experience to know that there are shapes to name and colors to fill the shapes in and make them shine.

As I grew older, Greta's cottage receded from me; the weight of her hand on my own diminished. When Ada told me the stories of her mother's life, all I saw was that they explained who I was supposed to be. I didn't see the knots in the floorboards anymore or the mammoth iron mouth that was Greta's cookstove. And I only had a faint, haunting memory of the last trip Greta and I took out to the forest, when she helped me climb up into a tree and together we hummed the river's song. I had some notion of the person who happened towards us and, hypnotized, scrambled up the tree to sit beside us.

That person was, I thought, my mother, Sara, with her dark hair and her almond eyes. She took our hands in her own and lifted to each of our lips a crust of bread fresh from the oven, watched me chew and swallow and open my mouth for another. And she looked at me, looked so reproachfully, when from either side Greta and I leaned in to kiss her cheeks. I remembered faintly the way the color drained from my mother's face and how her body fell like a rag to the forest floor. She got up and brushed herself off, walked away, but I could see that something was missing from her from that moment, and that I had taken it for myself.

"Now you'll be strong," Greta told me. "Like I was."

I put my hand on my belly and could feel through the taut skin the basic outline of a foot. I inspected it for toes and searched for a heel, but everything was still too indistinct, too much a part of me. Kara was sleeping, soothed by who knows what. The sound of my heart? The thrum of my blood? Something nourished and protected her. Some piece of me that lay beyond my control.

Interlude

As I learned at the age of four—leaning my rib cage against the window sash and stretching my neck into the dirty Chicago air—sound is a product of its environment. Anyone can test this with a pop bottle and a small amount of embouchure control: flatten your lips and blow across the top of the bottle. When it's full you get a whistle. As you drink the soda down, the sound deepens.

The principle is just as true inside your body as out in the world—a soprano is born, and you can see it in her silhouette. More often than not she's small, like me. Her thin neck means that her vocal cords are slender and tightly packed together. They resonate at a high frequency when air rattles through them. Her jaw is strong, the mouth an echo chamber. Every tuck and fold a part of the instrument.

As a singer you have to be careful with your body the same way you'd be careful transporting crystal or glass. When the temperature varies too drastically, molecules shift and expand. Things shatter. The pen in my purse spills ink everywhere during altitude changes; and after plane rides longer than two hours, I need to avoid citrus fruits for a week, drink only herbal tea.

Travel, then, has always been dangerous for me. It can affect a performance in unexpected ways—hemming my voice in with static from the dry velveteen seats on the train into a new city, and desiccating it with the train's hot, recirculated air. High elevation breaks sounds into brittle sheets of paper; the color and texture of grain bins in a city's street markets bleed through into my tonal quality. Resonance comes from a barrel of smooth red quinoa seeds you can stick your hand in up to the elbow. Sharp color from hard, ridged bulgur wheat. Airiness from vats of flour that feels like silk when you lay your palm on top—if the frowning merchant will let you handle his wares so freely.

A voice is spongelike. It can absorb, and it can be wrung out.

When I step off a plane, I need to take a long walk in open streets to shake off the tin can aura of my transportation. Without the walk, without the wind to flush me, my lungs remain compressed and I can't go onstage—I hear the atonal *ding* of the seatbelt sign when I should be hearing the key changes my accompanist is running through on the piano, and I become convinced that the audience in the recital hall will be populated by duplicates upon duplicates of my fellow airline passengers, shifting around their neck pillows and cricking their knees.

What I mean is this: sound is never described with the density or complexity that it deserves, because we imagine it as separate from the texture of the rest of our lives. Words like *crystalline* and *booming*, *full* and *sharp*, reduce music to decoration, something adjectival. When in fact it's more like an animal. Living. Hungry. It sucks up atmosphere, emotion, experience. Pushes you to feed it by doing things you wouldn't otherwise do.

It's the whole of life, round and plump as a planet. Ample as a memory or dream.

Mongolia held its first opera festival in Ulaanbaatar and unwisely scheduled the festivities in December to appeal to the singers' sense of a snowy Christmas. At least that's my best guess at their intentions. We arrived during what's called the Nines of Winter: nine sets of nine days that each hold a special place in a hierarchy of bitter chill. The nine days when vodka freezes upon contact with the air. The nine days when you can walk up to a baby ox and crack its tail off in your hand.

I was not yet pregnant. Back then, I was only vulnerable in the ordinary ways. I descended from the plane already wearing silk long johns, lined pants, a sweater, a scarf, and my Chicago winter coat, but the weather hit me like a frying pan to the back of the skull. A man named Zhenjin met me on the tarmac and immediately wrapped me in a fur cloak the size of a bear. He grinned.

"You need to gain at least two inches." His gloved hands indicated a bubble around his waist. "On all sides. Then you will be a proper Mongolian woman prepared for winter." The bearskin, he explained, would stand in as my two inches since I didn't have time to gain the weight *au naturel*.

I'd been invited to sing an aria from *The Snow Maiden*.

Rimsky-Korsakov. Very Russian in its sense of tragedy. The maiden in question seeks human companionship, a communion of souls, despite being unable to actually feel affection. Then, when she does find love—having begged her enchanted mother to grant her the capacity—it kills her. Some versions of the myth have it that she, a girl made out of ice, tries to impress her beloved by jumping over a fire. Some just say that her ardor brings forth the spring. Either way, she melts.

Standing there, freezing in my winter clothes, I felt for the first time that she made the right decision: anything for a touch of warmth.

Zhenjin ushered me into a car that smelled like diesel on the outside but was reasonably clean within and did not stutter when he turned the key. I held my mittened hand over the nearest radiator vent and then retracted it sharply—the air blasting from the vent was arctic.

"Have to wait for the engine to warm up," Zhenjin said, and then took my hand, peeled off the mitten, and cupped it in his own. He blew onto my skin. All this in a quite businesslike manner and with no hint of hesitation.

We sat that way for a minute or two, him occasionally switching my hands between his soft grip and my pockets. Finally the car heater coughed, and I felt warm air spill out over my wrist.

"Now," my companion said, "we are ready."

Ulaanbaatar is not a soft place. On the drive to the hotel, Zhenjin warned me not to walk around alone, especially at night, since many of the streets were still without proper lighting, and an unaccompanied white woman would be a target for muggings. Out the window I saw street merchants hawking yak-wool socks and camel-skin gloves, wearing what looked like felt booties over their shoes to insulate against the layer of ice on the sidewalk. Many muggers carry knives, Zhenjin said, but they will use anything they have at hand: some throw bricks or, in the time-honored tradition of men, just use the weight of their bodies to throw you against a wall.

We pulled up to a curb.

"Okay," Zhenjin said.

The hotel's exterior appeared to have been wrought by a civilization long extinct. *If anything's going to be dangerous to me*, I thought, *it's this*. Stucco crumbled from the façade; bare patches of brick were visible where the siding had calved off slabs large enough to kill a man in falling. I looked at Zhenjin. Over the course of our twenty-minute car ride he'd become important to me, arbiter of street chaos and purveyor of furs. He smiled. "You'll like it," he said. "Inside." He climbed out of the car and held a hand out to me, and we ascended the three steps to the door while the wind did its best to freeze off my ears.

With a cracking sound—icy rubber separating from icy rubber—the doors opened up and I let out a gasp. The interior of the hotel was a sea of marble, a pristine palace. I couldn't have been more surprised if it was made entirely of cut gems. There were no windows, just a cavernous well of veined columns, and without sunlight the brass bell on the reception desk shone only beneath incandescent lamps. But the room was so grand I could imagine candles, could almost see the bulb light lick and flutter like a flame. The bell was polished to a high gleam and seemed to be waiting there for someone to ring it and magically summon back the hospitality of nineteenth-century travel—diplomatic cocktails and colonial balls.

I shook my head, feeling out of place in my animal hide. Disoriented and savage. A dark corner of my mind turned to lineage: Greta, Ada, Sara, me; beasts into ballrooms. Something always lost along the way. I tucked my hand into Zhenjin's elbow, and this alone seemed to keep me from losing my grip on time and place. First I'd stepped off a heated airplane onto the dusty snow of tundra, and then into a car that whipped through streets blooming with apocalyptic decay. And now this.

A t the door to my room I waited for a moment, half expecting Zhenjin to enter ahead of me and clear it of any obstacles or danger. He could do that, it seemed. Keep me safe. Like a girl keeps safe her dolls, needlessly brushing their hair and caressing their cold porcelain cheeks. Brushing away an errant eyelash and saying, *Look, make a wish*. But he didn't walk in and undress me, fold my clothes in neat stacks on a chair. He didn't wash me with a soft, drenched sponge. Instead he bowed and walked away, his black hair wafting slowly against the back of his neck. His brisk steps those of a man acquitted of his duty.

I was surprised to feel a twinge of annoyance. *How dare he*, I thought. But then: how dare he what?

Once I'd showered I felt better for a while. More myself. At home I take two baths a day, and if I go swimming in the magnificent pool at the gym I might take three. As I stripped off layer upon layer of clothing, I began to feel giddy, unwrapping the gift of my actual form, scrubbing off even the thin film of grit and sweat. But when I was pink and dry, I made the mistake of tunneling into my bed to read through the libretto and then the score of the role I would be singing. I'm very susceptible to the instinct of hibernation when I'm touring. Things started well enough—I marked emotional shifts in purple, suggested breaths in blue, and used red to let myself know that a troubling passage was upcoming.

The blanket weighed down on me, melting over my shoulders and breathing hot air onto my back.

But the thought of getting up brought dread, increasingly. Especially the thought of Zhenjin, his low bow at the door, his antiseptic eagerness to please. *What are you doing*, I asked myself. *What do you want from him?* Not his embrace, his mouth on mine. I just felt that he was holding something back from me—that beneath his crisp shell beat a heart I could not reach. And that was a problem. At home I could count on John to feed me his intimate secrets and stories. But here, I would get out of bed and things would spiral out of my control. Instinct would take over, pushing me to show my good side for photographs, smiling with teeth as sleek as sculpted ice.

Zhenjin had warmed my hands in the car, held them very gently. But he also walked away instead of being asked to go. What if, then, I walked onstage and found myself without the strength to sing? Wouldn't it be better to stay here, where I needed nothing? To jump up just briefly and lock myself in with the duvet curled around my neck? I could remain in the bed until the fire squad— if such a thing existed in Ulaanbaatar—came and axed my door to smithereens, dragged me to the airport. I could walk into the hall and discover I'd been transported home, that John was in the kitchen cooking risotto.

A knock stirred me.

"Yes, hello?" It was Zhenjin's voice, polite and inquiring. "Am I disturbing you?"

"One minute," I called. *Look at yourself.* I ran a hand over my face. *You're just jet-lagged. Put on a sweater. Put on pants.* Slowly I pieced my outer shell back together and recovered my gown from the closet, where it had been transported from the car by unseen hands, still zipped inside the whispering black garment bag. I inquired at the mirror—I was more or less composed—and threw open the door, nodding to Zhenjin.

"Good," I said. "You can keep me honest." I tossed the garment bag over his shoulder and buttoned my coat. "Let's walk to the opera house."

"We have a car."

"No, I need the walk." I tugged on my mittens. "It'll bring me back." I paused. "I mean, wake me up." Zhenjin looked at me, stern, and I thought, *No, your job is to give me what I want.* I took his hand and pulled him down the hall, feeling the soft catch as his shoulder extended. Zhenjin made no move to resist, or hold tighter.

The festival organizers had planned well enough to book rooms in a hotel mere blocks from the National Academic Theatre of Opera and Ballet, a pink Romanesque building studded with white colonnades. The Opera House, as they called it, was another surprise: an Easter egg shell filled with a Samarkand mosque. The doorways were embellished with gold filigree and the lobby was filled with arches and domes. Inside, I released Zhenjin and sent him, blushing slightly while he opened and closed his hand, to deliver my gown to the dressing room.

Singers are not ballet dancers. We breathe into our bellies. Expand the diaphragm and keep it expanded. Do not be afraid of a little pot belly, because it indicates power. This type of breathing also affords you the feeling of appetite.

I walked through the Opera House hallways and ran the pad of my index finger over a crashing, cascading loop of gold painted onto the wall. It appeared to be flecking off, so high was the glisten, and I rubbed my finger against my thumb, looked at both, surprised for an instant to find no golden powder there. Butterfly wings. John sometimes catches moths off the dandelions that grow up through the cracks in the sidewalk, presenting them to me as a magic trick—*ta-da*. His hands are always dusted, after. But John wasn't there, and in his place was a hollow orb I had to fill myself. I breathed in the gold, imagined myself licking the entire hallway clean, gobbling down the sugar cube façade of the Opera House in hungry gulps. To eat something is to absorb its power. Many cultures have thought so. I strolled around taking in everything I could see and everything I couldn't, all the music that had ever shown there: inhale Handel, exhale Liszt.

The stage itself was familiar, as stages tend to be worldwide, the ceiling hung with acoustical beams and curves, the flat dark wood of the stage floor swept clean. I took in the scent of dust and polish. The wire tang of the piano.

I fished my phone out of my purse, warming the near-frozen electronics against my chest, and turned on the metronome application so it ticked and tocked like a clockwork heartbeat. To sing, your breath must be steady and controlled. You must always be shoring away air for later use, never expending yourself to the last gasp. This keeps your voice from becoming vulnerable. You have something on hand: a socket of oxygen, the smile of a near-stranger who warms your fingers and has thin eyes and skin like wrinkled paper.

That night I stood before an audience of colleagues in tailcoats and gowns, plus locals who bought tickets whether they were interested or not, to encourage the Ulaanbaatar city council to organize more international festivals. All day I had been keyed up by fear or exhaustion or desire for something that I couldn't name. But now everything that had filled me rushed out. Rinsed off. As simple as that. I sang the dirty gasoline smell of the snow, and the holes in the road that Zhenjin swerved casually to avoid. I sang the cold that leeched up through my shoe soles like water and froze the balls of my feet, the tips of my toes. I sang the broken outer windows of hotel towers and the gold light of the lamps within, the silver brads on the uniforms of the bellhops who lined up in the lobby on the way to my room. I sang the gruff mumbling of the bear I imagined was furnishing me with his skin, and the snowy backsides of yaks I was told were kept on farms on the city outskirts. I was relieved, so relieved to sing. I sang Snegúrochka the snow maiden. I sang her fifteen years of winter, and then I sang her melting into spring.

I look back now on that period of my life with terrible jealousy. So recent, and yet so distant. Three years ago I was in Mongolia, and my body was still the body I'd been born with, tightly packed. Tightly wound.

Because sound is so rich with texture, it is endangered by travel through time as much as it is by travel through space. Look at me: once all I wanted was to have enough energy for my own life, enough control of my lungs to make each note clear. Now my body has changed allegiances. Now my heart has. There is Kara to contend with, and instead of wanting to take something from her, I'm afraid of all I want to give.

Part Two

11

Taking me to the opera was my mother's last attempt to make me her own. Like everything she does, she went about it in a strange way: not many parents would choose to bring their daughters to witness a tragedy to which they are namesake. But whatever her insufficiencies, my mother understood my sense of pride. She knew that seeing the name *Lulu* on the tickets would thrill me more than the character's death would undo me.

The show was a matinee on one of those magical Chicago days that are clear and bright, so the cold doesn't seem so punishing. Walking outside reddened our noses, and my mother pinched mine with her gloved fingers—I could feel the faint pressure from her long manicured nails beneath the leather.

"Let's pretend we're orphans," Sara said to me. "Only not really orphans. Children abandoned at birth who discover that they're really royalty."

"And magic?"

"Yes." She smiled. "And magic. This will be our first time out in the world in our new clothes, and no one will recognize us. They'll all be impressed with how pretty and fancy we are, and even people"—her face darkened—"who've been terrible to us and shunned us because of our orphanhood will love us and sing our praises. And we'll be kind to them." The darkness lifted from her like a cloud in the wind.

We took the O'Hare line to the Loop, then transferred to get to Washington and Wells—it was a long ride, but to us each train was a royal carriage. My mother and I pointed out all the special touches that had been left inside for us: the clean blue pair of seats in a beam of sun, the advertisements for a local jeweler showing pictures of a diamond-studded necklace and bracelet. We might consider getting our tiaras refitted there, we said. If the store had sufficient dignity upon inspection. The other passengers received our scrutinizing attention as well: there was the café owner who'd refused to sell us hot chocolate because the gold coin we'd found to pay with was dirty. Beside her, the spoiled twin girls we always saw in the park whose dresses and hair ribbons threw us into fits of jealousy, which we quelled thanks to our superior breeding.

A blind man with a cane and a threadbare hat sat in the handicapped seats a few feet away from us, and he rocked with the rhythm of the train, singing softly to himself.

"That," Sara whispered to me, taking off her gloves, "is the royal madrigal. He recognized us for what we were long before anyone else, but he couldn't tell us for fear of retribution from the evil queen. She wanted to keep us poor and wretched. But she couldn't fool the madrigal: he sensed our greatness through the sound of our voices. He can tell a prince from a hog farmer by hearing them speak a single word."

We were quiet, listening to the madrigal sing. He changed

tunes after a minute or so, and my mother tilted her head to the side so her long hair fell away from the ear that faced him.

"Well, of course he'd want to honor us with a song." She raised her eyebrows at me gravely. "Shouldn't we honor him back?" My mother could be as great as I wanted her to be, sometimes. When she wanted it too.

I nodded, and she put a finger to her lips. *Hush.* She walked over to where the man sat and placed herself beside him while I watched. Silently. Hushed. At first I couldn't distinguish the sounds she was making from the man's singing, so low were the notes and so well intertwined with the music that was already in the air. But as the man raised his voice my mother made hers more audible, and they began to play together: his legato with her crisp stutters, his baritone with her alto-soprano.

The song was sad, but somehow between them it sounded triumphant. Like they'd found one another after a long search. Ended a long loneliness. She bobbed her head as they tossed lines back and forth, trading phrases from "Body and Soul." I leaned my chin against the cold metal headrest on the back of my seat and watched. The grinding of the train against the tracks rumbled against my jaw as my mother and the man spun the air into an earthy, rasping exultation. They were harmonizing now, and my mother put her clean, beautiful hand on the man's, which was thick with calluses. I loved her then.

Together, they sang about the spirit and the flesh. Together, until they ran out of words.

As the train pulled up to Washington and Wells they hummed a few last bars, until the conductor made a scratchy announcement, breaking the spell. I held my mother's hand and we hopped off onto the wooden platform. The blind man stayed where he was and smiled.

I almost broke into a run towards the front entrance of the Civic Opera House, home of the Chicago Lyric Opera, but my mother snagged the back collar of my dress and pulled me around the building. We approached a side entrance where a man stood smoking in a tuxedo and tails. My mother nudged me.

"*The gatekeeper*," she whispered. I had the tickets.

"Hello," I said to the man. He peered at me through a cloud of smoke that he puffed in and out of his mouth without removing the cigarette. Then he turned to Sara.

"You Jimmy's friend?"

My mother nodded and I silently offered up the tickets in my palm. They were delicate slips of paper with careful calligraphy, unlike any theater stubs I'd seen before. The smoking man picked them up and inspected them, smirking.

"This all seems to be in order," he said. With the gesture of a ringmaster, he extended his arm towards the door, then opened it just slightly so we would have to slip inside. I looked hesitantly at the tickets.

"Are you just going to keep them?" I asked.

I wanted to pin them to the wall beside my bed and teach myself how to write my name in similar sweeps and flourishes. I'd expected an usher to glance at them and hand them back, maybe adding a minuscule tear. But the man in the tuxedo had other plans.

"How right you are," he said, and removed a lighter from the inside pocket of his jacket. The paper was extremely thin; they were gone almost as soon as the flint in the lighter struck metal.

"Come on, Lulu." My mother pulled me through the slender entrance by my elbow.

"Oh, *Lulu*." The man stayed outside and laughed. "This is the famous little *Lulu*. Well, it is an honor." If he said anything else it was lost to me behind the steely slam of the door.

Inside we wound down a series of dark hallways before emerging in the empty lobby. We wove through the columns, clattering against the marble floor, and Sara explained to me that it's the gatekeeper's job to make your passage more difficult, so I shouldn't be offended.

"Nothing worth doing should be easy." She scanned the room for a sign that would point us to our seats, though I realized that without the tickets I had no idea what to even look for. "And nowhere worth going should be easy to get to."

"Why is everything weird?" I asked. "Where is everybody? Baba took me to the opera before."

My mother saw someone lean out a doorway and wave to us a level above our heads. She put her hand on my shoulder.

"Not like this," she said.

We walked out onto the first balcony, and the same woman motioned us towards the front. She was wearing a black gown, waves of loose fabric hanging off her arms like wisps of smoke. When she saw me, she put her hands over her mouth and giggled.

"Oh." She stifled the laughter but still seemed electric and intense. "She *is* a young one. You're sure about this?"

I mustered all my royal pride and raised an eyebrow at her.

"Who are *you*?"

She drew herself up. Her eye makeup was also black, and

with a shadow across her face it looked almost as if she had no eyes at all.

"I'm Lulu," she said.

I sucked in a little surprised air, but kept myself together and held out my hand.

"Me too."

After making introductions, the adult Lulu led us to our seats: dead center, front row, so we could lean against the railing and see the entire stage below us. When I looked down I noticed that the ground floor was completely empty—after glancing around, it was clear that only a few other chairs in the audience were occupied, and no one was sitting near anyone else. Before I could ask Lulu about this, however, she disappeared out the door.

Sitting in the Civic theater is like sitting in a mouth full of gold teeth, red velvet tongues periodically unfurling into aisles. Though the theater was not bright, an occasional patch of warm light glimmered off the embellishments on the walls and hung around me like hot breath. I felt the theater's mouth yawning out from the stage and leaned into it. I wanted to throw myself down the room's golden throat.

Beside me my mother peeled off all her outer layers and laid them on the unoccupied velveteen chair next to her, tucking her gloves into the pockets of her coat. She smoothed her dress out: red, square at the neck so her collarbones emerged gracefully and created chasms whenever she swiveled her head. I had no idea what our "tickets" must have cost, the favors my mother would have had to call in to procure them—*Jimmy's friend*, the man at the door called her. The house wasn't full, but the audience, apparently, was selective. She scratched the back of my hand lightly, and I let her weave her fingers through mine. But I didn't look up at her. The bells sounded and the remaining lights went down. Even in pitch-blackness my eyes didn't leave the stage. My mother was magical, but this was more.

At the time, *Lulu* hadn't been performed anywhere in the world in its entirety. Shows were gearing up in Paris and—oddly enough—New Mexico, rumors being murmured into the ears of the highest society. It was shocking, people said. Adultery and misused sexual power and love wielded like a whip. A woman so desirable she can only destroy herself. And the music is also a challenge: it plunges through discordancy into positive aggression; the orchestration calls for a vibraphone and requires an onstage jazz band in addition to a pit orchestra. The sound expresses a complex network of psychological wounds and perversions.

As most of the world chugged on blissfully unaware and most opera lovers waited in painful anticipation for the Paris premiere, a small subclass of aficionados surfaced and groped their way towards one another. These were people who couldn't be satisfied by seeing the new opera—with its mysterious backstory and dead composer, in addition to its salacious libretto—performed on television in a foreign country. They wanted *Lulu* immediately, and they wanted to inhabit her.

Anything can be had for a price: at least, if the right person is willing to pay. Even a piece of music that is being held hostage for reasons of propriety, bereavement, and force of law. So musicians were assembled from Chicago's jazz underground, singers invited through a series of secret handshakes and lucky misunderstandings. Costumes were borrowed from the mothballs of old shows—a dress here, a coat there. And though no one asked how she accomplished it, the soprano showed up at the very first rehearsal with copies of the complete score and libretto for every participant. They were to be kept secret on pain of death or humiliation.

Here is the thing you must understand: to know an opera you must be part of it. You must emerge into its world and lose yourself there with no hope of ever escaping completely. No matter where you go, the pitches and tones will follow you. The arias will pop up at inconvenient moments, and you'll see the characters ducking into alleys years after you last met them onstage. Letting some other company have the world premiere of *Lulu* would've been, to the performers I saw in the darkened, near-empty Civic Opera House, like watching strangers parade around in their stolen skins. They didn't care about having an audience; they cared about the thing itself.

My mother was not invited to be a part of the secret show. But she knew enough people to finagle two of the precious seats in the theater when almost no one was allowed in. She brought me there to show me what it meant to have real passion. What she didn't anticipate was that perhaps I already knew.

In the first intermission the entire small audience crowded together in the hallway and passed around bottles of champagne: I was allowed two tastes myself and laughed to feel how strangely the bubbles sipped at my throat. Lulu's second husband, The Painter, had committed suicide, and she had convinced Dr. Schön to throw off his fiancée and marry her instead. She looked dark and foreboding onstage, but throughout the first act had worn a red cloth heart pinned to the front of her dress, which was occasionally singled out in a lone slender spotlight.

Sara put her hands on my shoulders, leaned down, and gave me a quick kiss on each cheek. She was lightheaded from the champagne, like me. I could tell: she bobbed from foot to foot as though she was standing behind a microphone, and her expression was moony.

"What do you think?" she asked me.

I regarded her seriously.

"It feels real."

"Yes." My mother gave me a strange look. "It does."

By the second intermission the champagne was all gone, but Sara procured a bottle of whiskey, which she shared out in nips amid the nervous laughter of the small crowd. Lulu had become heady with lovers in this act: lovers hiding in closets and spilling out from behind divans. Lovers accusing their own sons of treachery and emerging from under tables like ghosts rising from ill-dug graves. Dr. Schön, played by the tuxedoed gatekeeper who'd burned our tickets by the door, encouraged Lulu to shoot herself to atone for her perfidy, but she shot him instead. When Lulu was sentenced to life imprisonment, the jurors tore her red heart in half and left her with only the wound. She fell ill.

I had a new admiration for the gatekeeper after hearing him sing. In the hallway I tugged on Sara's arm to ask her who he really was, but she was busy laughing with a man whose face was completely hidden behind his beard. Without looking down, she offered me the bottle of whiskey, and I was so confused that I backed away and waited by the wall for the bells to direct us back to our seats.

At the end of the second act, Lulu escaped from prison by letting her lover, a beautiful countess, rot there in her place. She left for Paris with Dr. Schön's son, Alwa, a strange and desperate look painting her face.

The third act was the real premiere: the composer had died before finishing it, leaving behind the sordid tale and a series of complex notes and ideas. His widow forbade anyone to complete the opera, then changed her mind, changed it back, and finally capitulated to a full production through the simple expedient of her death.

Sitting in the darkness waiting for the music to recommence, Sara mumbled that she was cold and started fumbling with her coat and scarf. One of the gloves fell out of her pocket and she swore, feeling past my feet for it and finally giving up.

"Shit," she said. "Shit shit shit." I bit back the urge to shush her.

The act opened with a scene of opulent destruction: the police continued to pursue Lulu as she and Alwa made toasts at a party. The smile on Lulu's face was false and men tugged her from side to side, whispering items of blackmail into her ears until finally they pulled off the sleeves of her dress, leaving her shivering in the middle of the room. Everyone's wealth was consumed by a stock market crash, and Lulu managed to escape only at the last moment by tricking the police into arresting a waiter instead.

My heart was beating so loudly in my ears that it nearly obscured the voices of the singers. With one exception: Lulu's could always reach me. The notes she sang carved the room like a guillotine blade. I reached out and tried to hold my mother's hand, but she'd thrust it into her pocket and refused to budge. She sniffed slightly, watching the jazz band onstage. The bassist was a man she sometimes worked with. She seemed to be sizing him up, her lip curled back with derision.

Finally, reduced to prostitution, Lulu took in a string of clients who eerily resembled each of her dead husbands. The loyal Countess Geschwitz reemerged with a portrait of the fallen beauty at the height of her glory, and Lulu and Alwa stared into it, hypnotized. There was a full round heart apparent on her painted breast.

But the spell didn't hold. More clients tumbled forward: Lulu's first husband, Dr. Goll, then The Painter, The Acrobat. Everyone she had abandoned or to whom she had done harm. She killed Alwa with a blow to the back of the head and then sat down in the dark, her hand to her chest. Again there came a single beam illuminating the broken red heart, with Lulu's fingers trembling above it.

The doorbell rang. At first I was confused, thinking it was Dr. Schön, but Sara leaned down to me and whispered savagely: "*Jack the Ripper.*" Lulu didn't seem to know the difference either, though, for she ran into his arms. The two left the stage together hand in hand, and her scream resounded from the darkness into the empty theater. Jack the Ripper returned, carefully wiping his fingers clean with a handkerchief, and casually stabbed the beautiful Countess as well. Then the red curtains fell, half of a giant black heart pinned to either side.

When the lights came up, I blinked in the sudden brilliance of the room. I'd focused so long and acutely on the stage that having a whole broad world to look at made me somewhat dizzy. I took a deep breath to clear my head and then sneezed. Turning, I saw Sara smoking a cigarette in her seat.

"I don't think you can do that in here." I rubbed my nose and looked at her accusingly, hoping nonetheless that her smoking would give me time to get my bearings.

"Oh, please," she said. "You still don't understand about being clandestine? It means you can do anything you want. Just like being a princess. So come off it." She stubbed the cigarette out on the polished arm of her chair, leaving a black circle of singe and the poison odor of burning varnish.

"Come on." My mother tugged on my hand, and I hurried to thrust my arms into the sleeves of my coat. Having outfitted herself for the chill winter air over an hour before, she didn't seem to notice that I'd barely had time to stand up. I took a last look around the theater, which still seemed to throb with the opera's final notes.

"Can we go see the orchestra?" I asked as I fumbled with my coat buttons. "Or say good-bye to the singers? I really want to see the singers."

Sara rubbed her forehead, pinching the skin between her thumb and middle finger. Her wooziness had taken on new dimension during the show's finale, and I could see her debating the wisdom of sitting back down and closing her eyes for a moment while I ran around and had my fun. Today was the first day I'd been able to identify her tang of maple syrup and wood smoke as whiskey: the bottle she'd waved towards me in the second intermission had solved the long mystery of my mother's most peculiar perfume.

Lulu—her real name, I learned later, was Rosalind DeLaney—sashayed onto the balcony and, spotting me, threw her arms open wide. They were bare now that the sleeves had been torn off them, but five or six new cloth hearts had been pinned haphazardly all over her remaining strips of dress. I ran over and tucked myself into the crook of her neck and shoulder, smelling the tacky sweet makeup caked on her face, cut with the salt of her sweat.

"My understudy!" She picked me up and twirled me around in the air and I laughed, making the sound purposefully melodic so she would hug me tighter. Then she set me down. "You have some pipe organs in those lungs, I hear?"

I nodded and beamed.

"Well, you take care of them." She put a hand over her mouth to stifle a giggle. "And someday you'll be here too, singing secret shows for no money."

"Do you think so?"

I had no reason to trust her encouragement and, having never heard me sing, she had no reason to give it. But still the moment glowed between us: she, shimmering with the light of her success, and me, burning brightly from the heart out.

"Lulu."

We both looked up at the sharp sound, but it was clear that my mother was talking only to me. She had another cigarette between her fingers—this time, thankfully, unlit.

"Let's go," she said. "I have to get out of here."

I gave Rosalind one more squeeze around the neck and then ran after my mother, who'd disappeared into the hallway. If Rosalind was confused about Sara's behavior—ignoring her, absconding before the party I now know must have followed—she didn't show it. There were other guests to greet and preen to.

✦❧ • ❧✦

We pushed out the back door into the alley and Sara immediately began flicking her lighter at the cigarette. She was talking to herself quietly—*should've known, pretentious assholes*—and couldn't get a flame, so she threw the lighter against the side of the building opposite.

"Whoa, sunshine." The gatekeeper pushed himself up from the wall against which he'd been leaning, puffing smoke into the sky. "Let me get that for you."

I frowned at him, though I also had the urge to reach out and touch him as he casually ignited my mother's cigarette and gave an ironic bow. The front of his tuxedo bore a bright red flower that had been used to simulate Dr. Schön's gunshot wound.

"You shouldn't smoke," I scolded, thinking of his voice.

My mother rolled her eyes and tugged my arm again, waving vaguely at the man.

"What do you care?" She moved quickly towards the subway platform. The sun had disappeared behind a new head of clouds while we were hidden in the theater, and the cold felt less pure now, more invasive and wet. "He's nobody."

"He's the gatekeeper," I said, no longer sure.

Back at Washington and Wells, we waited for the train on the creaking cold boards of the platform. A sheet of newspaper blew around, never quite kicking off onto the tracks or down onto the street but tumbling up and back, shushing against the advertisements and occasionally tickling someone's legs. Waiting for the train, I knew we wouldn't be calling it a chariot or a royal carriage. But I couldn't help feeling a shiver of hope, of electricity, as we retraced our footsteps.

The train slowed down, stopped, and lurched slightly forward again before the doors opened. My heart hiccupped into my throat and I hopped on board, accidentally pushing into a teenage boy, who told me to watch it. There was an old man sitting in the handicapped seats by the door clutching a cane with both hands. The madrigal, I thought; he would recognize us. The madrigal would wake my mother back up into the woman she had been that morning, putting a smudge of lipstick on my mouth before we left the apartment and entrusting me with the tickets, tucking them into the secret inner pocket of my coat.

I sat down in the pair of seats closest to the man, and Sara set herself beside me with a sigh.

"Shouldn't we sing him a song?" I nudged her and indicated towards the man with the cane.

"What?" My mother followed my gaze and then looked up at the ceiling for a long moment. She said something that I couldn't quite hear, using mostly the back of her throat.

"What?" I parroted. She closed her eyes.

"I said, can you give it a goddamn rest."

My mother slept until we had to change trains, and I watched the blind man, studying him. He couldn't possibly be the royal madrigal, I decided. His hat was different. He was no longer humming along with the train but just letting it throw him gently back and forth as it turned around the Loop. Anyway, I assured myself, it was too much of a coincidence.

When we reached our stop, I shook Sara gently by the shoulder and she blinked at me, then stood up and walked off without saying a word. I hesitated in front of the blind man.

"Good-bye," I said.

He tilted his chin in my direction, and a mask of something approaching recognition came over his face. *He sensed our greatness through the sound of our voices,* my mother had said. The madrigal knew the orphans to be more than they appeared.

A metallic *ding* sounded and I ran through the doors of the train before they closed and locked me in. But when I looked through the window, I thought I saw the madrigal wink at me— wink, that is, at the ground on which I'd been standing before I ran after my mother into the world.

12

History is like any other story—it depends on us, it feeds on us, on our desire to get it right. But what if there is no way to know exactly how something was, what it meant? What if an event is too complicated to make sense of, to ever put your finger on?

Most people vaguely remember Fryderyk Chopin to be French. His father hailed from Lorraine and his compositions were Romantic, so it seems aesthetically appropriate to tie him to the City of Love and Light. Indeed he died in Paris; his body was interred there in Père-Lachaise Cemetery after he drowned in the fluid of his own lungs. So he is called Frédéric François Chopin, and listeners feel *haute* and *beau monde* when they put their children to sleep with his nocturnes.

But in fact he was born on a small country estate in Żelazowa Wola. He was christened in the same church in central Poland where his parents had been married, and he grew up under the watchful red turrets of the Warsaw Barbican. His family lived on the grounds of the Saski Palace, and as a boy Chopin played a small piano with heart-shaped legs under a window that looked down on trimmed trees and lawns as slick as seal's fur.

Is it just the glamour of Paris that makes audiences wish it was the musician's home? What about the romance of something star-crossed? Chopin left for France just before Poland rose up and was crushed down by the hand of the Russian Empire, making it unsafe for him to return. In all his time in Paris, Chopin never sought fluency in French and always kept a silver chalice filled with soil from his homeland.

Still, when he died the Parisians didn't want to give him up. They collected their most buxom women and had them throw armfuls of roses over his grave to bury him deep below the French streets; their nattiest gentlemen poured out decanters of wine to confuse Chopin's spirit and keep it happy in the company of Théodore Géricault, Dominique Vivant, and Vincenzo Bellini.

They kept his bones. The distals at the tips of his fingers that stroked the keys of his instrument; the elegant tibia; even the skull. An artisan made a death mask of his face, and reproductions of it hung in the best houses of Paris. But Poland, with all the power of the *rusalka* residing in her wet, rolling hills and icy streams, called his soul back. By decree of his sister, Chopin's chest was cracked open and his heart removed to a marble pillar in the Holy Cross Church in Warsaw.

I used to imagine this with a hysterical vividness: the organ resting on a velvet pillow stuffed with down, surrounded by slick satin lining. All the fabric was red and glistened like exposed muscle tissue, a new warm chest for the heart to inhabit, with wooden ribs and an ivory clasp. And because a child's imagination knows no boundaries of taste and is never stilled by fear of excess, the heart reposed with piles of rubies. There were holly berries and pomegranate seeds and the flesh of ripe figs burst open by their own internal weight. The heart was beating.

"No," said my mother when I told her this fantasy. "Actually it's preserved in cognac. Probably inside a glass bottle. I wonder"— she paused and wet her lips with whatever was in her cup—"how that affects the flavor of the cognac." The sparkle in her eyes was truly indecent.

Sara sighed and leaned back in her chair. She closed her eyes and I shrank away from her, my nightgown brushing against my ankles. "It must be exquisite." She laughed. "Or disgusting. Repugnant. Repellent. But still. A completely unique experience."

W as Chopin Polish or was he French? You could say both and be satisfied. But people always want to tell a story that has loyalties. They want you to form a hierarchy of love.

A s a child, I listened at night for dark clickings. The sound of heels with the tips danced off, a whiff of cigarette smoke curling under the door. I wasn't allowed to stay up waiting for my mother, but sometimes I would snap awake in the middle of the night and know she was there, her key easing into the lock, a breathy curse echoing when she turned a heel. I could picture her routine perfectly: making her way to the hallway table and balancing on one foot, her weight bearing down with one palm on the table. One shoe slid off, then the other. Tucking her hair behind her ears in the dark mirror.

I was not a part of her routine, a kiss good night was not usual. Most often I would drift back to sleep while she was running the bathroom tap; she liked to fall asleep with legs freshly shaved, which is a habit I have stolen from her. Sara's nocturnal behavior was animalistically private—you might make educated guesses about what she would do, predictions based on observation. But her motivations were always her own. She ignored me often enough to lead me to expect it. She loved me just enough to pit my stomach with yearning.

Most nights she would leave the bathroom and go straight to her bed, bare feet making sticky, quiet steps back down the hallway. But sometimes this: my door opening a crack, letting in a slim line of moonlight that leaked from the windows into the hall. And my mother's figure looking down on me. Often I would pretend to be sleeping, and she would tiptoe to my bedside, lay the back of her hand across my hot cheek. If she happened to come in following a nightmare, she would crawl into my bed and hold me, sing a lullaby against the rhythmic gulping of my sobs. "Swing Low, Sweet Chariot." "All the Pretty Little Horses." Her songs were gravel, loneliness, a puff of smoke. The most beautiful songs I'd ever heard.

"*Lalka*," she would whisper. "Come on, you know the words."

The dark wrapped around us as Sara shifted and settled, and we kept our voices quiet so that Ada wouldn't hear us and wake up. It was more than politeness that kept us hushed: we were swaddled by the delicious notion of being alone in the whole black world. Two sailors singing a private language on the night's inky sea. I felt her breath warming the back of my head and fell asleep, her child, her star.

At some point she would slip out the door and back to her bedroom and be swallowed up until ten or eleven or noon the next day. She would emerge with a flowered silk dressing gown pulled around her, toenails visibly crimson when she sat down and propped her foot up on a chair in the kitchen. She would already be smoking as she walked from her room, and when she looked at me I felt like a stranger. A blank.

"Your girl's got that face again," she'd say to Ada. "Why don't you take her away for a little while."

Poland is sometimes called the Christ of Nations because of the number of times her borders have been invaded, her land divided by conquering hands. Germany, Russia, the Bohemians, the Mongols—no muster of troops ever abandoned its chance to slice the country up and take a bite. At times Poland has existed nowhere but in the hearts of her remaining people, and so she shone brighter there than she would have in the hands of real, imperfect kings and ministers. And the damage that was done to the nation became, in its own way, a holy thing. A sacred basis for offense.

It makes a person dangerous to love their own trouble. My mother is the best example of this that I know. Like Poland—her homeland of conception, if not of birth—she blazed with glory through her young life. She strutted into the Green Mill jazz bar at age sixteen in full light of day and told them she was there to audition for a job. There were no open positions, but they let her sing on a lark and she walked out with the promise of an opening act on Tuesdays.

She painted dark lines around her eyes like Cleopatra, and dark red onto her lips like blood. She vamped. She dressed to precision. If she wanted a man she blew in his ear and he would follow her anywhere. Then she'd abandon him there. I never knew my father, because she wanted it that way. Whoever he was, she just didn't care.

Ada stood behind Sara with pins in her mouth and refitted her clothes to give her the dimensions of architecture. When Sara tilted her head to the side in a gown her mother had sewn for her, a person saw the Leaning Tower of Pisa. Ada curled Sara's hair. She laughed with her about the women whose jobs Sara usurped with a wink. And she told her how she was a credit to Greta. A person worth making a sacrifice for to the devil.

When I was born, Ada took all these gifts back and one by one she gave them to me. It happened almost immediately, the transfer of love, the replacement of the legacy on my still-soft head. How can I know this? I was only a baby. I should think that pampering and love is simply my due.

But I know my mother. She's the one who taught me the phrase *Christ of Nations*. She's the one who taught me about war and invasion. Every story I ever heard from my baba Ada about Greta, I heard again from my mother Sara another way. For one thing, what Ada called our family's gift, Sara assured me was a curse. My childhood was different in her eyes, and her mouth.

"**W**as there really a piano factory?"
During the years of Ada's lessons and excursions—to the Green Mill, to the beach—I also sat on my mother's wine-colored Turkish rug and braided the fringe. It was my secret responsibility: if left unbrushed, unbraided, unattended, the fringe collected weeks of dirt and dust. Once I ran my fingers through it and a beige spider trundled up from the tangle of scratchy strings and hurried over the back of my hand before disappearing again under Sara's bed.

My mother didn't leave until I was nine, and that gave me plenty of time to grow accustomed to laying my head against her knees in the early afternoon; to being the silent partner squeezing her hand as she talked and cackled into the phone; to giving my opinion on the shoes and jewelry she chose to highlight the flecks of gold in her dark eyes. I liked to listen to her talk about Greta too—not as an authority, like Baba Ada, but as another aficionado. Her versions of Greta's stories gave me a shiver of frightened pleasure. They'd been drained of one type of blood and infused with another.

One November day, she lay on her stomach in bed with light streaming in through the long scarves she'd fashioned into curtains. I was seven. The cup of tea I'd carried in as currency sat on the squat cherrywood table beside her, a red lip print glazing the edge of the secondhand china. When I knocked on my mother's door, I was obliged to wait, sometimes to give her the opportunity to touch up her makeup before allowing me entrance, sometimes so she could tell me to go away.

"Of course there was a piano factory." Sara frowned at me, as if I'd gone a bit too far. "You can still buy those pianos. They're antiques now. But good ones—like a Stradivarius."

"Why don't we have one?"

She laughed at me.

"Because they're expensive, dummy. Like a Stradivarius."

"I know a Strad is expensive." I did know this, vaguely, from Ada and from trips to the library. I called it a *Strad* with tired self-importance, thinking that was the right way for a musician to speak. "I was just asking. I could take lessons. I could learn sight reading."

Sara reached a lazy hand out to the table and picked up her teacup. She sipped it and grimaced—as usual my tea was too strong for her—and then drained half the cup so quickly it could scarcely have brushed her tongue.

"You don't need sight reading. Good lord. You need a childhood."

I loosened the fringe braid I'd been working on and combed the strands neat.

"I need sight reading to be *adaptable*."

"Whatever you say." Sara stretched out her fingers and regarded the polish. "What were we talking about? How did we get on this subject?"

"The piano factory," I said. "In Poland."

"Oh, that's right. The fucking piano *fabryka*." My mother's use of Polish in my presence was haphazard at best and expletive at worst. If it had been up to her, I'd only ever have learned the terms she used in public to mask my need for a toilet: *dupa, siu-siu*. But she loved storytelling every bit as much as Baba Ada. She was compelled by it, telling with inventive precision even the tales she claimed to regret ever having known. "Where Greta the Great sold her soul."

I looked at her uncertainly.

"To the devil?"

"Sure," said Sara. "If that's how you want to put it."

My mother described Greta's world to me in a way that felt familiar but askew. The orange foxes there did not whisper messages, and the boys—Andrzej, Fil, and Konrad—only went with their father into the woods to learn the basics of his trade. But there was still the feeling of something unseen lingering beneath the surface of everyday life, a coded danger. Perhaps there were dark messages written in the trees?

On one side of town was an area that Ada had never mentioned, with a synagogue. If I'd asked, Baba Ada would probably have said that those people were irrelevant to her because they didn't come to church and hear her sing. Their children didn't compete with her for solos in the choir. Sara had her own thoughts on the subject.

The buildings in town stood close together, like men lined up side by side so their shoulders hunched up slightly towards their ears. At ground level, slabs of window glass glinted before stacks of brightly colored cans, dress dummies swathed in wool, and posters extolling aperitifs and local pilsner. The skin of the world was composed of cobblestones and careful storefront displays, its spirit written in gossip and hunger. There was a broad plaza next to a railroad track. Naked rabbits hung upside-down in the window of the butcher's shop, ruby red like lipstick.

On the village outskirts, where Greta and Saul lived, a person could get by on their wits—that is, their wits, a small farm, and a gun. For a house in town, however, or even a small flat above the shops, one had to be willing to give his time away for money. Some people owned the shops themselves and lived in slender buildings along with their bolts of cloth or tack and feed or even mortuary tools. There was also a fruit processing plant to which blue-suited workers walked each morning. One could recognize them from the sweet gummy stains on their clothing and from the way their wrists swelled up to the size of persimmons after ten-hour days fixing lids onto jars.

But the jewel of the town was the piano factory.

The *fabryka Łozina* sat on a hill above the streets and always had an aura of pitch about it: the place stank beautifully with the blood of trees. Men walked out after a long day's work laughing, sometimes singing, with grit adhering to their shoes. They picked sticky slivers off their shirts as they unrolled the cuffs and descended home into the warm light of the town.

Saul was a woodsman. He understood the weight, the grain, the flexibility of different types of wood with the instinctual ease most people use to differentiate wholesome milk from sour. By placing his palm on a tree trunk, he gauged its usefulness in building a home, carving the headboard for a bed, or amplifying keystrokes—housing hammers and wire. Łozina instruments were of the highest quality, meant to accompany symphony orchestras across Europe and teach young aristocrats the value of perfection. And although he was not officially employed by the factory—Saul liked to keep his own hours and his options open—Greta's husband was sought after by the buyers there because he brought them the best lumber, simple as that.

W as it the house of the devil? Was it full of fire and brimstone, I wanted to know?

"Don't be so stupid," my mother said. "Do you really believe everything that woman tells you?"

I frowned. "Don't you?"

Sara brushed the question aside.

"Here's what was inside the factory." She waved a hand out past her head, nearly toppling her teacup and a jam jar full of makeup brushes. "A handsome man."

"Saul?"

"No," she said. "Not Saul. He couldn't give Greta a daughter, remember? He didn't have what she needed."

This was something I'd always wondered about but had been afraid to ask Baba Ada. She was so fervent in her tales of Greta's encounter with the devil in the forest that even my heart didn't dare question their reality. But I was curious anyway. I wanted to understand the stories from every angle, until I could close my eyes and sculpt them with my own hands.

"Why was that what Greta wanted? A girl?"

Sara closed her eyes and laughed at me. It always delighted her when I asked her a question she knew I'd never have asked my *babenka*, brought up a line of inquiry that ran contrary to Ada's version of events. Then something occurred to her; her smile froze and retreated into a straight line.

"It's very painful, to lose a child. A daughter. You'd do anything to get her back, get another chance with her."

I smoothed the fringe of the rug beneath my fingers. Separated the strands into threes for new braiding. From where I was sitting, I could see the small of my mother's back, the place where the satin of her kimono robe collapsed.

"How do you know?" This too was a question I would never ask Ada. "You don't have any dead babies."

She kept her eyes closed.

"No, but I have you," she said. "Isn't that enough?"

My mother, by nature a performer, shrugged something off when she fell into a story. Yes, she still had a tendency to brood and, yes, she was mercurial—I might easily be kicked out of her room for an offhand remark, no matter what we were doing. But her eyes grew bright. Like Baba Ada, she told it all as if she'd been there. And Greta especially intoxicated her, as wine would, or a puff of opium, or her tongue's first taste of salt.

Greta had dreams of working in the piano factory. Not as a secretary, stirring cream into coffee and shuffling paper into files. She was grander than that, and her dreams were grander too. She wanted to be a doctor of music.

Sometimes Saul was called to Łozina when a special-order

instrument wasn't behaving—falling out of tune or echoing. On occasion a board would warp and the keys, which were so precious as to have been cut from the mouths of elephants, refused to fit evenly in the slip. Saul described it to Greta: they undulated like waves in the river, cresting over one another and yielding banshee twangs. He would bring in boards so fresh they fairly dripped with the spice of their sap and plane them fastidiously, sanding the wood in broad concentric circles. These would be used to replace malfunctioning elements, and Saul would leave with a new happy weight in his pocket.

But what if, Greta asked herself, *the problem was smaller, more subtle?*

Then they would need a subtler solution. They would need someone for whom music was language, and medicine. They would need the Doctor of Łozina.

The images ran through her mind while she was kneading bread dough in the kitchen, punching gasps of yeast out into the air. She would wear a white coat. Why not? She would wear quiet white shoes, slippers of cotton that hugged her feet and slid against the slick factory floor. Men with dark, serious faces would usher her over to an ailing instrument and wail, "No one knows what to do!"

She'd smile. Place a hand briefly on a quaking shoulder and then turn to the patient. The Doctor of Łozina would run her fingers over every inch of the piano, then open the lid and smell the interior, judging health or sickness from its bouquet. *It's the wires,* she would say. Then take a small silver hammer out of her coat and tap around on the soundboard. *There's a murmur. A break in the vibrations. A misplaced damper. It needs someone to spend the night here with it, taking its pulse at regular intervals.* And the dark, tense men would drink in her every word, writing it all down and thanking her profusely. They would hold Greta's hands in their own and squeeze them.

"Thank you," they'd say. "*Thank* you."

And she would wince, drawing back and flexing her fingers. Smiling once more before she withdrew.

Maybe it was this (*maybe it was this*, Sara said into my ear, the warm air hissing against my skin. I'd climbed onto the bed and curled into a ball before her, wrapped her arms around me and held them there by the bulb of her fists), maybe it was this unrequited dream that brought Greta to the factory gates one morning not long after the loss of her fifth daughter. In this Ada and Sara agreed: it was after the fifth.

She was in town for some small thing: negotiating a price on a bolt of cloth, replenishing her store of baking yeast. (My mother snorted as she said this, though she was a fine baker too.) Perhaps acquiring poppy seeds to make *makowiec*, rolls of white and black cake for her sons. (*For her brats.*) This small task was her outward purpose, the sense of volition that allowed her to get out of the house in spite of the fact that Fil had just hit Konrad in the head and the latter was crying; despite the fact that laundry needed to be hung to snap in the wind. Her inward purpose crouched in the lacuna of her mind, until a pinch in her calf muscles startled her out of a daydream and she realized she was walking uphill. *Well,* she thought, *I guess I'm going to visit Łozina.*

It was a surprisingly cold morning; the sky was the sharp blue of ice. The iron gate was open to allow for the influx and egress of craftsmen and guests, and Greta slipped through casually as if she was meant to, walked up to a window, and peered inside. Her hand idly ran down the rough scratch of the bricks on the exterior wall.

The window was fogged up, crystallized with condensation—the accumulated hot breath of so many men.

Greta peeled away the fug of ice with her hand to provide a better view. Her belly still felt raw and carved out, and somehow this formed a delicate thread of logic. If she could be changed instantaneously from a mother into an empty bowl, then it was her right of transformation to become a person who belonged at the *fabryka Łozina*, instead of one who simply wished to. She did not press herself for specifics. Something inside her simply said to wait.

Two men strolled out into the day, one pushing the doors open bombastically with his palms and exclaiming at the cold. The other ran a hand through the salt-and-pepper of his hair. Neither of them turned to where they could easily have seen a misplaced woman peeping into their factory. Spying. Greta froze in place and in her momentary fear heard only some of what the men said to each other: one enumerating points on his fingers as though he were trying to teach someone to count, the other laughing. She caught a few words: *exhibition, showroom, certain failure, mad*. She came back to herself just in time to hear, "*All right,* Gustaw," just as the men passed through the factory gate and descended out of range of her sight and hearing. The name echoed in Greta's head: *Gustaw.* She considered it for a moment and then shook it away; in its place she formed a plan.

(*Desperate people,* Sara told me, *always make the most interesting plans.*

Was she desperate? I asked.

You'd better believe it.)

The factory's bustling central room was kept warm with four masonry heaters, stationed one in each corner. Greta walked purposefully towards the nearest one and held her hands out, savoring

the light burn on each palm. Although Saul was called to the factory for work, Greta hadn't been inside since the night so long
ago when the *fabryka* had been opened up for a dance. It was as
alive now with industry as it had been then with youth, and Greta
soaked up the energy of it, the noise. She looked around herself,
keeping close to the heater and its embellished ceramic legs, made
to look like the paws of a blue lion.

Raising his eyebrows from across the room, a young worker
walked up to Greta and said, "Yes, hello?" making the greeting
into a question.

She turned to him with a brilliant smile. Yes, she belonged
here. She had always belonged here.

"Good morning, sir," she said, winding the shawl off her neck
and shoulders. She was wearing mourning blacks, her small outward concession to loss, and she knew that these clothes—kept
pressed and stored in a chest in her bedroom, hidden away out of
sight until necessity demanded them—looked much smarter than
her everyday dresses. "I'm here for the tour?"

The worker leaned in as if he hadn't quite caught her words.

"The what?"

"The tour, of course. For the exhibition guests? I was told it
would be starting sharply."

It was a gamble: he might easily have remembered Greta from
town, but as luck would have it, the worker's natural nervousness
eroded his attentiveness to detail. He started to blush up over his
collar, craning his head around for some possible authority.

"I'm not—" he said. "That is, *I* don't . . ."

"Yes," Greta said. "Quite. Well, anyway, if Gustaw is
unavailable—"

"Gustaw!" the man cried. Really, he was no more than a boy;
his relief was almost embarrassing. "Yes, Gustaw! That is, Mr.

Lindemann." A frown spread over his face. "I'm afraid he's gone, for the rest of the day."

"Hmm, how like him." Greta was really enjoying herself, despite a small twinge of pity for the boy in front of her. "Well, that's no trouble. I'll just look around myself. Unless"—she eyed the nervous youth and turned her mouth down into a mock sulk—"that's against some sort of regulation? I promise I'll be as quiet as a mouse."

"No." The boy deflated gently back into his socks. "Quite all right. As long as it's no trouble to you."

Greta gave a nod and slid away before he could change his mind.

The air buzzed with conversation as men walked past, the top buttons of their shirts undone, rolls of paper tucked under their arms. Some of them seemed to recognize her, their eyes lingering on her face with momentary curiosity. But she was lucky. Whether because they were too busy to stop or whether they thought she was there on some errand for Saul, no one did more than nod hello. Greta took deep breaths to keep her heartbeat even as she had in preparation for giving birth, when the first sharp pains shot up her spine. But she found that she wasn't nervous. Her body moved smoothly and her mouth remained kinked into a small, smug smile. She was looking for something, without knowing quite what.

(*She wanted something*, Sara said, *that she couldn't admit to herself that she wanted*.)

To her left, a pair of legs extended from the bottom of a discordant, groaning instrument, one bent at the knee and tapping its toe. Farther off was a tunnel. Could that be right? Greta approached and saw a man reaching up and making pencil markings on an arch of white wood, and realized the tunnel was in fact a caterpillar queue of grand piano frames, lined up with their bottoms in the air.

Everywhere around her were sounds. Not just factory sounds, but echo chambers, hollow demi-music. A fist connected with a keyboard on the left side of the room, and the dissonant chord stormed across the warehouse like a wave. When it passed, Greta could hear wire coiling, stretching, snapping, and below this the great rumbling of boxes being moved on wheeled trays with a rhythm all its own. She felt she was being tugged in all directions at once, and the effect was familiar somehow, that yearning, gnawing urge. A high trill here, a rough scratching there, as pianos were pulled and warped into life.

Greta tried not to stay in one place for too long, silently imploring the men (*everywhere, men*) to ignore her, to pass over her with a glance and move on to more important things. She reached a hand up to rearrange the curls of her hair. Back home the oven temperature would soon puff them out into a shapeless, floating floss, or else sweat them down in rivulets along her neck. But she was here, a part of the factory machinations, and she knew that for once she looked the way people expected a lady to look.

As she walked towards the showroom in the factory's rear, the tinkering fell away. First the pallets of raw materials were shed, then the sand-shaved, pretreated wood that still retained its faint scent of needles and leaves. Greta felt she could see all the detritus—the tools, the wood chips—being swept backward away from her, though in fact it was she who moved away from it. Her eyes were keyed on the sleek floor before her, peopled by a black herd of perfect glassine surfaces. At last even the sound of conversation died away, so that stepping onto the polished showroom floor was like walking into a world where everyone held their breath.

Greta felt a pinch in her abdomen, and wondered if she would find another small trickle of blood on her leg when she went home and stripped off her town stockings. The thought made her nauseous, and she sat down before an imposing baby grand piano— her back was turned to the piecemeal beasts in the workshop, but her mind strained towards them. *Not so different*, Greta thought, as her stomach clenched. *How many unfinished things have I abandoned?* Her left hand found its way to the keyboard, and she suddenly felt very angry and foolish. A cough resounded behind her.

"Excuse me?"

Turning sharply, Greta found herself staring into the face of the gentleman she'd seen outside the factory, the one who'd laughed so freely when his graying companion said *failure* and *mad*. He had white blond hair and a strange smile on his face, his hands tucked carefully behind his back.

"My name is Gustaw," he said. "Gustaw Lindemann. I'm a senior designer here at Łozina." He stared up at the ceiling for a moment, as if uncertain how to proceed. Greta noticed that he rocked gently back and forth on his heels. "I heard that there was a lady looking for me on the showroom floor. Would that lady by any chance be you?"

Lindemann smiled at her, gently now. His suit was made of tidy pin-striped wool, and Greta supposed his was the sort of polite society that noticed when a woman was wearing mourning blacks, that made a point of knowing the difference between fashion and funereal garb.

"Oh," she said, blushing. "You design these?"

"Yes." He gave a slight bow. Or perhaps he was still just rocking back and forth. "Well, that is to say, not all of them. Not alone. But I do have a degree of oversight over the direction of our movements. Glandt and I share a certain, shall we say, particularity about the way our instruments sound. But I'm also interested in their longevity, so—" He stopped. "You don't really know what I'm talking about, do you?"

Greta frowned.

"How can you design a piano? Doesn't it already more or less have its own design? Built in?" She stroked the keys of the instrument in front of her like they were little finger bones.

His hand going lightly to the nape of his neck, Lindemann laughed again. His fingers were clean, scrubbed pink.

"Well, I can't say it's the first time I've heard that question. Let me put it this way: I believe there is an ideal piano out there"—he gestured vaguely, into the distance, not the factory—"somewhere. A fixed form, if you will, which if you found it would allow you to make a perfect piano every time, without fail. But at the moment, you see, no one knows what it is. So when I say I'm designing pianos, what I mean is I'm trying to shave away all the mistakes that the other piano makers—and, well, also that I—have made." Lindemann grinned. "Trying to get closer to that piano in the sky."

Greta looked out over the gathered instruments. Was each one different? Each one an infinitesimal improvement? Were they lined up, then, in the order of their creation so that discerning buyers could easily select the finest or choose, with greater consideration to price, the third from best? Fifth from best? Perhaps it gave Lindemann a pang of regret to depose each glorious princeling with the new generation. After all, each of them began with him. "You must be very well known for your work. You speak about it beautifully."

She was worried that he was growing tired of her, as he had his back to her, strolling through the instruments and striking a note or two on each one. But then he turned and shrugged.

"Ah, well, there's the rub. If I'm doing even a passable job, most people don't have the faintest idea who I am. They all think like you, don't they?" He nodded at Greta. "A good piano has no maker. It just is."

"But Łozina? Surely people look for the name?"

It was a point of pride for Greta, when she thought of Saul cutting and warping the boards. When she dreamed of sussing out the faults and illnesses of each instrument in a peerless white coat. Somewhere out there a woman in finery was asking specifically for a piano from their town, believing nothing else would do.

"Oh, certainly, the manufacturers' names have a certain caché—Łozina, Steinway, Petrof." Lindemann waved a hand. "But most people still don't know what those names mean, who's behind them. I suppose they imagine Łozina as some great mother instrument, trailing baby grands behind her."

Greta and Lindemann looked at one another for a moment, sharing in this strangest of images. Then Greta shook her head, trying to dissipate it. Her hair was pinned back, but a few strands fell over her ears and she felt slightly indecent, like Cinderella shedding her finery at the stroke of midnight.

"I should be going," she said. "I'll be needed at home."

Lindemann looked once more at Greta's black dress, its creases carefully ironed, her shoes with a high polish. His face was soft, and he crossed the room to her, taking her warm baker's hand in his own.

"*To była moja przyjemność*, my good lady. My pleasure entirely. I hope that I see you again."

Greta stood still, feeling the pace of the man's heartbeat through his palm. Small moves change you, she thought. A small twinge in a piano wire to make a note come out clean. A smile at one man or another at a dance when you're young, yielding daughters or sons. She looked into Lindemann's eyes, each with a crease trickling out from the corner, his head tilted to one side. When he ran his finger over the keyboard of a piano, he noted every small catch, every minute imperfection with a tenderness that astounded her. To be master of your craft, like Saul, was one thing. A beautiful one. But it was another thing to be overwhelmed by your work. Consumed by your love for it.

A recognition flashed between them.

"I should go home." Greta flushed up the back of her neck.

"Yes." Lindemann didn't let go of her hand. "You said."

I stared at my mother, something hot and sickly mixing around in my stomach. My spine felt rigid and my heart too high; I slid onto the floor from the bed and scooted backward towards my mother's bedroom door.

"So you see," Sara said. "Greta cursed us all because her heart was untrue. She didn't love who she was supposed to love."

"You're wrong," I said. She folded her hands primly over her knee, sitting up now with her back against the wall.

"Whatever do you mean?"

Her eyes searched mine, and though she held her mouth in a perfectly neutral pose, there was a smile hidden behind the cool mask of her face. Escaping through the seams.

"You know." I squirmed, feeling my tailbone scrape against the floor. "Greta wouldn't. Do that."

Sara picked the dirt out from under her fingernails, making a sound like a cat testing its claws. *Flick, flick, flick.*

"I know one thing," she said. "You're just like her. From everything Mama says about Greta, you're her little double, aren't you? You take everything there is to have and don't give a damn about the people who give it to you. You always want more. You can feel the wanting under your skin right now, can't you?"

I shivered. To this day I can't be sure whether it was, like my mother said, the fingers of desire I felt. Or whether it was just the flicker of recognition that the stories my mother told weren't meant to instruct or entertain me. They were meant to destroy something. Meant to infect.

13

Every day now, John comes home and sits across the room from me. He doesn't look at me. And I think, *Good*.

We used to come home together and race to the door so we could begin taking off our clothing, running as fast as we could up the stairs so no one would see us unzipping, unbuttoning, shrugging out of shirts and shoes. Or if I got back from rehearsal before him, he would pick me up off the couch and give me a kiss. Hold me in his arms like he was carrying me over the threshold, and then set me back down. Put a blanket over my knees. Kiss my toes.

He wraps Kara into a papoose and walks around the kitchen, cooking for one. The scent of sautéing onions drifts through the door while I'm taking a bath and I dip my head under the water just to escape it for a moment. I get out and drip all over the floor to dig around for a handful of bath salts, which smell like heather. It's a quiet enough scent that it won't make me immediately drunk, the way rose would, or patchouli. But when the salts are absorbed into the water with a patter and a hiss, I still get momentarily lightheaded. Slide gratefully back into the bath so I don't have to stand on my own two feet.

I hear him eating alone at the dining room table, silverware scraping, ice shifting and cracking in a water glass. He babbles to Kara in a light voice but won't say a word to me beyond the necessary—*excuse me, pardon me, are you going to be in there for much longer?* And again I tell myself, *This is good*, when I think about how he used to talk to me almost without ceasing, memories crowding one another to get out of his mouth. Always reaching for the next story, the one that would really explain who he was.

J ohn once described to me a camping trip he took as a child. He grew up in Virginia, in a town surrounded by farmland, with devoted parents who drove him to Blacksburg and later to Richmond and D.C. for voice lessons. It was a safe place, he told me, and so at the age of ten he was allowed to wander and sleep out of doors with only the supervision of a redtick coonhound, Rabbit. She was named for her ears, he said. Long ones, and soft like velvet. In the morning John woke early to the sun leaking milky through the canvas of his tent. He let Rabbit out and stood in an empty field to pee, staring into the morning light with his face upturned. Bold and certain of his place in the world.

After sharing a Pop-Tart with the dog, he proceeded to explore. His parents wouldn't expect him home for hours. And even then they wouldn't worry too much, knowing how close he was to the house, how easily they could drive out and find him. Rabbit loped beside him, sometimes pausing to flop into the dirt and wagger around on her back, scratching head and spine. Her tongue lolled out into the pebbles and dried leaves, picking up both indiscriminately and not bothering to shed them when she sprang back up to trot again beside her boy.

Soon they reached a collapsing barn, old bones of a building, cracked and withering wood. John had to step over broken boards to get inside, push aside the remains of a door that still hung on a single rust-bitten hinge; the sky was visible through the holes in the roof. He should have been more careful, he told me. It could all have fallen on his head. But he wanted to see what there was to see. Wanted to know what the barn's husk looked like, how it felt, from the inside. In his mind, he said, he could have made a second home there. A secret one. And so in a vague gesture of housekeeping, he picked up an old rusted rake and dragged it across the dirt floor, collecting pieces of debris and leaving thin schisms in the dust.

Rabbit was sniffing near his ankles when John used the rake to flip up a piece of corrugated metal and surprised a velvet-tail rattler below. A black-banded snake, coiled up like rope. They all three startled, but while John staggered backward, the snake and the dog both leaned in. John scraped his ankles on a pile of decaying lumber, and as the snake struck Rabbit lunged, so the venomous fangs sank into her leg high up, near the chest. Then the snake was gone. And Rabbit lay on the floor, breath heaving. Leg starting to swell.

I remember we were at a café when John told me this, in public, but he still started to cry. Or at least to tear up. He said it was too far to run back home and get his parents, or so he'd thought at the time. The swelling was so immense and came on so quickly that he could only watch, transfixed, as Rabbit ballooned in front of him. The bite was near her heart. *I should have tried,* he said. But she was so big, compared to him. He couldn't carry her, couldn't drag her behind him without hurting her more and perhaps getting bitten. So he took her big skull in his hands and lay it in his lap and watched her die.

John told me this story not long before he asked me to marry him, and sometime later that same year his parents visited us, passing through Chicago for a night on the way to somewhere else. Over celebratory drinks, while John and his father huddled together at the bar, I asked his mother about Rabbit. Was it hard for John to lose her? Did they ever think about getting another dog?

She grimaced while I recounted an abridged version of the tale, then took a sip of her gin and tonic. I could see her holding it on her tongue to give herself a chance to think before answering.

"He told you that?" she finally asked.

"Yes." Her tone surprised me. "He got very emotional. Why? Does he not usually tell that story?"

"Well, honey, let me ask you." She put her hand over mine. Manicured nails, white French tips. "Do I look like a woman who's lived on a farm?"

I sat back, my spine straightening with a crack. We'd never visited John's hometown, so I hadn't seen his house firsthand, his neighborhood or childhood bedroom. But what had I imagined? To be honest, not the dried birds' nests and pine cone collections of a country boyhood. His father was a cellist. His mother a socialite, masquerading as a stay-at-home mom. Not exactly the type of people to pick up a coonhound pup.

"No." I was breathless. John's mother threw her head back and laughed.

"Let me give you a piece of advice, honey," she said. "John likes telling a tall tale from time to time, but he's not really *good* at it. Always pushes things a little over the edge, you know. For atmosphere. That's how you can tell."

"So no dog?"

She waved her hand and picked the lime off the side of her drink, tossing it in among the ice cubes.

"Pug. Ugly little thing he begged for. But it got hit by a car after a couple of years, and no one was too sorry." She smiled. "Doesn't make for quite the same effect, does it?"

Why did he tell me that? I remember leaning in towards his words, elbows grinding crystals of sugar into the tabletop. It must have meant something to him, or else he'd have laughed to see my face so earnest and interested. Maybe I asked a question about his childhood and he didn't have an honest answer he thought would hold my attention. Or maybe it was simple inspiration: a dog walked by outside, healthy and smiling with the heat of July. Why not?

When I come out of the bathroom wrapped in a towel, John is dancing with Kara in the living room, slowly shifting his hips and shuffling his feet, adding the occasional moonwalk. His romance with her grows daily more intense. Sometimes he holds her out in front of him, cradling the back of her head where the skull is still knitting together beneath the skin, and smells her forehead. Long and deep.

For now he has her balanced against his chest, and I can see her face over his shoulder, eyes open wide, stunned by their own existence. I can't help worrying that she likes him better than me. And why wouldn't she? I would, if I were her. He's much more solicitous.

I'm surprised to see crackers and Brie laid out on the coffee table, next to a bottle of mineral water and two glasses. Kara's face gives no indication about what kind of motives might be attached to them or whether there is a time limit I need to be aware of—*I'll be nice now or never,* that sort of thing—and so I slip into the bedroom and throw on some clothes, taking my time, brushing out my hair with my fingers to keep it from drying in bunches and snags. Look at the bruise on my hip, a deeper purple now. Does that mean it's festering, or healing? When I emerge, the spread is still there, untouched. The Brie has melted a little bit, oozing out its own sides.

"For you," John says. And all I can say in reply is, "Oh." But I sit down in front of the plate and smear a buttery wedge of cheese onto a cracker, licking a little bit off my thumb. I watch John, who settles into a chair on my left and pours himself a glass of water. A few companionable minutes like this are enough to break me of my own determination not to speak.

"So," I ask. "How was your day? Is Stan giving you hell?" Stan is John's vocal coach, and he's a real son of a bitch, though we love him. His heyday was in New York, and he likes making fun of John for being based in Chicago, the Second City. But he's a wonderful stickler for the emotional power of music: he once held John for an extra hour of rehearsal because he claimed, *If it was right, I'd be crying by now.* "Is he teasing you very much about Parpignol?"

John's role in the upcoming production of *La Bohème* is small, a toy vendor at the beginning of Act II. It is, he says, a new father's role. For a couple of years now, he's been making excuses for being cast in smaller parts—*I'm stuck between young hero and mature; I like playing soldiers; I don't want to travel*—but this time I think that what he says might be true. He's been staying at the Lyric well past his meetings with Stan just to chat with the designers making Parpignol's toys. That's what I've deduced through snooping. There were crumpled sketches on the table yesterday, brightly colored balls, marionettes, wooden ducks on wheels. Maybe he wants to bring them home for Kara at the end of the run.

"Who cares, right?" John shrugs. "He's just an old gasbag."

Although it's true, I don't know what to say to this. It seems to be the kind of statement designed to preclude reply. I crunch through a few more crackers.

"It's nice to have soft cheeses again." I gesture to the baby, who caused a nine-month moratorium. John nods, knowing.

"Yeah." He hefts Kara to the left and squints at her, doting. "Remember how we used to argue about what she'd look like?"

I laugh. "Argue is a strong word, but sure. I said she was going to have blond hair, like I did when I was a baby. And you said she was going to be covered in little golden scales, and have pearls for teeth."

"Hmm," he says. "We were both wrong." He draws her close and nibbles on one ear, as if it were gold and he was checking it for purity. She squirms. "You know, though, I think she looks like me."

"No she doesn't."

I've spoken before I can stop myself. *Shut up,* I think. *Shut up, shut up.* But John doesn't seem to care.

"Well, you know." She has so much hair, so unexpectedly much, and so dark. John was surprised because he'd been born bald. All the baby photos in his family show perfect Gerber mouths and plastic-smooth Kewpie heads. Now he spins the small tuft of Kara's hair around his index finger. "I called my mom, and she says Kara looks like my dad did when he was a baby. They have all those creepy formal portraits."

"What about her eyes?" I ask. It's a little hypnotic, hearing how hard he's willing to try to make this true. A storyteller to the bones.

"Nordic blood."

I raise an eyebrow.

"That's what she tells me," he says.

From the day she was born, we have politely referred to Kara's blue eyes as a puzzle. There's still a chance they'll turn brown in her ninth month—I was surprised when the doctor told me this could happen, as though babies routinely shed their skin and emerge purple or green. Then I was surprised I hadn't heard it before, that it isn't invoked more often as a grand metaphor for how human beings are adaptable and all the same even in their differences. When I was in elementary school, we divided up the world into blue-eyed people and brown-eyed people. Some of the blues called the brown eyes common, but I told them it meant we had a more solid base of power. Kara's eyes are waterways. Mine are the stony ground.

John stands up and carefully passes the baby to me.

"I'm going to take a shower," he says, "now that the bathroom's free."

I nod, and am just about to sit back, quietly baffled at our conversation, when he turns back and asks, "Is your mother going to be at the christening?"

His tone is so casual I almost don't hear the way it's laced with ice. But he says the word *mother* with such emphasis that I cannot miss it. He is still angry about my outburst then, Brie or no. I pale a little. The christening's in three days, and the last two people I want in a room together are John and my mother. I can't see how it will help to lie now though.

"I told her about it. So, maybe."

"That's just great, Lu." He's going brittle again as he walks away. "Because now it'll really be a celebration."

"She might not come," I say to his back. He barely shrugs an acknowledgment, which is just as well. We both know that Sara will do what she wants. I can't be certain about anything with her, except that she likes to stir the water. Even now, just the mention of her name causes ripples. What will happen when she sees my daughter and my husband, side by side? Eye to eye.

I shiver, thinking about the wave of chaos I felt chasing me down the street, away from the florist's shop. And the chaos of my own making that I feel chasing me now.

14

All throughout my pregnancy I sang furiously. My agent was concerned for my health, but assured me that audiences would love it. "Like a cellist who throws their bow because they're playing too passionately," she said. "It's kind of *weird*. Aficionados like that stuff." So I booked small concerts and private performances—the birthday of a Japanese seafood exporter, a party celebrating the IPO of a software company in Silicon Valley.

I did seem to inspire a strange sort of passion. As soon as my belly began rounding out, I heard whispers in the audience when I walked onto a stage. Michelle shrugged when I told her. "That's what you wanted, I thought." She sent me designer maternity wear on loan, favoring pieces that accentuated the bulge Kara elbowed ever outward. The only one I refused to wear painted me up like a bull's-eye, with a dot of red at the pregnancy's crest.

"This is crude," I said. "People will find this really vulgar."

But on a night not long after I sent that dress back, I stepped out next to the piano in a simple black smock—my favorite accompanist, Rick, was with me, on loan from the Lyric—and a wave of enthusiastic gasps broke out, inspired by a problematic spotlight resting momentarily on my stomach. It had been contracted down to the size of a single face, and as it dilated out from my navel I felt uncomfortably vaudevillian. The applause—the frenzied, wolf-whistling adulation—nearly knocked me over. I hadn't yet sung a single note.

Rick must have seen me going green, god bless him. He whispered, "They're not here to look, they're here to listen. They'll remember."

And I made sure that they did. In the early weeks of my pregnancy, my body had made a few adjustments without my say-so: unexpected notes popping out of my mouth during warm-ups; hands growing numb in the late afternoon as if a smaller set of fingers were rooting around in them, looking for a way out. But at this point, seven months in, the inconsistencies had quieted down, and I instead gained a modicum of power and range. Sometimes I felt as though no one was in my stomach at all and it was a hollow bell made to resonate like a gong.

Nodding to Rick, I rapped my thanks onto the piano and breathed as deeply as the changed real estate in my lungs would allow. We have a little code, Rick and I, in those knocks. We use them to alert one another to changes in tempo or octave—or even our choice of song. He looked at me, a question in his eyes, and I answered with a curt nod. *Yes.*

No one ever begins a performance with the *Reine de la Nuit* aria, because after that there aren't many places to go. But this audience made me angry. In the dark, I could imagine them rooting around for popcorn or munching on candy smuggled into the ballroom at the bottom of overlarge purses. A warm, bland mass.

The first notes cracked through them like a foot through spring thaw—I was the chill in every spine, the soft "Oh!" bitten back between freezing lips.

Death and despair blaze all around me! I sang. *Disowned forever! Forsaken forever! Shattered forever!* No one breathed. *My daughter never. Nevermore!* My audience for the evening was comprised of investment bankers. Maybe five among them spoke German, and one or two had familiarity with opera that extended beyond attending *Carmen* from a sense of guilty obligation when a boss lent out his box at the theater. In their experience, music was an excuse to wear a tuxedo or, if they were saucy, a fitted blue three-piece suit. The women wore gowns.

I undid them by the buttons. I burned off their clothes. The ones who understood the words I was singing looked at my belly and took it the worst, drained completely pale by the time the aria ended. The piece has never been outside of my range, but that night I felt my tessitura stretching and my throat throbbing like a frog in front of those thin-skinned business faces. If I'd tapped them with an egg spoon, the lot of them would have shattered into unusable fragments.

When my voice died away, the air in the ballroom felt thick. There was a shell-shocked silence in which one man adjusted his tie; a lady in the first row slipped her shoes off her heels. I certainly wasn't going to be the first one to move, and held my show posture—air sucked carefully into my diaphragm so my shoulders wouldn't visibly rise and fall. For a second I was worried that nothing would happen at all and that I was still invisible. Nothing but a belly. Then there was a small creak from the back of the room and the door popped open. A head peeked in, a small head. It was a tiny girl, no more than six, and after sweeping her eyes back and forth she blinked at me. Like an emissary from the future, or the past.

"Wow," she said. And, as if they'd been waiting for her opinion, the audience burst into thunderous applause.

I thought Ada might disapprove of my continuing to sing when she heard my choice of repertoire. But she was happy as a fat seal in the sun. She fed me up on rich oils and leafy greens and a weekly glass of wine that she claimed would stir the baby's blood. Once she sat with me in my living room, stroking the foot I'd placed lazy on her lap, and suggested stretching headphones out over my stomach.

"Oh god," I said. "No Baby Einstein."

She raised an eyebrow and, when I explained, swatted the idea aside like a gnat.

"Don't be ridiculous," she said. "I just mean for her enjoyment. All the rest of that *curriculum*"—the word boiled on her tongue—"is for people who don't already know what their children are going to be."

I laughed, but inside my heart shrank back. Better than me: that's what she meant. Although she wouldn't have said it quite that way, I could hardly miss her meaning. She might have said the same thing to my mother, once.

I say that Sara loved her troubles, and that's true; she didn't have to tell me the stories she did, didn't have to try and splinter my heart. But I should also be fair: Sara had plenty of troubles to love.

I think that she wanted to take care of me. Wanted not to fall asleep so often in the middle of the day, pulling a pillow around her ears so she couldn't hear my footsteps. Wanted not to ruin her voice with whiskey and cigarettes, wanted not to throw me with disgust at her mother and go moonlight in Italian bars in the Loop where they'd give her glasses of cheap red wine to drink as she sang and put her in a cab at the end of the night.

But I made it difficult for her.

My mother enjoyed feeding me. Little bites of strawberry into my mouth right off the knife, pieces of hot bread with butter and honey. Greta's talent for baking skimmed over Baba Ada's surface—she could do it sufficiently, it just didn't hold her interest—but embedded itself in my mother, deep. I remember how happy she was every time I took a mouthful of something, like the use of my incisors was a miracle, the plunge of my throat an expression of love.

One Easter when I was about five years old, my front two teeth dangled painfully loose, and I couldn't eat the chocolate or jelly beans or gummy worms stashed for me in plastic eggs. Ada was impatient with holiday traditions that did not involve church, but that year Sara wouldn't let her take me, and I think Ada saw my situation as a piece of minor divine retribution. She sat sanguine, trying to distract me by painting eggshells. But my mother was wretched.

"It's not Easter if she can't eat candy," she said. "Here, Lulu, try this." She handed me a marshmallow rabbit. I bit down on it and grimaced, shaking my head.

"If your hands get sticky, you'll muck up the *pisanki*," Ada said. She removed the disemboweled pink bunny from my hand with two fingers and covered it with a piece of newspaper. "Lick them like this, *lalka*, and then you can try again." Ada stuck her tongue out at the tips of her fingers and I giggled, following suit. She craned her neck at Sara. "There, she got some sugar. Are you happy now?"

"Yes, obviously," said Sara. "My concerns were purely chemical."

She kept trying different concoctions, chopping gummies into a near paste and holding chocolate kisses up to a flame, letting me drink the melted liquid out of her hands. I wasn't really hungry, and would have forgotten about my candy in minutes if I'd been given a chance, but Sara pushed more and more options towards me—marshmallows microwaved into fluff and hard candies crushed into powder that dissolved on my tongue.

Finally, her Easter eggs shoved by the wayside, Ada got up and washed her hands, then returned to her seat in the kitchen and folded one leg carefully over the other. "Well," she said, "that is enough. You've ensured the child will never sleep again, and she looks like a Chinese panda." Indeed there were smears of chocolate all across my face, rimming my mouth and daubing my cheekbones like war paint. "*Mamenka* would never have allowed this kind of nonsense on a holy day. She put my hair up in special curlers the night before Easter Sunday so that I would be perfectly uniform, and I spent hours embroidering a new dress, because I wanted to be the most beautiful, perfect little girl in church."

Sara raised an eyebrow. To invoke Greta was to pull a hidden card from your sleeve, not really an argument but a firm "Because I said so." The effect on me wasn't punitive, it was just unstoppable. Once tossed a crumb of Greta lore, I would do anything to get another taste.

Immediately my hands went up to my face and started wiping the chocolate away. Sara *tsked* and tried to help me, but her fingers were also spun with sugar and I shrieked when she grabbed my arm to pull me just a little bit closer. "*No no no,*" I cried, squirming and retracting. "No, please no, stop it, I can—" But she clamped down harder and dabbed at my cheeks, licking her thumb and scrubbing my skin in a huff. I twisted away, knocking over my chair, and when I picked myself up off the ground I saw a shadow of chocolate on my Easter dress. My ears started ringing and I collapsed into sobs.

"Why did you do that to me, Mama, why did you do that?"

Ada scooped me up off the floor and grasped my chin between her forefinger and thumb. She shushed me and nuzzled me and took me over to the sink, where a quick swipe from a damp cloth scoured my face pink and removed the worst damage from my dress, while Sara remained in her chair, ash silent. She picked up a hollow painted egg and rolled it back and forth in her palm.

"Now, *słodka*, it's not so bad, is it?" asked Ada. "You know, we could still curl your hair with the curling iron. Would you like that? Hmm?" I nodded reverently. "And then maybe we could paint a couple more Easter eggs, and I'll buy you a nice, soft piece of cake. Soft as a cloud. You know, Greta loved to have cake on Easter Sunday. She would bake a cake that was so tall! Like a man!" Ada held her hand up flat, high above her head. "And we would eat it with custard, and I always knew that if I finished Easter that way I would fall asleep and dream of a clockwork girl, of braided gold and a beating garnet heart. A whole child made of jewels and shining rings and chains."

Sara sighed through her nose, peering at the egg in her hand. I watched it and her from Ada's arms, the slow rhythmic nature of their movements. The egg was red, struck through with lines of yellow and black, and it matched the crimson of Sara's fingernails, though its pattern was much more severe. I remained cosseted in my baba's arms but willed my mother to look at me, ashamed of myself without knowing why. Sara's eyes were partially hidden by her lashes, but I could see them growing darker, edging towards black. If she would only look up, I thought, I could smile and everything would be all right again. We could all eat cake together and tell stories, bundled onto the couch under a blanket. But my mother set the eggshell on the table and slowly crushed it under her palm. Then she stood up, brushing off her hands, and walked out of the room.

"Well," said Ada. "How about that cake then?"

Sometimes I forget that Kara is a real baby, that she isn't just a manifestation of my own difficulty with *babyness*—that in fact when her pupil dilates, her nostril flares, it is a genuine person's experience of something outside itself. Which means there is something inside itself as well. Not just blood and a shining purple liver the size of an apricot. Though that too. Organs glistening in miniature, and then somewhere inexpressible, unidentifiable: awareness.

I wonder if my mother ever saw me this way, as a whole thing, someone outside her own game of trials and errors, wracking points up for themselves. When she put her hand on my head in passing, did she somehow feel a brain beating beneath it or did an idle part of her just think *girl*? The shadowy form of *girl* that lived in her mind instead of the hungry-thirsty-needs-to-pee version that lived in her house. The shadowy form that came to eclipse her.

I lean into my baby, I surround her and drink in her scent of milk and straw and butter. The clean smell of ironed cotton and her own slightly rancid spit. I always want to be touching her, examining her, to remind myself she is there, she is she, but I still have this terrible time knowing it. Separating the she that has a smell from the me who smells it. And so the fear I feel is transposed onto her, the fear that singing to her will make her a part of my family's strange and imaginary history. Draw her in like my mother's mouth draws in smoke, like I draw in oxygen. When in fact the truth for Kara is that a song would be rhythmic to her, a song would just send her to sleep.

15

Ada never returned to the town where she was born after coming to America—there was no town left to return to. The war swept through Poland while she was on a ship, traveling steerage, weighted down with pregnancy and seasickness. It brought a rigid structure of death, organized in small cabins on vast, endless fields. It spilled people out of their homes, dragging furniture to train stations so they could furnish the new houses they'd been promised, but there were no houses. Just trains, pushed full with bodies. And stations, piled high with abandoned chairs and divans and mattresses that got soaked in the rain, stained and ruined.

The rain itself was ruined in Poland for a time, each drop marred with bodily grime. Chimneys stretched up into the clouds and populated them with the smoke of burnt hair, sizzling bones. And the rain that once fell on Greta and Saul's wedding turned soot black, marking the ground where it fell. Marking the trees.

In spite of all that, I'm not sure Ada ever forgave her mother for sending her away. Or, for that matter, for being dead. I've seen the thought cause my *babenka* physical annoyance: closed eyes and breath in counts of ten, shoulders bunched up towards her ears until *nine, eight, seven, six, five,* she could release them back down into her perfect posture. Once I found her and Sara in the kitchen, talking about the town in quiet tones. My mother stood behind Baba Ada, arms around her waist, chin on her shoulder. When they heard my footsteps they both turned around, and I never forgot their eyes: frightened, glass bright.

Baba Ada treated her grief like an oyster treats a grain of sand. By working it over, covering it up. Just for instance: instead of fighting Greta's death, she told me about it every chance she got. More often than she told me about Greta's wedding. More often than she told me the dark color of her mother's hair, or described the crackle of stones under her own feet as she walked down the road between her home and the town.

But she told the story differently every time. It was the one Greta story that really changed, and when a new version came to her, it came with urgency. Sometimes she'd grab my arm in the hallway, leaving fingerprints of flour on my sweater sleeve. Sometimes we got stuck on a slow-moving train and she'd tell me three different stories in an hour, circling above Greta's death like a bird as the train clacked slowly over the Chicago streets. Each new version made the others harder to believe, and that was her weapon: the multitude, the manifold, made the very fact untrue.

All the different versions of the city's death that I'd heard commingled in my mind, giving birth to new permutations. Hydra-head history. Did Ada tell me that lightning struck the town, burning a path from the woodpiles of the piano factory straight to Greta's door? Or did she say that a shard of fire fell from the sky and pierced Greta's heart directly, burning her up between the ribs but leaving everything else untouched? Chopin's heart was removed, after all, by the mere hands of man. Why should God be less specific?

Perhaps the lightning came from inside Greta. This version of the story is easy for me to imagine in Ada's careful enunciation. She would have rubbed my belly as she spoke about the spark in Greta's chest, leaving my skin uncomfortably warm.

"Think about it, *lalka*," Ada said. Must have said. "At first Greta wouldn't have worried at all, because it would only have felt like a bit of congestion. A little nausea, maybe. She'd had babies. Heartburn was nothing to a woman like that."

The lightning tumbled around in Greta like an acrobatic child, testing its musculature, pushing against the tensile strength of her skin. It tickled her, vibrated in response to her songs, delighted her with its vivid newness.

Perhaps it even loved her.

But fire can't escape its tendency to burn. Not even for a beloved. It crackles and consumes; it wants to be the only thing breathing. Soon Greta began to spy light shaking out between the chinks of her skin, illuminating the creases worn in by time. A cough released smoke curls, and each inhalation fanned the heat: flames rose and fell in time with her shoulders.

Next the electricity made itself known—her hair standing on end, kinking out, crackling. Folds of her dresses sticking together in errant attitudes. At this point, it was still possible to hide her condition by excusing herself to the restroom during a surge, blaming her mood on the monthly change. It would have hurt Greta to turn away from Saul's embrace, but how could she let him near her when a single touch could engulf him in flames? When the core he was reaching for was molten?

(And after all, I can't help thinking, she'd turned from him before.)

One morning she woke up with her heart on fire, and she knew the time had come. Gathering her skirts up, she rushed out the door, sparking against metal buttons, doorknobs, the teeth of a rake. Outside she shook her hair down around her shoulders and swiftly walked into the forest—the leaves on the ground would cover her tracks, she knew, and keep her from being found until it was already over.

On the moss bed of a clearing she sat, thinking about the day she'd met the devil and feeling her body vibrate as her veins hardened into wire. They twanged. And then they began to conduct.

She felt heat. So much heat. It broke her apart until the shards of her flew in every direction: pinpoints of fire exploding up and out and through the woods like the devastation of an earthbound star, unseen except by the sky above her and the animals too fool to flee.

Her miscalculation, of course, was going into the woods. Did she simply forget that they could burn? Or was she compelled to go there and complete the deal she'd made so long ago? (*First I wanted your sons*, the devil whispered. *But now I want more. Now I want everything. Your girl is safe. Who are you to deny it?*) The force of the explosion pushed her underground and lit everything else up with a flash and a boom.

Saul was consumed. The boys were consumed. The *fabryka* was full of blinding piano-shaped auras, articulated skeletons of fire. Houses in town were reduced to black dust. Black roads led out towards the untouched world.

"Yes," Sara told me once. "The town and the forest both burned down. A lot of people died. But not because of a storm. It was because of the war."

"How do you know?"

She batted my question aside like a fly. "Because of history books. Anyone could know what I know. Just by looking."

To understand the death of the town, Sara said, you have to go back quite a ways and tell a story that seems unrelated. One thing leads to another. It always does.

There was once a little boy, Sara told me, who lived in the same town in Poznań where Greta's family made their home. His father worked in the fruit processing plant—he was unimportant, but the family got by. They had socks without holes in the winter, and if they were sometimes hungry, they were never starving. On special occasions they opened a jar of fruit from the plant, and the boy was allowed to pluck out a black plum with his fingers, letting the syrup run all down his hands.

As the boy grew older, his mother let him ride a bicycle to the church, where he was an altar boy. He liked swinging the censer and watching the haze of incense billow through the sanctuary; it made him feel that he was in charge of something important. He was present at the birth of clouds, which would grow and grow into unimaginably large shapes and fly through the air to be seen all around the world: in Egypt, Indochina, France.

The boy liked to be important.

Sometimes, after helping the priest clean up after the service, the boy would ride his bike through the streets and towards the woods. He would abandon it at the edge of the trees and hike to his secret places, where he stored beautiful stones and saw fish talking to each other in the river. On other days, if the priest had given him a coin, he rode to the Jewish side of town and bought a pickle, crunching through the first bite to the burst of garlic and vinegar inside.

And on some days he let himself get lost, for the pleasure of finding his way home again. His mother didn't worry, because he told her that he'd been setting out candles in the church, polishing the confessional booth, sweeping between the pews. She patted his head and told him that he was a good boy but that he should remind the priest he needed to be home before the sun went down.

One day after eating his pickle and playing a brief game of tag with some children in the streets, the boy decided he was not yet ready to go home. He ought to have gone and asked his mother's permission to stay out a bit later, told her that he was going on a ride and pointed in the direction he was intending to pedal. But he was ten years old. He felt strength ripple through his legs as he drove his bicycle faster and faster. He felt his first little glimmer of power, and he didn't want anyone to know where he was going.

At the woods he tucked the bike underneath a flowering bush and ran with abandon through the patches of sun and shade cast by the treetop canopy. The river was running fast and deep, but the boy found a narrow bend and leapt across it, his shoe just barely finding purchase against the far bank. Rooting around in the dirt and leaves, he gathered a supply of smooth, flat stones and tried to skip them over the surface of the water, but the current was too fast and they all sank, cast forward a few feet by the force of the waves.

After a while, the boy got tired. He wanted to go home, but the river looked terribly wide. Had he really jumped across it just a little while ago, he wondered? The sun was beginning to sink towards the hill, but it wasn't yet late enough to give the boy pause. He decided to rest against the trunk of a tree and make the leap once his strength was regained.

But, of course, he fell asleep.

Meanwhile, his mother was starting to get worried; her son had never stayed out so late after the church service was over, though the time he spent helping the priest had been stretching out longer and longer. She decided to go fetch him home and ask the priest please to not keep the boy for quite so much time.

When the boy's mother arrived at the church, the sun had just dipped below the horizon, and the woman was alarmed to learn that her child was not there. *He left a few minutes after you did*, the father told her. *I gave him a coin and he rode off on that bicycle of his.*

Which way did he go? the mother asked, wringing her hands.

With a frown, the priest shrugged—the boy told him he'd go straight home. After that, he hadn't thought to watch.

A few hours later the boy awoke. He called out to his mother for a glass of water, as his throat was sore and dry, and he seemed to have kicked the blankets off his bed. Then he started. He was not, he realized, in his bed at all, but on a soft mound of dirt, leaned up against a tree. He'd fallen asleep, and now his mother would be angry.

The moon seemed to howl down at him, a terrible white and open mouth. Something with soft feet shuffled through the shadows deeper in the forest's bowels. The boy sprang to his feet and jumped over the river, landing on his knees and tumbling through the dirt. He ignored the scratches and scrapes on his hands, the mud on his pants. With his heart pounding up through his tongue, the boy ran to his bicycle without looking back and raced through the dark streets towards his home.

His mother was pacing in front of the door, and his father was sitting at the kitchen table, sighing. He had just arrived home from work, hungry, his hands and knees sore. When the boy rode up on his bicycle, his mother gave a cry, and both parents ran out to the terrified boy.

What happened? his father asked, picking him up as if he were an infant and carrying him inside the warm, bright house. The boy's mother ran her fingers over his dirty clothes, then hurried to get a warm washcloth to clean away the blood and grime.

Where did you go? she asked.

The boy's head was buzzing. He was exhausted, frightened, and also concerned. If he told the truth, he knew, he would be spanked and sent to bed with no dinner. There was a chance that his father would take away his bicycle and tell him to walk to church with his mother from now on. His parents would be angry if they knew how long he'd been lying to them.

He opened his mouth. Out came a whimper.

They took me, he said. And then it began.

The boy wove a fabulous story, picking up his cues from whatever came into his head. He remembered buying a pickle from the Jewish grocery, remembered seeing boxes of crackers on the shelves, and remembered the stern, dark eyes of the shop owner. The ringlets of hair.

The Jews took me, he said. When his father looked unconvinced, he said, *They wanted my blood for matzoh,* and his mother—holding tight to his bleeding fingers—began to cry uncontrollably.

I had to fight them off me. The boy looked up at the ceiling to avoid his parents' eyes. *And then I escaped and I ran through the woods and I just barely got home alive.* He began to cry and threw his arms around his mother's neck. *I'm so happy to see you. So, so, so happy to see you, Mama.*

Although his father remained somewhat dubious, the boy's mother spoke to him in a voice so low it was almost a growl. She told her husband to go find his friends and to bring the Jews some kind of *justice*. She hissed this at his back, as he walked reluctantly out the door.

"Wait." I grabbed my mother's hand. "No one did anything to him, though."

"I know," said Sara. "But that's how it was. Sometimes little children do big, bad things."

The boy's father got into the spirit of things once he saw the outrage in his friends' faces. They drank brandy to put a little fire in their bellies, and then they picked up large sticks, fireplace pokers, bats. They smashed the windows in every Jewish house and store and burned the synagogue to the ground. The little boy got to stay in bed the next day and eat sweet plums. He licked sugar syrup from his palm and nibbled the soft plum flesh out from where it stuck underneath his nails.

"So is that how the town died?" I was horrified.

"No," said Sara. "But people remembered it. Even once the boy had grown up and moved to a different town, they told the story to their children. They told each other around fires at night. So even if they did business with the Jewish side of town, or were friendly, people always remembered."

"But that's stupid," I said.

Sara shrugged. She leaned close to me.

"The things people say have the power to change your life, whether they're true or not."

I kept my face upturned towards her, and we stared at each

other, both of us seemingly waiting for a kiss. Instead, my mother said, "Ada lied too, you know."

"About what?" I shrank back just a bit, because her breath was fusty, and I didn't like the glint in her eyes. My mother didn't blink as I recoiled. She just stood up and walked over to her closet, pulling out an indigo dress that was cinched at the waist and fell off of one shoulder. She removed her robe and started to dress for the evening, tugging and tucking her body here and there.

"Mama?" I said. She came over and placed herself next to me, looking at me over her shoulder. She lifted her hands.

"Zip, please."

I stood up on the bed and obliged, the zipper clicking sticky teeth.

"Mama?" I tried again. "What did you say?"

"I said she lied. You heard me." My mother checked the zipper and then opened the window, lighting a cigarette and blowing the smoke outside. "Someday you're going to understand." She inhaled. "About Greta. And all that." She exhaled. "I'd be doing you a favor, telling you. But you wouldn't see it that way, I don't think."

She dropped the cigarette in a jar she kept on the outside sill. It was half full of rainwater, so the other butts were tinted green and black from stagnation. The new one expanded just a bit when it hit the liquid, slowly coming to resemble the rest.

"So I'll do you the favor you think you want."

She kissed me on the cheek and walked out of the room, slamming the bathroom door behind her. A week later she would be gone, but I didn't know that yet. Maybe she did though. Maybe it was in that moment, and with those words, that she formed her plan.

I didn't see Ada's stories as lies, but some part of me knew that their truths were separate from the truth of the war offered up by my mother. They felt, in my hands, like two sides of history: Chopin in Paris and Chopin in Żelazowa Wola.

It didn't bother me. The split seemed as natural as having two bedrooms in a house: you could walk into one and see a single life laid out, then close that door and open another. But in either room you knew the larger home, the larger truth, was still around you.

The real problem was that neither story was complete—they didn't tell me what I wanted to know about the end. What shape did Greta's sacrifice take? And who were the men and women who came to the town and burned it? How did they get in? How did they leave? And how could they possibly hurt Greta's family?

The truth lay, as it so often does, between the two stories. In the cracks and crevices where they seeped into one another. At least that's what I've decided.

When my baba Ada was a girl, she could have swallowed the whole world and no one would have tried to stop her. She was the only child her mother ever gave birth to laughing, smiling through the grit of her tears. Greta the bear. Greta the she-wolf. Greta the lonely who craved a pair of ears to recognize music when they heard it. Her other girls had died being born, and she had battered herself over their deaths, wondering, *Why them? Why not me?*

Ada was sprightly, dark, and small. She bounced unstable from place to place making up songs, pulling on her brothers' hair. They were all besotted with her, especially Konrad, who was not much older. He followed her everywhere. When she was learning to walk, he shadowed her with such a look of serious concern—that furrowed brow, those blue eyes clouding—that Greta and Saul could not help but laugh. They clutched one another behind his back, tears streaming down their cheeks. *Look how he loves her.*

How can I know this? It's nothing Ada would ever tell. Nothing she has the authority to know. But I know. I've spoken to Greta in my sleep, and she fills me in on the secrets that my mama and my *babenka* kept close to the chest for reasons of their own.

Ada was her mother's image reflected back, slightly smaller, slightly oblique. The pair of them were a walking discourse on the evolution of proud Polish blood. Is it impossible to improve on a good woman? Or inevitable?

Saul could refuse the child nothing. Poor papa. He saw his powerful wife transformed into a creature he could pick up with two hands and toss into the air, and the vision turned his heart on its side. *Here is someone to protect,* he thought. Little knowing what he was dealing with. Little knowing how headstrong a body can grow when given unlimited access to satisfaction.

"You'll spoil her," Greta warned.

"If she turns out like you," he said, "I can't see how I'd call that spoiled."

And so she grew. A laughing, twirling dervish. A girl beloved by her whole town, who looked so much like her beautiful mother that no one thought to question why she didn't really look like her father at all. No one held her hand in check, no one watched her, because everyone was confident that no one would hurt her. And

Ada. Well, Ada wasn't a foolish girl. It just didn't occur to her that ministrations, attention, could have consequences. That they were anything other than an end in themselves.

This is the beginning of my mother Sara's story. Some night after a dance in town, the summer darkness. These things happen. The fields near the church were covered in soft grasses, a spray of flowers. And the young boy, drunk on love, told Ada over and over again how beautiful she was, and how precious.

A s my mother loved to remind her, Ada was ushered out of town before the war fell. But of course my mother always fails to mention that it was because of her that Ada agreed to go.

"We all have to give something up," Greta whispered to her. Then she gave her a gentle shove onto the train. "So our daughters can grow."

Ada's eyes filled up with tears. She couldn't even pronounce the name of the city to which she was being exiled. The word *Chicago* made no sense in her mouth—her hard *ch* and soft *sh* always blended together; she confused her sibilants and places of articulation, her tongue tied into knots. But she clutched her visa to her chest and took a step forward into the world.

She must have felt much smaller in transit, more like the soft toy that Saul always imagined her to be, tossed from side to side by the steam engine, the waves and their methodical pounding, the second train from New York to Union Station in Chicago. Her cousin Freddie met her dressed in a dark suit, like a funeral man. He took off his hat to her, but once home in his small apartment he made her sleep on the couch. Instead of opening his arms in welcome, he was curt and always in a hurry. He seemed annoyed to keep having to explain her presence, to clarify that, no, she was not his wife.

As if I'd want you, Ada thought. He was fat, almost enormous considering the little that they had to eat. Any weight he'd lost since the war began still hung off him in folds of skin. *As if anyone would want you.* The thought was Ada's one cruelty, her unspoken revenge. Everything else was fear: troops mustering in the newspaper. Boys in Germany with bright blond hair.

And so it was little comfort to be cruel to Freddie, because he was suddenly, breathtakingly, all that she had. Every Monday, and sometimes again on Friday, Ada sent a letter to Greta or Konrad, and even once to the boy she'd met in secret behind the church. But she received nothing in return, no replies. Not even a note from the post office explaining that most of her letters had been lost in transit. The growing hysteria of one young girl was not a priority in a time of war.

So she didn't know that back in Poznań, the piano factory had been requisitioned as a bunk and barracks manufacturer. Greta ran into Gustaw Lindemann one day when she was coming out of the alleyway that served as a meeting ground for black market exchanges. He was going in. His face was grim, his suit still gray, as always, though not so crisp.

"It's a lucky thing," he whispered to her, "that we got the girl out when we did. I wouldn't be able to do it now. My money's no good." He ran a hand over his hair, as if to reassure himself it was still there. "I'm trading ivory keys for food. God knows what they're doing with them."

Lindemann slipped Greta a key, *Just in case you need it*. And she did need it. She and Saul were going hungry more often than not lately, trying to keep their sons in food. The boys, in turn, snuck their own portions back onto their mother's plate. But there was little enough to shuffle around. Potatoes from the garden, all turning black after a deep frost. Plums from the local trees, mostly gone rotten. The good ones were canned and shipped out to feed the soldiers who were amassing in anticipation of an invasion by Germany.

"We should have sent the boys to America too," Greta said to Saul.

"Couldn't do it." They sat on the porch, feet hanging off into the air, and he gnawed on a piece of dry venison jerky from a hunting trip the previous year. Even game was in short supply these days, with too many people going in to thin the herds. "You know it. We had the money for one ticket, and I don't even know where you got that." He didn't meet her eyes. "You made a choice. And we all agreed. The boys want to stay and fight, anyhow."

That was the truth. If she had pleaded with them, and had the means, she could maybe have gotten one to leave. Maybe one. To spare himself for her sake. But Greta's resources were limited even with a powerful friend, and she couldn't stand the thought of another one of her daughters dying. Especially not when the girl had her own child brewing, a new innocence growing within her. So the boys remained and made it clear that they saw it as their duty to fight.

"It's a damn devil's bargain," Saul said. "Choosing one child to go."

He put his hand on Greta's, and they stared into the woods, where dark shapes shuffled off on their unknowable errands.

16

One morning in my ninth year, I woke up to find the apartment silent but full of smoke. It didn't worry me the way it might concern most children: I recognized the scent as cigarettes, not fire. I was annoyed that my lungs were going to be scratchy for a day or two—usually my mother smoked out the window so I wouldn't have to worry about this—but the haze lying over all our furniture made the rooms seem new and distracted me from working myself up into a snit.

It was like finding oneself in the middle of dense fog, or waking up on an airplane that was rising or descending through cloud cover. There was that sense of disorientation, and that feeling of being followed. I sat up in bed and felt the smoke waft around my hair. Darker and lighter curls wormed their way through the mass and I slipped onto the floor, my feet scudding against the hardwood.

"Ada?"

My voice was thick and dry. Before speaking I had no choice

but to breathe, and the smoke coated my throat and tongue. I wandered down the hall half expecting to see a dragon's tail disappearing around a corner, but I reached the kitchen and found it empty, light bleeding through the windows and diffusing in the clouds. There was a note from Ada on the table: *Gone in to work. Find something to eat. Do your homework.* It was Saturday, but Baba Ada often worked on weekends, altering party dresses and adjusting the cuffs on tuxedos. Rush jobs for an event that night, a debut, a premiere. Costume changes between cocktail hour and after-dinner drinks.

It wasn't until I read her note that I realized I was hungry, and that I wanted pancakes. It felt important to follow my instincts in a house where everything was suddenly so indistinct. For a moment I considered tackling the cooking myself, but I was still sleepy and didn't quite trust my eyes in the smog. It seemed all too possible that I'd end up knocking the pan off the stove, burning my hands and legs and face with hot batter.

A few weeks earlier my mother had made me pancakes from scratch—a peace offering after our trip to the opera—adding cornmeal to give them grit and bite, trying to form each cake into the shape of a foreign country. They looked like blobs, failed mouse ears, but they tasted wonderful. She smiled at me and sucked on a cigarette while I ate.

I thought, *I'll help.* So I took down the grease-spotted *Joy of Cooking* from the shelf and dug through drawers until I came up with a few measuring cups, a Pyrex bowl, and some flour, butter, vanilla, and baking powder. I couldn't remember exactly what went in the batter, but I figured Sara would tell me what to keep out and what to put away. Whispers of smoke hung around my head and followed my hands; it was starting to make me cough, but I didn't open a window. The smoke didn't seem like something I had the right to control.

The day before, my mother and my baba Ada had gotten into a fight. I thought it was lucky that Ada chose to leave so early today: it gave us all a chance to calm down, forget what was said, and move on. Sara had been telling me about how Ada came to America: That she was pregnant and refused to name the father. That she left just before the Second World War reached her town in Poznań, so she wasn't there to fight against the Nazis, to protect her family or hide the Jewish children who were being rounded up and sent to death camps. In death camps, Sara told me, a child might be picked up by the ankles and swung around in the air. Around and around, arms dangling in front of them.

When I tentatively suggested that this sounded fun, Sara laughed, and asked if I thought it would be fun to have my skull crushed against the side of a brick building after swinging for a circle or two.

Your grandmother was a coward, Sara told me. She abandoned her country and her parents and her brothers and ran away to live in America and never heard from anyone ever again. Her mother saved all the money they had to get Ada out of Poland. Her brothers signed up for the army to help pay. They died because of her. Everyone died because of her. She and Greta had no mercy.

"And I suppose you're sorry?"

This is when Ada walked in, her face completely composed. She ran a hand over her hair, smoothing down invisible flyaways.

"After all," she continued, "who do you think I was pregnant with? Some stranger? Are you sorry we didn't all die? That you didn't die? That Lulu is here?"

She stood next to me and put a hand on my shoulder. My mother grasped me on the other side. But neither woman looked at me. They had eyes only for each other.

The red measuring cups stood in a row, lined up by size. Each one was full of smoke: a cup of smoke, a half cup, a quarter cup. In school sometimes on Halloween, the teachers filled a plastic cauldron with punch and dry ice which they doled out in single servings, and I had the urge now to pick up one of the measuring cups and sip from its billowing bowl.

My eyes streamed tears and yet still felt like they were full of pepper. Maybe, I thought, if I lay down on the ground there wouldn't be quite so much smoke and I could just go to sleep.

I shook my head. The smoke backed away from me, made tentative by the sudden movement, but soon swirled back, ran its fingers through my hair. I scrunched up my nose and stretched the cotton from my pajama sleeve across my airways.

"Mama," I whimpered.

It took longer than usual to get to her bedroom. Our apartment wasn't very big, and on an ordinary day, if I was full of energy I could run around it at top speed and bang my fist on every door several times a minute. But today I kept getting lost. Every few steps I paused to get my bearings and found myself standing by an object that I'd never seen before. True, we had a hallway table, but did it look like this one? Was that our coat rack? Those abandoned shoes couldn't belong to me, so did they fit some other, unknown child?

When my hand found the knob on my mother's bedroom door I nearly sobbed with relief. She would be irritated that I was getting her out of bed, but she would know what to do, how to clear the air and cook me breakfast. She would make some noise, put on high heels, tell me I was a real pain when I wanted to be.

I knocked. There was no answer.

This wasn't unusual. More often than not, if I disturbed my mother's sleep before ten a.m. she would throw heavy things against the door until I went away or started throwing things against the other side. I knocked again and leaned my cheek against the wood. I could feel the incipient splinters, and the resonant sound of my knuckles against the board.

"Mama?" I knocked harder. "Mama, are you awake?"

Still there was no answer. Since these were unusual circumstances—my coughs were beginning to come up caustic with phlegm and I kept hearing shuffling, scratching sounds behind me in the clouds of smoke—I turned the cold knob and fell into the room, planning to jump into my mother's bed and throw the blanket over my head. If I was lucky, she'd wrap an arm around me and ask, thick with sleep, what on earth was wrong?

But the room was empty.

In my memory, Sara's dresses bloom out of her closet like mushrooms, a living profusion of brocade and tulle.

"Beautiful," she would say when I wrapped them around my arms and shoulders, cinched them about my waist, and tried to sashay in place. "You know they wouldn't look the same on anyone but me. They're tailored to fit."

She wore a new dress for every performance, every booking at the Green Mill, even when she was hired to sing a jazzy radio jingle for Caramello candy bars. It didn't matter to her that no one could see her clothes through the radio; her music and her beauty were linked inextricably, and she never left the house without lipstick and a freshly pressed skirt. Together, she and Ada were a sight to behold.

Sometimes, if she lay in bed for long enough dipping toast into the wet yellow yolk of soft-boiled eggs, I was allowed a few precious minutes to throw myself into her wardrobe, with its immersive lexicon of sensation. Unlike the wedding dresses at Marshall Field's, these didn't frighten me so much as intrigue me. They smelled like Sara. They were built in the shape of her body.

The fabric rustled in the closet of its own accord, even when I backed away and jumped onto my mother's bed to join her underneath the twisted sheets. Looking at the dresses gave me a shiver—where did they come from? No one could sew that fast, buy that much. I'd learned that cats produced more cats, birds produced more birds, even if I was unclear on the particulars. Looking at the closet I saw no other explanation than that this finery too was self-duplicating, breeding rapaciously just out of sight.

If someone had walked up and slapped me in the face with a cold palm, I could not have been more shocked than I was to see my mother's empty bedroom. The white paint on the windowsill was peeling slightly and marred with sticky red circles of wine. I watched a dust bunny lift on an unseen wind and drift across the floor. I nudged a stray button with my toe: it was cracked, and left a thin scratch on the floorboards. My stomach filled up with ice water that flushed up my throat and dripped down through my veins, from my heart to my fingertips and toes.

All the furniture was gone, right down to the bed frame, though I could see a faint line where each object should have been. Already the dust was beginning to explore its new terrain—everywhere—with no rug or table or stack of books to impede it. I walked into the closet and took a deep breath. Two thoughts hit me as the air hit my lungs. First, *no smoke*, and then, *she's gone.* My mother's room was completely unpolluted, the closet bare of dresses, hangers, and shoes, and the air as clean as evaporation off a glacier lake.

Considering the comprehensive nature of her wardrobe, I'd always assumed Sara's closet to be immense. But emptied out, the space was surprisingly shallow—just a rectangular box with a bare hanging bulb and an extra bar shoved in to fit more hangers. Standing there I began to feel dizzy. The cold water in my blood mixed unpleasantly with the smoke in my head, and my heartbeat grew so loud in my ears that it seemed to echo in the hollow space around me. I closed my eyes, and for a moment the sound was so large I believed I'd been mistaken: that the closet was big enough to hold a very empire of dresses.

Then the dizziness overtook me, and when I lay down on the closet floor I couldn't even stretch my limbs enough to straighten out my elbows or knees.

It was dark by the time Ada came home from Marshall Field's, and she found me exactly where I'd set myself down hours earlier. I could barely account for the time. My nose was running, a small puddle having collected on the floor by my head. It seemed probable that I'd fallen asleep, but I didn't remember any dreams save the image of our apartment on a mountaintop suspended in clouds.

The smoke that had haunted my movements all through the morning was gone, and I know Ada would have called it a dream too if not for the scent that lingered over our upholstery and curtains. All the cooking equipment I'd set out remained on the counters, the butter long since softened but everything else completely unchanged. Baba Ada trod around me delicately. That my mother could have removed every scrap of hers from our home between the time when Ada slipped out for work and I awoke stretched plausibility. It spoke of a desire to flee so swiftly and so unimpeded that my knees grew weak just thinking about it. She didn't want to say good-bye.

"Was there a loud sound, *lalka*?" My grandmother sat me down at the kitchen table and gave me a mug of hot chocolate. "Any sort of bang or clang, or a voice maybe?"

I shook my head. "Nothing. Just the smoke."

We both quietly gripped our mugs and avoided looking into each other's eyes.

"She thought I was cursed," I said. "That's why she hasn't been getting so many shows."

"No." Ada looked intently into her chocolate. A film of marshmallows melted on top and she dipped a finger in, bringing it up coated in white. "She thinks *she* is cursed."

"By me." My voice cracked. "Same thing."

"Oh darling, she didn't say that to you, did she?"

Ada came and picked me up out of my chair as easily as if I'd been two years old. I wrapped my arms around her neck and my legs around her waist, crossing my feet at the ankles to stay secure. I could feel that I was too big for this, but I also felt that if Baba Ada set me down I would fall to pieces on the floor. An arm here, a knee there, fingers scattered under the refrigerator.

"She didn't have to say it," I mumbled into Ada's shoulder as we careened into the living room to sit on the couch. "That's what she thinks. That Greta cursed us and she's dead and I'm bad luck."

"No," said Ada. "No."

But she did nothing else to contradict me, just stroked my

back with her fingernails until I fell into sobbing and began to cough. I ran into the bathroom and up came balls and balls of dark material. They hit the toilet with sickening plops. I cried and spat, sick at myself, as if I were contaminated with something I couldn't define. As if the smoke had gone inside me and turned solid, and only by hacking my throat red raw would I ever get it back out again.

17

If events begin long before they seem to, does that mean that the future and the past are linked? In fact, it must. A small move, a kicked stone at the top of the mountain leads the landslide into the houses below. Slip of the rock, slip of the shoe. But take the argument one step further: if the past must exist *just so* to cause the future, then doesn't the same principle suggest that the future also causes the past?

What I mean is, was Ada's death my fault? Was it Kara's? She's so light in my arms, her skin so sweet-smelling, that I think it can't be so. But what about Greta and her boys? All those baby girls born blue, who never breathed air, never felt the sun on their skin. Never had skin, some of them, to speak of. What about the children dead during one of the rehearsals for *Kristallnacht*, lying in the street on beds of window shards? What about a girl on a table being given a shot of poison slowly, into her spinal column? And another shot of poison, and another? All those girls. Did we reach our hands between their ribs, between the sinew of years and bones, and take their heartbeats for our own?

If they had to die so we can live, then yes, right? Somehow we did.

Today is the day of Kara's baptism, when she becomes John's child officially enough that nothing is likely to change things. A festive atmosphere is called for, despite the fact that Ada is missing, and my husband is being so cold to me that sometimes I forget I haven't told him about Finn at all. Despite the fact that I haven't sung in weeks, but today am meant to open my mouth and sing Kara welcome as part of the choir. At least it's funny, so many problems at once.

Under a sky the white of dirty cotton, I step into a cab with my husband's hand gripping my shoulder. Kara is curled against John's chest, wrapped up in as many layers as an onion. Beneath the ergonomic blue baby carrier, and the fleece blankets, and the pink hooded coat adorned with kitten ears, is a dress as frothy as egg whites whipped up for a meringue. She has been alive for ten weeks, her soul in ostensible jeopardy for all that time.

"Christ, what time is it?" John stretches his elbow upward to try and get an angle on his wristwatch without removing his hand from the baby's backside. "We're going to be late, you know."

I slide into the taxi, which is cold beneath me, the gray vinyl squeaking. I'm not in a hurry, and I've gotten used to John's tone. Proprietary. Wounded.

"Well, damn," I say. "Then they'll just have to christen someone else. Who do you think they'd choose? Out of everyone?"

John looks at me blankly. Another joke. That we can do

anything, choose anything, without consequences. He situates himself beside me, peeking at Kara under her hood.

"Remind me again why we're doing this?" he asks.

I hesitate, then lean against him. He lets me, and I'm grateful. It's been so long since we touched easily.

At the christening, a baby is given her name. She's made a part of the world, and she is announced to it. Past and future. Ada never met Kara, not really. But she planned this event, and so we'll go.

"You really have to ask?" I say.

John looks helpless.

"We don't even go to church," he says. "It's not such a crazy question."

It isn't, for him. The language of institutional faith is foreign to my husband—seductive, maybe, but incomprehensible. He was raised with Sunday morning cartoons and trips to the swimming pool on summer weekends. John's parents told him he could be whatever he wanted to be, as they zipped him into a rain jacket and walked him to the museum. Cathedrals were pointed out to him in terms of architecture and design, the glint of stained glass and the turn of a spandrel.

The first and only Communion he ever took was with me, one afternoon in Sacré-Coeur not long after we met. It had been five years since my own last confession, when I'd admitted to the sin of vanity and decided that I could presume that sin for myself going forward. Instead of going through the fuss of attending Mass and asking forgiveness, I began saying preemptive Hail Marys each week from my bedroom at home. But ignoring the rules is not the same as forgetting them.

We met in Paris, both of us twenty-three and singing our first roles at the Palais Garnier. The city's new modern house, L'Opéra Bastille, had opened several years before, but the director of our show wanted what he called "an antique feel" for the sound.

"An imperfect feel, he means," John said. He wore a blue vee-neck sweater with a hole at one elbow over a crisply ironed button-down shirt. He kicked stones as we walked down the street, and spoke in importunately loud English. I liked him because his shirt had soft pink stripes, and because he was blunt and a little bit proud of it. "A crappy feel. A boxy feel."

"You have no sense of history." I bumped him with my shoulder and he bumped me back. We tottered along through Montmartre this way, bobbing together like buoys in a tide. Both our voice coaches had somehow double-booked the afternoon, and our sudden freedom elevated us up off the street, almost out of our shoes. "Spaces carry memories! Singing in the Palais is like singing with Maria Callas!"

I flushed. The air was cool, but spring cool. Sorbet. Chilled grass.

"You know what?" I said. "I'll show you."

His hand felt soft and dry, the palm littered with an embarrassment of lines and wrinkles.

"Where are we going?" he asked.

I tugged him forward, keeping my eyes on the street signs, because I suddenly knew that if I looked back at him, my happiness would overwhelm my sense of purpose and we would fall into kissing against a wall and never leave. The possibility filled my head with soft bees, grumbling against one another and tickling me with their wings. Though he couldn't see it, I smiled.

"Wait and learn."

At the top of the hill that houses Sacré-Coeur, we both leaned, breathless, over our knees. It takes a special kind of fitness to run up so many stairs without getting winded. While trying to straighten up I stumbled into a stone barrier, and when John laughed at me, I pushed him to watch him wobble back and forth, and to feel the warmth of his chest underneath his sweater. We both giggled in between deep ragged inhalations until we heard the gong of bells and fell solemn.

"Okay," I said. "Do you believe in God?"

John searched my eyes, as if to measure which answer was more likely to impress me.

"No."

"Right," I said. "No. Not now. So follow me."

The Basilica bubbled white behind us, a lure of light. I tilted my chin towards the entrance and we walked inside.

We were in time for the end of afternoon Mass. I dropped to one knee in the doorway, crossing myself, and then stepped in line for Communion. John followed me with a look of game incomprehension. He raised an eyebrow. I mouthed, *Do what I do.*

So we shuffled slowly to the front, looking up at the golden mosaic in the apse and the Latin lettering hammered into the walls. When my head turned, John's head turned. When I put a hand in my coat pocket, he did the same. There were two priests up at the altar, splitting the line to more efficiently deliver the sacrament. *Bless me, Father*, I thought, *for I am about to sin.* I turned to the left and signaled to John that he should go right, hoping he'd better be able to see me and mimic the two-fingered motion of crossing myself, my bowed head before the priest and the silver dish of Eucharist wafers.

Around us rumbled the lowing chants of the monks, and

through them rose the ivory spires of soprano voices. I've never been able to resist the drunkenness inspired by the church smell of candlewax and incense. The vegetable taste of old paper, the masked sweat of old women, the polished wooden pews—as a child in tow to my *babenka*, these mingled aromas made me feel both minute and infinite. As an adult, the combination of them hitting my senses still humbles me with the feeling of being in God's presence. Bashful and in awe.

I presented my tongue and accepted the host. I had swallowed so many of these tasteless wafers that one more should have made no difference, but it called to mind every Communion of my life with its unflinching sameness. The priest blessed me and turned to the woman behind me in line. Across the altar John closed his mouth on his own bit of Eucharist, holding his lips in a pinch as if to keep the wafer protected by a buffer of air. He looked around but didn't see me, turned a whole circle before starting for the exit. I watched him watching the rise of the walls, the eggshell sheen of the dome above us. The river of bodies moving up towards the front of the Basilica to receive a bit of that same bland bread.

I followed him at a small distance. Outside I took a deep breath and stretched, letting the wafer melt into glue on my tongue. Then I walked up behind John, the shivering entirety of him, and tapped him on the shoulder.

"Now," I said, "how do you feel about God?"

He turned, and if I could not read his smile, I still fell into his arms as he lifted me into the air by the waist.

"Let's go sing with Maria Callas!" he said.

Because I wanted to, and because I was distracted by the pressure of his hands sliding onto my hips, I felt that I had been understood. We laughed and ran down the white steps of the Basilica, laughed all night as our bodies knocked together and we reached our fingers towards each other's faces. I laughed as John fed me vanilla bean ice cream, as his arm got stuck in the rolled-up sleeve of his shirt when we tried to pull the shirt free from his body. Laughed when his mouth brushed my belly, my ribs, because I realized this was what it meant to share a secret. We would look at one another in rehearsal the next day and smile and no one would know why. No one but us two, and the God who saw us take Communion unpurified by anything but our new love.

The question that nags at me is: was I understood though? Really? It makes a difference to me whether John saw what I meant, felt what I felt. Jumped into that passion with the same resolve and abandoned himself to it. It is a question of the possibility of faith.

The problem lies with Rabbit, you see. His false dog. The future, causing the past to crumble. It's a good story for getting a girl to fall in love with you: the mistakes you've made and how you mourned them. But when I found out it was not true, it became something different to me. A fable that explained why John thought a girl—any girl—might fall in love with any boy. A pretty package with nothing inside it but tissue, tissue. Layers of tissue and air.

I wanted to laugh it off and forget. But instead I peered backward at all the things about John I'd believed. There are many such things, when you're in love. Each day, new ones—a favorite flavor of tea, or a dislike for getting up before seven in the morning. He always told me he thought granola bars were tawdry, the downfall of a civilization too lazy to prepare real food.

Was that true or did he just say it because he thought I'd agree? And was there any one truth that I could pull away without the rest crumbling down around me? If too many tourists pocket white pebbles in Montmartre, after all, the city will be made naked of her temples.

18

"Where's Mama now?" I asked Baba Ada. For months after Sara left I pestered Ada with this question.

"I don't know." Ada, curt, looked at her watch. "Who knows. It's only ten o'clock. Wherever that woman is, she's probably still sleeping."

"Don't you think"—I wrapped my hands around Ada's wrist—"she's probably wearing a dress as dark as the ocean? Don't you think she's walking through a long hallway that's only lit by fireflies?"

"Don't you listen, child?" Ada shook me off. "She's in bed somewhere. That bad bed she always insists on keeping, with those terrible pillowcases she never remembers to wash. They smell like they're fermenting."

I sat down on the living room couch and pressed my knees together hard, so the inside skin of each developed a distinct patch of red.

"If Mama was in some kind of maze, she might not be able to

find her way out." I peeled my knees slowly apart and pressed the red spots, leaving momentary white fingerprints. Ada didn't seem to be catching on, but this was important. "Say it was a really tall maze made out of bushes."

"A hedge maze."

"Yeah, a *really* tall hedge maze. Maybe there are flowers in there that she's allergic to, and she sneezed so many times she *had* to fall asleep." I considered. "Or else someone poisoned her. It's possible."

"Is it?" Ada rubbed her face with both hands. "Listen, *lalka*, I need to do the laundry."

"No." I crossed my arms. "Tell me a story."

"What kind?"

"A story about Mama. A Sara story."

But Ada just sighed.

"You already know everything about that woman that you need to know."

In spite of Ada, I didn't stop imagining stories about my mother. It was a habit too deeply ingrained to let go. Her disappearance smacked of Greta—both were great queens, kidnapped somewhere, asleep. Or scheming. Both were dangerous and powerful and full of misbehavior. Both were missing, and in neither case did I understand quite why.

At night, after Ada left my room, I lay with my eyes closed and imagined her still there, holding my hands and telling me this:

"When your mother left here, she went to live in a castle, and all around her were battlements and gargoyles spitting hot oil and men with guns. She brought in women from all over the world to brush the hair off of the deer in her bestiary and card the fur into usable material, spin it into thread. Sometimes they spun thread from shining gray cats instead, or thoroughbred horses. Sometimes they plucked feathers from tropical birds and snipped them to pieces and wove that into the fabric, so the colors were always changing under different angles of light.

"Her dresses were golden and brown and littered with white spots, and sometimes she wore one that had a long tail. Not a deer's tail, but a lion's tail, which switched back and forth while she walked through her castle's stony hallways to a great room filled up by an admiring audience. They listened to her singing and threw roses at her feet.

"When she had sung, the fawn most recently born in her forest would be walked into the great room on trembling new legs, a lead of silk around its throat. Sara stroked the animal's head and slit it open from belly to sternum so that its organs scattered on the floor and mingled with the shining silk. The servants struck up a fire to roast the animal's body, and when Sara had feasted on tender deer meat and fruit and fine wine, she would recline onto the piles of pillows that her servants carried into the room, and people would ask her about her beautiful daughter. She would smile.

"'My daughter is so small that she can stand on my thumb, but her voice is as big as a cloud surrounding a mountain. It wraps around your body and shields you from the world, so you can't look out and no one else can look in—not while she's singing. Of course, a voice like that is a dangerous gift, and she can't completely control it, not yet. Sometimes it will lash out and tie a man or woman up with its cords, and before my daughter knows it that person will be choked blue, as still as a statue forevermore.

"'That is why my daughter isn't here with us now, even though together we could make music that would freeze the air into crystals of ice. She has to tame her voice, become one with it, so that the power it contains is hers to wield, and no one will be harmed by it unless she intends them to be. I miss her,' she would say, 'with all of my heart. And when we're together again we'll be happy.'

"Then the audience would applaud your mother again, and they would all talk late into the night while the animals outside tiptoed around the grounds, dreaming of giving their fur to Sara's dresses and their children to her table."

Instead, when I really bothered her, Ada told me that we couldn't see my mother because she lived in a bad part of town, somewhere I wouldn't want to go.

"Or would you, *złota*?" She tilted her head, gave half a smile. "Do you want to go someplace full of cigarette smoke and see your mother from a distance? Would you like to beg her to come home?"

When I heard this, my face grew cold and pale. The blood trickled out of my cheeks down into my stomach, into a hot and gurgling bowl.

"No," I said. It was a misunderstanding. All I really wanted was to hear stories about my mother. That was how we fixed things: with stories. Anyway, that was how we tried.

But once I got her started, Ada was relentless. She wrapped an arm around my waist and told me to go grab my coat, we'd take the train right away, absolutely.

"You can get down on your hands and knees." She rubbed her palms together. "Tell her how sorry you are that she's gone. How much *harder* things are now. How much worse, *lalka*."

"We can't." I stomped one foot. "She was kidnapped."

"She wasn't."

"She *was*."

I started to cry, tugging my body away from my *babenka*'s, curling up into a tight little ball. Ada watched me for a time, and then leaned down and put her arms around my shoulders. With great heaves, I wept.

"Oh darling," Ada murmured. "What do you want me to say?"

As John, Kara, and I approach the church, I can see a figure that must be my mother, from an almost impossible distance. She is the first point my eyes focus on in the horizon, the dark mark on the road, the glint in the glare. I watch her grow from a featureless manikin into a woman. Her hair emerges, combed into a bun. The curve of her hip issues out from her waist. As we get closer, I can see her fingers, the blink of her eye. Our driver stops the cab with a lurch at the corner.

"Cortland and Hermitage, right?" he says.

She was kidnapped, I think. *Taken by pirates and sent around the world in a galleon with only old burlap to make into dresses. Life with the pirates made her hard. Too much salt on her skin. Too much sea rum.* Even with no one to contradict the story, it doesn't much satisfy. Sara idles on the sidewalk, one foot atop a pile of calcified snow. She looks like she's waiting for us, but I think she's just smoking. My mother. She's here.

Leaving John behind in the cab to handle the payment, I step carefully out and stand beside her. Without speaking, I breathe in the scent of her cigarette smoke, which hangs around us like a cloud. It smells sweet and like dirt, with a bit of canned tomatoes underneath it, a trace of peat. I can tell right away it will stick in my hair and on my clothes, clog my throat. So that's real enough.

"Mama," I say. "Hello."

She's looking at me. No, she's looking past me, for the baby. She won't quite meet my eyes. I, however, cannot look away. I take in every inch of her. So different. So the same.

My mother's cigarette has burned down almost to its base, and it's only when the heat reaches her fingers that she realizes. She lights another from the glowing tip, tossing the spent one onto the sidewalk and grinding it beneath her boot. Her hands are stained orange between the index and middle finger. Now that I'm next to her, I can see that her skin is loose in odd spots around her face—not uniformly, like an old woman shrunk into herself, but here and there. A sag near the left eye. A few too many lines by the mouth to be accounted for as the product of old smiles.

And yet for all that she's held on to at least a modicum of her beauty. She's managed it well, with dark lines around her eyes and a professional dye job in her hair. Still dark, almost black. Shining against her shoulders.

I feel a stab of impatience. Isn't she even going to speak?

She fought the pirates and came home, brandishing her sword. They let her go when she kicked a chest full of treasure off one side of the boat, then jumped into the water and swam the other direction. The pirates all dove after the gold, stuffing coins in their mouths for safekeeping so they could grab more and more, until they sank. Too heavy with treasure. My mother was picked up by the coast guard of a small island nation and flown back to civilization, and now here she is. But she has a heavy coin in her mouth, too.

"So," I say. "You came."

"Can't get anything by you." Sara sucks in her cheeks to pull the smoke in deeper, faster. She flicks her ash onto the toes of my shoes but then, surprisingly, looks sorry. "Hmm."

"Why, though?"

My mother glances up, at last, into my face. Her eyes are softer than I thought they would be. If I didn't know better, I'd say there were some tears there. But of course it's cold. The wind makes you cry, too.

"You're kind of a mess, aren't you?" Her voice strains towards indifference, clipped efficiency. Not quite reaching its goal. She licks two fingers and sticks a flyaway piece of hair down to my skull—I inhale sharply when we touch. Part of me wants to hit her hand away, and part of me just wants to hold it in my own, run the tip of my finger over the hard sheen of her painted thumbnail, as I did when I was a girl. She's so close. I can smell a little something acid on her breath, maybe juice and unbrushed teeth. Maybe vodka. "You know, I went to see my mother in her goddamn grave and there weren't any flowers there. I mean, dead flowers, yes, but not real ones."

"I haven't been back yet," I say. "Since the funeral. I told you, I tried to go." John has finished with the cab and is beside me now, holding Kara. He has a look on his face of unbridled morbid fascination. I ask, "Why didn't you bring her any?"

"Ha." Sara goes in to touch Kara on the cheek and then looks between her and John—fast, just a flash of appraisal. That's all she needs to know everything. "Well, you're right. I didn't."

My mother locks eyes with John, very casually. "When you're not invited to the funeral, these things have a way of becoming someone else's responsibility. Wouldn't you say," she asks, "that when someone takes matters out of your hands, that leaves you more or less free of obligation? To the results?"

"So you're Lulu's mom," he says. "It's nice to meet you."

I tug on his coat sleeve. "Let's go in."

He's still staring at Sara. "I can see the resemblance."

"Can you?" she asks. "Me, I'm not sure."

John balks, genuinely surprised—my mother and I really do look quite a bit alike. And Sara laughs a little, seeing him compare us. Looks between him and Kara. I hold my breath and wait for a wave to crash into me. To sweep us all away down the street, our voices lost in the roar. But my mother doesn't press. For once in her life.

"Yes," she says. "I'm sorry. I thought we were talking about something else."

As we walk into the church I want to hold someone's hand. The idea is so grounding—a hand, like a lightning rod. John's hand, with its funny wrinkles, or my mother's, once pristine. Now a bit dirty and tattered. What I need is a little warmth to keep me going. Someone to lend me a little strength. But everyone is all bound up in themselves right now, and I can hardly blame them.

Sara bends down and picks a piece of paper up from a basket by the end of the pews.

"Programs?" she asks. "At a christening?"

"Baba Ada planned all this." I take the paper from her and cluck at how it flops around, flimsy. "She wouldn't have been very happy. It looks cheap."

"She would have gone and burned down the store that sold it to her. Held the clerk's whole family captive until he agreed to a twenty percent discount."

"No." I fold the program and replace it on the pile. "She wouldn't have." I've tried to bring Ada back with stories. Since she died, I've been telling myself every Ada story I ever knew. But even the true ones just make it clear something's missing. False ones would be worse. Rewriting. Erasing.

"Are you cold?" my mother asks. I realize I'm shivering.

"No," I say. "I'm just nervous."

"To sing?" I can see how it would sound ridiculous. Me of all people. But whatever lurking danger has been following me since Kara's birth has crawled here, certainly. The delicate balance between my mother and my husband—secrets. The knowledge that what happens to me could happen to Kara a hundredfold if I sing to her. Good and bad.

She could have a better voice, a purer song. And. My fingers find my midriff, walk along the scar, which has been slightly weeping, so I have to dress it again. Beneath my clothes, a thin band of cotton wool. Am I to be ridiculed for worrying that the wound means something worse is coming? I move my fingers to my forehead. It's enough to drive you mad.

"About you," I tell my mother. "Wouldn't you be?"

She smiles. "Oh, definitely."

But the smile fades. She sits down in the last pew and drums her nails on the space beside her. I hesitate, but follow, and we both watch John at the front of the church, directing people around. There's something funny about the arrangement behind the altar, but before I can think too much about it, my mother asks, "Don't you want to know what I've been doing all these years?"

"What?"

"You know, *Hello, Mama, I've missed you. What on earth have you done to fill the time?* I've been waiting for you to ask any one of the sensible questions, but you never do. It's not your style, I guess."

"Huh," I say.

Sara plays with her bottom lip without realizing it and then sees the lipstick on the tips of her fingers. She pinches her lips together to smooth out the shade, and runs a nail along the line of pink and pale, to assure the definition. This is what she pays attention to as I sit beside her, not answering. I, *the daughter,* a vague notion she has carried in her head.

"Maybe I don't want to know." My voice, catching in my throat, sounds husky. "Maybe I have other things on my mind, or maybe I'm just not interested."

"Oh, you're interested." She takes my hands, both of them, just what I wanted, only times two. Too hard. "You've always liked to be told scary stories."

"Come on," I say. "You live in the city. How scary could it be?"

She tilts back her head to look at the ceiling and her mouth falls open, just a little. Puppet jaws, on a hinge. The inside of her mouth is just as dark pink as her lips, teeth pearlescent, but studded with aluminum fillings. One gold, in the back. Sara sighs, upward.

"You asked me, on the phone," she said. "About Greta? I mean, talk about your spook stories. Let me tell you something." My mother rights her neck and I hear a small crick. "About you."

"Okay," I say. Sara angles her head and indicates me closer.

"Well, doll." She used to call me *lalka,* like Ada did. Little doll. I guess I've grown up. "You were always looking for the curse. *Always.* Every little bad thing that happened to you, everything you did wrong, you asked me, *Was that it? Was that the curse?* As if taking five dollars out of my purse without asking is the kind of thing that you'd be forced to do by magic."

"No," I say. "I don't remember that."

"You were a child." Sara squeezes my fingers so they crush together. "What the hell do you know?"

"What's your point?"

"Sometimes," she says, and then stops. There's a sound up by the sanctuary. "Things happen just because we do them. Not for any other reason."

The sound comes again.

"What is that?" I ask. But Sara doesn't answer. She knows. I know.

It starts as a low moan. The keening of a child who is lost in the woods. And then the sound lifts mercifully, a feather on the wind, that same child looking up at the trees to see a familiar face through the leaves. There is an element of sobbing that I can feel in my own chest—the phlegmatic stickiness and heaving—but also something of joy. I feel my body unsettle as though it had been covered with six feet of dirt and then suddenly dusted off. Light as air.

A violinist I recognize from the Lyric orchestra, the assistant concertmaster in fact, stands on a podium dressed in a dark blue gown. She tilts to one side with her instrument cradled under her chin, bobbing back and forth. Her hair, chopped short against her ears, shakes against the movement of her body. If she tilts right, her hair falls left. Beside her sits Rick, looking at her with suspicious eyes and wearing a tuxedo. With tails. I didn't expect that from him, today, though I knew he would be here. The godfather. Apparently Ada planned something more for him and didn't tell me. I put a hand over my mouth and bite back a bit of sudden laughter at the seriousness of his dress—I don't want to interrupt the violinist. She's practicing an accompaniment to "Ave Maria."

The song is so common that it's almost a rite of passage for singers—everyone must record an "Ave." Jazz it up or dress it down. And it's a rite for musical audiences too, performed so often that people like to pretend the song bores them. Like to think they know the story of it. But they're usually wrong—ask almost anyone on the street and they'll tell you the piece is a song of worship, in Latin, when in fact it's Schubert, and the words are German.

It's not a prayer. It's an appeal. A young woman, called the

Lady of the Lake, asks the Virgin Mary for help and peace in a time of war. Families fighting one another, families perishing. And a man who loves the singing lady leaves for battle, realizing he will never hear her voice again. But the lady doesn't sing for this warrior, she sings for her father, who has declined to fight and has therefore made himself terribly vulnerable. *Hear for a maid a maiden's prayer. And for a father hear a child.*

We haven't had very many fathers in my family, so maybe I'm not accustomed to them. What I hear is a girl crying for her mother. For a hand that soothed her in the night, and touched her cheek, and disappeared.

I look at Sara. She seems bored, or maybe just distracted. *Where* did *you* go? I do want to ask her. *How on earth* did *you fill the time?* But I think I missed my chance. Maybe I'm not supposed to know. Or maybe it's not fate, but just the choice I made. *Things happen just because we do them,* she said. *Sometimes.*

The violinist reaches the end of the song and nods to Rick, seated beside her at a piano that I'm sure he had brought in especially for the occasion. He's very particular about what he'll play on, sometimes going to the trouble of tuning an instrument himself if he's displeased with a damper or the tension in a wire. The two of them wait for a moment and I can hear them counting, getting into the same rhythm of notes per heartbeat. And then they begin to play together. The piano is the lake water. The violin plays the part of the wind in the trees.

As they run through it, the song begins to feel like a round, or a fugue. Repeating itself only to pick up more steam, to grow and expand. First there was silence, then the violin, and then the piano layered on top. I sway slightly, listening. Because soon the piece will end again, and if it picks back up, I could add my voice. Take the journey a little further.

I feel a bit nauseous in my desire to do so. To sing this song, and every song. To never stop, and damn the consequences.

The Lady of the Lake performs her "Ave Maria" in a woodland cave, and I can feel the forest floor beneath my feet, the soft bed of pine needles and birch leaves dried into a crackling path. I bite my lip and watch Rick's hands tremble over the keys, the violinist bob and weave like a river wave. *The past, and the future*, I think. *The past and the future.* Ada lying on the hospital floor, already gone while busy people touch and urge her. And Kara, my baby. Is it worse if she caused Ada to fall by being born, child of a curse made well before her reckoning, or is it worse if I let her become part of that birthright so that someday, somehow, she loses something too?

The answer is: both, both. Somehow I am the survivor of both deaths, if I believe all that nonsense that my grandmother told me. If I stand up and do the only thing I've ever known how to love completely. If I stand, and sing my appeal.

L ast night when I was dreaming, I sat beside Greta on a knoll in Poland and we shared a cigarette. A luxury for both: Greta chewed tobacco because the papers were expensive, and the absolute proscription on smoke coming anywhere near my throat has long been a contentious part of my existence. Sara once threw an ashtray at the wall when Ada asked her to take her filthy habit out to the fire escape on a cold day.

In the dream I liked the smell. It was more like pipe tobacco, sweet. Greta squinted and pinched the small rolled thing between her fingers, exhaling into the distance. She blew perfect smoke rings of outlandish size: as they emerged from her lips they were minuscule, but the farther they drifted away the larger they got, until several were resting on the treetops in the forest below us.

"What happened to you?" I finally asked. We might have been sitting there for an hour, ten minutes, several weeks. I was in no hurry, but it was a question I'd always wanted to know the answer to.

Greta's chin lay on her hand, and with the fingers of the other she passed me our cigarette. I inhaled with gusto, feeling the curls of smoke caress my throat, the mass of black breath coil and undulate within me.

"There was a war on," she said at last.

"Yes, but you were you." Greta was the size of a mountain, safe as houses. "At least," I said apologetically, uncertain how much I'd spoken aloud, "that was always my impression."

She stretched, and then looked at me. We both fell backward onto the grass, and I coughed a little puff of smoke out when my lungs felt the impact. From the ground, Greta reached out one hand and placed it on top of my head. Her palm moved back and forth across my hair, probably causing knots and tangles.

"Little girl, I ran and ran across the fields," Greta said, still stroking my hair. "I had a gun in each hand and I shot anything that moved. They were all bad ones. But that wasn't my concern. I wanted to get to my boys and feel their foreheads one last time. Fil had such a funny shape in his, a line right down the middle. Andrzej's was enormous, and Konrad's was so smooth. He never got," she gestured at her cheeks, "any spots. He was just a perfect child, except not what I wanted. It was hard to forgive him that."

I took a deep drag off the cigarette and moved it up to Greta's waiting fingers.

"Sometimes," she said, "it took my breath away."

"What?"

She exhaled through her front teeth. "The sheer cheek. The total lack of respect for what I had. For my husband, for my beautiful sons. And it wasn't just my sons, no, I wasn't content to give just them up. I gave up every son in every township. Every daughter I could have imagined a life for. What did I think the devil would want? Everything," she said, stubbing the cigarette out in the grass. "From everyone."

"Even me?" I asked, though I knew the answer. She moved the cigarette around in the dirt—I could hear the shuffling—and brushed my hair again.

"Of course."

I was silent. Wind whipped through the trees below us and dissipated Greta's smoke rings. Pine crests tilted and croaked under the strain, but where we were the blustering had no effect at all.

Finally I said, "That doesn't answer my question. Where did you go? Where are you?"

Greta sat up, and for a moment she looked so much, so achingly much like Ada that I cried out. But when she turned back to me, the likeness faded.

"You want to know where my grave is?" Greta asked. "The order in which we died? Whether we tried to save each other or sent people out to be slaughtered? I'm telling you, it doesn't matter." Her eyes looked for something on the horizon, something they couldn't seem to find. "Gone is gone."

"I don't know," I said. "If you can't show me your grave, how can I know you really died?"

But Greta just shrugged.

"For all you know," she said, "I never even existed."

I walk towards the front of the church as if in a trance. On the way I pass John and I gently peel my daughter from his chest and lift her up into the air. Her arms and legs dangle down towards me, and one leg gives a kick. A jig.

With only a bit of difficulty, owing to the fact that I can't use my hands for help, I climb up onto the podium beside the violinist and Rick. Rick winks at me.

"Nice to see you," he says. "Been wondering when I would."

"Hush," I say. And then, indicating the violinist with my chin, "Who put you up to this? It was just supposed to be the choir."

He smiles at me. "Wouldn't you like to know?"

The three of us—four of us—form a semicircle. I shiver again, with nerves.

"I'm not warmed up, you know," I say. "I'm not ready."

"That's okay." Rick cracks his knuckles and runs a few fingers over the keys. "We've got some time."

And so I listen to them run scales, first the basics at an even tempo, and then Rick adds in a little verve. Takes things into minor, adds trills. Generally tries to entice me into joining. This is always our game, but I'm not sure I can play. Already my pulse is quick. There are knots in my stomach, and I can't tell which are tying and which untying. I am, I realize, terribly unprepared for this.

Instead of the sensations in my own body, I concentrate on Kara's slack weight, and on what I see in front of me. John sits in the first row, watching me back, and a few rows behind him I see my mother. No longer in the rear of the church, she seems to have moved closer when I wasn't looking. My chest pinches whenever she catches my eye, and still I am silent. Waiting until the last minute to decide. The violinist shoots me a very sideways look.

At last the priest shows up next to me, nearly tripping on his own vestments. There are two altar boys lighting candles around the room, and I breathe deeply the fat-rich scent of melting wax.

I keep my voice steady.

"Is it time to begin, Father?" I ask. I want someone to tell me what to do.

He blinks at me. "It's your party."

"All right," I say. I fill my lungs and empty them. Bellows in and out, breathing over a fire. Then I give Kara a kiss on the cheek and hand her to the priest. I almost can't; it's like handing over a bit of my body. But I do.

I nod at Rick.

And I sing:

Ave Maria! maiden mild!
Listen to a maiden's prayer!
Thou canst hear though from the wild;
Thou canst save amid despair.

I feel a prickling behind my eyes, in my ears. The way blood builds up before you faint, when your head gets too heavy. I look at the door and for an instant I see Ada walking through it, and think, *No, you're not supposed to be here.* But I blink, and it's no one. Just a gray shadow come and gone with a trick of the light.

Safe may we sleep beneath thy care,
Though banish'd, outcast and reviled—
Maiden! hear a maiden's prayer;
Mother, hear a suppliant child!

The room is silent, listening. My tongue is an icicle, melting in spring. My throat is a river, rushing. My body is breaking. My breath is quick. Quick. Quick.

Kara's eyes are large white discs, shot through with blue. The pinpoints of her pupils focusing, watching my lips with hungry attention.

There is a merciful moment where I'm able to feel surprised, just before I lose consciousness.

The silence that follows a performance is a different silence entirely from the one that precedes it. Both are full—one with anticipation, the other with echoes, as if the silence itself were a vibrating bell.

I feel the tremors of sound before I hear them, and then I hear smears, snatches without meaning. As the sounds warm up and gain flesh, almost distinction, I'm aware of something physical: my hands are shaking.

Slowly, more leaks in. My hands in other pairs of hands, being held against a face that feels like ice. No. The face is warm. It's my own skin that's cold and pale as frost.

"Baba?" So I have a voice, too. I open my eyes and see my husband, looking concerned. "John." Only the people who are supposed to be here are here, after all.

"Lu, what happened?" John asks. "My god, you really did blow a gasket. I thought that was a joke."

"So did I." My hands find my abdomen, pressing gently against the schism of string and scar tissue that's been holding me together. "Sort of. Am I bleeding?"

"No, of course you're not bleeding," he says. Though even at that moment he's looking, touching me gingerly, finding the same thing. Nothing. But he keeps checking, placing his hand against my forehead and lifting my chin with three fingers. Moving my face from side to side, inspecting me with urgent eyes. Everyone else is standing, peering, but keeping their distance as John waves them back. "Do you feel like you're hurt?"

In fact, for the first time in several weeks I feel calm, and whole. My body is radiating a peculiar heat, so it feels liquid and elastic. Beyond the possibility of harm. I don't know if I can stand, but I don't care. I lie propped in John's arms, letting myself ebb and flow. What just happened? I can only half remember. There was a party. Or not quite a party. I sang a song.

"I'm fine," I say. "I just— It was too hot. I need something to drink."

John signals and someone runs to get something for me, bringing back a thick, riveted glass of cold water. I sip and it's the best water I've ever tasted.

"John, listen," I say.

"What is it?" His brown eyes find mine, and I think, *I chose you. I would choose you again.* John has told me many little lies, ones I know and ones I haven't yet discovered. But in his arms now, I feel there is a larger truth still. Montmartre standing. Sacré-Coeur. The lies seemed so significant to me that they've shrouded the fact that I haven't been better. Waiting for him to discover me. Waiting for him to call me out.

"Listen," I say again. "I've got something to tell you."

19

Kara—the real girl, the one who lives and breathes and probably has her own thoughts, though I cannot yet fathom the shape of them—she deserves a real baptism. It's a thing about the soul: even if you doubt it's real, even if you don't believe in heaven, you want your child to go there. To be invited, with or without you.

John shakes his head. "Why would you tell me that?" he asks. I take his hand.

"What do you want me to say?"

No one else is standing close enough to hear what we're talking about, but I can imagine what we look like, two dark faces shedding tears, and then nodding.

"You think this is the right place for this conversation?"

"I don't know." I lick my lips. I was afraid for so long, and now here we are. Talking. It's not so hard. I look at John, who doesn't seem to agree. "I don't want something to happen to me without you knowing the truth."

At this, he softens. Just a bit.

"Still though. Why?"

"Because," I say. "You're the right father. The one who loves her." I'm not quite brave enough to say *us*. "I wanted to make sure I told you that."

John keeps waving people away as we talk—they must think I'm very badly broken to stay so long on the ground, crying. And there may be some truth to that. But as much as I want us to be alone—two souls on an iceberg, together, at sea—I want to move forward with the ceremony more. For the moment at least, John agrees. To fix things. Keep them going.

Eventually it's established that I can stand.

"Who is the godmother supposed to be?" I ask. Realizing that I do not know. It was meant to be Ada, but if John has picked someone new in the meantime, I wasn't aware of it. Life goes on, despite our best intentions.

"Michelle said she'd do it," John tells me. "Pinch hitter."

"Can Sara?" My emotions are like bats, flying around my head at odd angles. I can't understand where they come from, where I'm getting my ideas.

"Your mother?" His hands in his pockets, John looks up at the ceiling. "That's what you want?"

I try to take it as a good sign that he isn't looking to fight me. So I nod and he goes over to talk to the priest, while I lean against the altar, smiling with what will I can at the little audience. John comes back with Kara in his arms, and the father with him. We look at one another as if to gauge tempo, all waiting for a signal from someone else.

"Haven't you done this before?" I ask the priest. He is gentler with me than I deserve.

"I wanted to make sure you were well, my dear."

John hands Kara over, her white gown fluttering around her and her face creased with confusion. The priest crosses his fingers over her head, raises a golden cup, and trickles it slowly over her forehead.

"*Ego te baptizo in nomine Patris et Filii et Spiritus Sancti,*" the priest chants, his voice high. "I baptize you in the name of the Father and of the Son and of the Holy Ghost."

He then calls for godparents, spiritual sponsors, to guide Kara's admission into the church. Sara, having been primed, comes up to stand with us, and one of the altar boys hands her a lighted candle. She tries to smile but gives up. Her face is serious. She raises one eyebrow at me, silent.

"And the second sponsor?"

From the audience Rick stands up and brushes off his tuxedo pants. The action is reflexive, as they're perfectly crisp and clean. His hands are white and manicured, as always, as if washed in boiling water and scrubbed with steel wool. I watch the flame of Rick's candle travel up with him to the podium. The side of the candle is emblazoned with silver paint, and a single drop of wax drips down its length only to be caught in the paper base.

"And now the child's mother and father will join me as we present her Christian name and invite her to join the society of God."

John stands by my side. His hand brushes mine but moves away, so we're close enough to feel heat radiating off each other, but not touching. The priest whispers in Kara's ear and her face breaks open, bright red with sobs. Addressing Sara and Rick, the priest gestures over Kara's form.

"Do you believe in the Holy Ghost, the Holy Catholic Church, the communion of saints, the forgiveness of sins, the resurrection of the body, and life everlasting?"

Ada always told me that Greta slept beneath the earth and would come forth if she was needed. Perhaps resurrection is another talent we all hold in common. I wonder what I might be asked to give up for that.

Rick and my mother assent to the priest, and hold out their candles as he crosses Kara three times.

"Receive this burning light," he says. "And keep thy baptism so as to be without blame: keep the commandments of God, that when the Lord shall come to the nuptials, thou mayest meet Him together with all the saints in the heavenly court, and mayest have eternal life forever and ever."

Later, in our apartment, John and I sit at the kitchen table drinking tea. Kara is asleep on the floor beside us, in her car seat. She cried all the way home—the water was too cold, or there were too many people. Or the music was too loud. Who can say?

"So we made your mother the godmother, huh?" John says. He has retreated back into himself, no more hand on my forehead.

There's wind blowing against the building, but it seems weaker than it has been, as if it's coming from farther away.

"Did you know?" I ask him. "Already, I mean, before?"

He shakes his head. Maybe.

"I don't know what I knew," he says. "I don't even know what I know."

"Yes," I say. I know the feeling.

There's a patter of rain, or perhaps hail, on the window. But just one wave, and then it stops. As if someone threw a handful of pebbles up to get our attention. A tree creaks. Quiets. John puts more water on the stove to boil.

20

Bright light and a lake as large as a sea.

As the months creep by after Kara's baptism, heat leaks back into Chicago and we all begin to unbutton our jackets. Slowly, because sometimes the heat is sucked back out. Sixty degrees followed the next day by thirty, a light rainstorm turning into a shower of snow. Like always during this transformation, I have been imagining a giant sleeping in the ground. He breathes out and the city is flush with warmth, but when he breathes back in we all shiver again.

Or put another way: the residents of the city are dancers glowing with effort, sweat on our napes. We spin until a girl in red strolls by and then we all freeze like popsicles, bent at odd angles depending on how the music has melted us.

Chicago is full of joy with the onset of spring. People smile at one another walking down the street, and tulips push crazily through the soil. Garden plots in front of apartment buildings turn barbaric with color. We all guzzle water and fruit and wine.

I t's late May, and Kara and I are at the lakeshore. I perch
on the concrete steps, Kara propped up on my lap, and
point out the boats far from shore. I'm not sure she can focus
across that distance yet, but she follows the direction of my hand
and then gazes up at me with wonder. The boats themselves are
not even looking at us. We are nothing they care to see.

For the past months I've been a shorebound creature, keeping
a modest radius from my home. But tomorrow I will wake up and
be a traveler again. I leave for Milan at five a.m. and won't come
back for two weeks. There are gowns bagged up and ready for
me to throw into a taxi, and a suitcase full of cotton shirts, iron-
pleated skirts, and sandals. It will be warm in Milan, and I will be
singing Violetta Valéry from *La Traviata*.

There is a tinkling and a rumbling behind us. A cart pulls up
behind a bicycle, parking in the half-full lot I walked across to
reach the lake. The bicyclist, dressed all in black, jumps down and
hops inside the cart, which is painted to look like a stage. In fact
there is a real red velveteen curtain, and when a gloved hand pulls
it back, a rabbit-shaped puppet appears. The little stage has my full
attention by now, and a few other giddy sunbathers amble over to
watch.

A light crackling precedes the music. The sound has the war-
bling quality of an old record player, but how, I wonder, could a
record player fit inside that silly wooden box? The song is ragtime,
two-step, soft-shoe. The rabbit puppet is joined by a green snake
with a hissing pink tongue, and they hop around each other, dipping in time to the shuffling beat.

John is going to stay home with the baby.

"Take the trip," he said to me. He pointed out that he went to New York a month ago to sing in *A Midsummer Night's Dream*. "Have fun. Live a little."

"Have you been reading pamphlets from a travel agency?" I asked. "Come Visit Picturesque Italia! Be the Envy of All Your Friends!" We are playful. It's something that we're trying out.

Somehow the puppeteer manages to keep his hands invisible for the entire song. This doesn't seem like it should be possible, and so I applaud when the puppets bend at the waist in a bow. In piping voices they welcome donations, and a little girl runs up with a dollar from her father's wallet, which the snake accepts in his mouth, speaking a garbled thank-you.

The music begins again and I lift Kara up by her underarms, placing her feet down on the pavement. They don't yet lie flat— the logic of putting her weight on her own two legs is still the dream of a dream. But as the rabbit and the snake bounce against each other—*rag-mop, shoe-bop*—she toggles up and down, hilarious with her own mobility.

A vessel cannot be judged separately from its contents. They change one another—the beautiful glass decanter bloody with dolcetto or sparkling with water over lemons and ice; the jar of pennies a different thing than the jar when it was full of apricot jam. When a crevasse in the earth is filled with salt water it's called an ocean. Filled with fresh water, it's called a lake. Even though to the seasick eye, the horizon might be just as distant, ruptured with waves.

The genius of music is that it makes the internal external, ferries the heart into the mouth or the fingertips, then into the ears of passersby. What was inside me moves inside you, yoked to both. In this way we share blessings and curses and affairs of love. The puppets mock and punch one another and then hug furiously. They butt heads and mouth along with the song's gentle nonsense—*pin-drop, clue-hop, do-wah-de-laddle*. Kara's feet shuffle against the ground; she is like an ice skater, slipping, except that I keep her aloft, and we both laugh with delight.

John hasn't asked about my plans for the trip. He has told me about it, weaving magnificent stories in advance. I listen with interest. Try to hear nothing in his stories but the pleasure of them, the dips and turns. No meaning, only voice.

"You'll probably meet some rich count, who will of course fall madly in love with you," he said recently. Sara was at our apartment, playing with the baby. That is something we're trying, too. I still haven't seen where she lives, but once in a while she will come over and stay for a short time. Eat a meal with us. Hold Kara in her arms. We talk sometimes about Ada, but neither one of us yet knows what to say about that. Ada weighs heavily; she always will.

As John spoke, Sara and I glanced at one another askance.

"Sure," I said. "Who wouldn't?"

But John wasn't really listening to me. "And then you'll have to break his heart. But he'll tell you that his love was just for your singing, and send us magnificent presents until his untimely death at age sixty-seven, since he can't be close to you, but his gifts can direct the course of your life."

"Will he send gifts to you?" I asked.

"Oh, yeah." John splayed on the couch, watching my mother pat Kara's belly and help her scissor-kick from her back. "He'll actually send me the best ones. He'll think we have a bond, and then eventually we will. Because I will be forever bonded with the man who buys me a really fine Swiss watch. A silver watch. Because gold is a little, you know"—he pursed his lips—"*too* too."

I squinted at him.

"Do you need me to leave you alone with these fantasies? Because we girls could just step out for a minute, if you like."

"No," he said, swatting at a fly. "But just, you know. Tell him I am partial to those watches with moon dials in them. Those are pretty nice."

I felt a little ill, but when I looked at him he was smiling. He was inside the story, it seemed. Nowhere else. It is my job to believe that is possible.

The sun is hot on the back of my neck, and I loosen my hair from its elastic band so it can provide some shade. I sweep Kara up into my arms and fish around in my pockets for some money. A couple of quarters and a five-dollar bill. I give Kara the bill, closing her fingers around it. She is not to be trusted with change yet. It always goes immediately into her mouth. I am forever making spitting faces—*pew pew!*—and sticking out my tongue to get her to mimic me.

She sniffs the five-dollar bill and rubs it against her cheek, but I'm successful in maneuvering her towards the rabbit. The soft puppet hands clap together around the money and then the rabbit bows. The top of its head brushes Kara's arm. She gasps and grabs at it, but it easily eludes her, as does the snake. I wonder how the puppeteer can see beyond his curtains. There isn't any evidence of a peephole or mirror.

Soon I'll be on a plane, shrugging and squirming to try and find a comfortable position. Then pulling out my headphones and falling asleep listening to Verdi and maybe Puccini, for fun. And when I step off the plane, I'll stretch my arms wide to open my lungs, wide enough that I can inhale the whole of existence.

All the Italian exhaust fumes and espresso oils and the musk dabbed behind women's ears. Pomade on men's hair. I'll walk briskly to baggage claim and let a kind stranger with my name on a placard pick up my things and place me in a car.

Kara will stay behind and learn things and I will scramble to catch up when I return. Not her first words, her steps, but maybe her first taste of mashed pears and the thoughtful way she considers them. Sometimes at night she looks up as if yearning for stars, and I wonder what it is she sees. The sky is mostly blank in Chicago—too much pollution, too much light. But if her vision is still blurred by newness, maybe the streetlamps and headlights look to her like distant suns. A motorcycle rocketing by, like a meteor.

This has become my wish for her, though she is daily more delighted by Mozart and Handel: that she sees things I cannot. The more she looks like me, her face resolving into my own baby pictures, the more I dream she will grow up to be blond and blue-eyed and inscrutable. I imagine her leaning over a microscope, a telescope, handily bandying a screwdriver or pipette.

I imagine her dreaming about Greta, huddled by the stove in that warm wooden kitchen while the scent of bread dough intermingles with cook smoke. Or about Ada, the great-grandmother who will perhaps loom larger in her childhood imagination. A foreign princess exiled in an unfamiliar land. A woman whose hair was soft and dark until the day she died, who knew just how to lay her hand on my cheek to help me fall into sleeping.

I don't try to keep Ada alive through storytelling. But she does come up almost every day, in my words, in my thoughts. The soft sock I feel in my gut when I hear her name. When I speak it.

Tomorrow I will put on a purple gown of silk that has been steamed smooth, so the skirt flares liquid like the arms of an octopus. I will use my lips and tongue and teeth, my lungs and belly and throat and spine. I will bend into notes and make the very windows shake. Make women and men in the audience cry.

And someday Kara might wear scuffed sneakers. She might sneak out to watch meteor showers and trick me into learning the names of false constellations. Come home from science camp bursting with data about skeletal formation and the sound wave-lengths in various parts of my chest. Blood thumping through my arteries carrying chain upon chain of unreadable DNA.

When she is ten she might run ahead of me in the park, the soles of her shoes flashing *white-white-white* as she goes. Jump up and tumble into the grass to pinch clover flowers into a necklace, a chain. And if I turn my back she'll scramble up into a tree. Her toes finding secret purchase where the bark puckers. She'll sit on a branch several feet above my head, swinging her legs and leaning her weight on her palms, laughing at me as I stand resolute below her holding out my arms.

Acknowledgments

Immense gratitude to Peter Turchi, Mike McNally, Melissa Pritchard, and Tara Ison, who saw this book through many strange permutations, and always offered generous guidance and love. Thank you for being my teachers.

To Branden Boyer-White, always my first reader and mind-twin: I have no idea what I would do without you, and I never want to find out. Appreciative adoration also to Angie Dell, Rachel Andoga, Lyndsey Reese, Sarah Hynes, Laura Ashworth, Sam Martone, Corie Rosen Felder, Beth Staples, Mairead Case, and Molly Backes. I am lucky to have such brilliant and talented friends.

To Katie Henderson Adams, an editor whose value and charm cannot be overstated. Your careful insight and infectious enthusiasm made this a much better book, and I cannot thank you enough. Much gratitude to everyone at Liveright, especially Cordelia Calvert, Will Menaker, and Peter Miller.

To Emma Patterson, a true friend as well as a wonderful

agent. You have been a delight from the very beginning, and I look forward to working (and emailing) together for many years to come. Thank you for being my work's greatest advocate—even to me, sometimes. Thanks also to Sarah Cornwell for bringing us together.

To my coworkers at Google, for their unflagging support—

To the Ragdale Foundation and the Willapa Bay AiR, for providing time, space, friendship, and sustenance (of every variety)—

To the Jewish Studies Department and the Virginia G. Piper Center for Creative Writing at Arizona State University, for awarding me fellowships that allowed me travel to Krakow, Warsaw, Singapore, and Montreal in pursuit of this book—

To Caitlin Horrocks, Kevin McIlvoy, Antonya Nelson, and Andrea Barrett, for their generous readings and advice—

To Kara Hitchko and Lucia Ballard, for the use of their names, and for their friendship—

To the friends whose emails and phone calls I doubtless neglected while working on this book—

To my family, for believing in me and loving me always—

Thank you.

And finally, thanks could never be enough for Dave Clark, who not only loves me but also knows when to be close and when to give space—which is an invaluable gift. You are pretty great, sir.